VIVIAN
VERSUS the
APOCALYPSE

VIVIAN
VERSUS the
APOCALYPSE

KATIE COYLE

HOT
KEY
BOOKS

First published in Great Britain in 2013 by Hot Key Books
Northburgh House, 10 Northburgh Street, London EC1V 0AT

A CIP catalogue record for this book is available from the British Library.

ISBN: 978-1-4714-0217-3

1

Typeset by Palimpsest Book Production Limited, Falkirk, Stirlingshire
This book is typeset in 10.5pt Berling LT Std

Printed and bound by Clays Ltd, St Ives Plc

FSC

Hot Key Books supports the Forest Stewardship Council (FSC),
the leading international forest certification organisation, and is committed
to printing only on Greenpeace-approved FSC-certified paper.

www.hotkeybooks.com

Hot Key Books is part of the Bonnier Publishing Group
www.bonnierpublishing.com

For Kevin—bluest eyes, kindest heart

Prologue

The Book of Frick 5:13

There came a time when the American people began to forget God. They turned away from His churches, and grew arrogant and stupid. God needed a Prophet, and He chose a man called Beaton Frick. Frick was pure of heart and mighty of resources; he lived in a Kingdom called Florida. The angels appeared to Frick and said,

"Build a Church in your name and tell America the good news: God loves them best, and will welcome them into the kingdom of heaven when the time comes."

Frick did as the angels instructed, but the American people did not listen. They fornicated and listened to rap music instead. God was made angry at this, and He Himself appeared to Frick, saying,

"You have done as I asked and shall be rewarded, as will those who follow. But as America has turned from me, so I shall turn from them. Let the Blessed be taken into heaven, and the rest suffer torment until the world finally ends."

So God let America go. And temperatures rose and tornadoes ripped apart the heartlands. Terrorists flew planes into buildings and young men walked into schools and shot children. The country was dragged into interminable wars. The people lost their jobs, their homes; they watched their children go hungry. They knew the end was nigh. They knew America could not be saved.

And Frick said, "Follow me, and be taken into heaven."

And the people of America began to listen.

Part One

Chapter One

Just before midnight that night, I stand barefoot in the grass in a borrowed dress, drinking champagne out of a plastic cup and looking at the stars. There's a party going on in the abandoned mansion behind me, organized by my best friend, the indefatigable Harp, the one who loaned me the dress and secured the champagne. It's late March, and a little chilly. I can hear Harp shouting over the music inside, trying to get everybody to count down, like tomorrow is just the start of a new year. *Ten nine eight.* I know I should be celebrating, too, but I don't like the countdown. *Seven six five.* I think of my parents. I wonder if they're counting down, too. I picture them, hand-in-hand in the middle of our street, waiting. *Four three two.* In this moment, the one they believe will be their last earthly moment, are they thinking at all of me?

One.

Inside, there's a whoop, then laughter. "Where's Viv?" I hear Harp shout. I half-turn to go in, to drink and dance with my best friend, both of us vindicated, still alive. But then something black flashes against the moon. It looks enough like a human body that I freeze. I think, *This is it.* In the three years since Pastor Beaton Frick first predicted

1

that the Rapture was approaching, I've never once thought he was right. But in this moment, my eyes wide open, my body taut with worry, I know I'm doing what I thought I never would. I'm believing.

Then I see the thing again, and recognize it to be a bat, darting and swooping in and out of my line of sight. And suddenly Harp's at the front door, saying, "Vivian Apple, what the hell? Are you trying to ascend? In the middle of my party?" And I'm rushing towards her, my cup of champagne sloshing onto my legs, laughing harder than Harp's quip warrants, because I'm trying not to feel the belief still shivering in my bones, like a new, unshakeable part of me.

I've lived next door to Harpreet Janda all my life, but she'd always seemed a little wild—this was the girl who at twelve pulled out a pack of cigarettes at the bus stop and hacked her way through four of them for no apparent reason while the rest of us looked on in awe. And anyway, I already had friends, good girls like me. But when high school started, nationwide Rapture Watch began to hit its stride. Pastor Frick had already made the prediction—that in three years, the most devout Church of America congregants would be plucked into heaven, and following that would be six months of hell on Earth for all that remained, ending in absolute obliteration. It wasn't until a series of catastrophic events in the weeks immediately preceding my freshman year—an earthquake in Chicago that killed hundreds, a massive bomb detonated at a Yankees game, the sudden and unnerving death of the entire American bee population—that people became convinced. My old friends turned

2

Believer; they retreated to hidden bunkers with their families. While I made SAT flashcards and waited for the weirdness to blow over, my old friends were getting married and having babies, populating the Earth with more soldiers for Christ's Army. So by last year, Harp's wildness suddenly resembled sanity more than anything else, and we became an inseparable team, a fiercely Non-Believing unit of two. Three months ago, when her parents finally converted, Harp packed a bag and walked the two miles to her brother Raj's apartment in Lawrenceville, where he lives with his boyfriend, Dylan. She's made no secret about wanting me to move in. It'll be like a slumber party, Harp's always saying, one where we have to pool our earnings from our minimum-wage jobs to pay the rent that seems to increase each month at the landlord's whim.

At Harp's apartment our main source of entertainment is reading out loud articles from the insipid Church of America magazines for girls sold now at every drugstore ("*SPRING into the eternal kingdom in this sweet pale gold romper! Only $145 on the Church of America website!*"). This is what we were doing two weeks ago when Harp had her idea.

"We should have a party on Rapture's Eve," she said.

"You think?" I said sarcastically. I'd seen this coming for weeks. In a lot of ways I'm still getting to know Harp—our friendship is less than a year old—but if I understand only one thing about her, it's that this girl loves a party.

"Something classy," Harp continued. "Wine. Music. I'm talking a Bacchanalian orgy."

I laughed. "Well, that does sound classy."

3

Harp grabbed a notepad from the table beside her bed, and started jotting down ideas. "We'll get Raj to buy the beer, and then, and then! We'll break into one of those abandoned mansions on Fifth Avenue, in Shadyside. You'll have to scope them out for a few days, to see which ones look dead."

"Just in case you're not keeping track, your plan already involves the breaking of at least three laws," I said. "And anyway, why Shadyside? Why not have it here?"

"It would be easier for you," Harp shrugged. "You could walk there from your house."

"If my parents let me go."

"Vivian." Harp frowned at me. "You know, and I know, that the world isn't ending in six months. But let's pretend, for the sake of argument, that it is. And then let's let that hypothetical guide our answer to the question, 'Will we be asking our fundie parents' permission to attend an alcohol-fueled gathering of heathens?'"

"You know I don't like lying to them," I said. "I don't like sneaking out. I just want it to be two weeks from now. I want everything to go back to normal."

"There's no normal anymore," said Harp. "There's never going to be a normal again. So now's probably as good a time as any to start acting like you're the hero of your own story."

"Yeah, yeah," I sighed. Harp's always singing this song. When we first started hanging out last year, she said she'd only deign to be my friend if I quit being the obedient prude she'd spied from her bedroom window—the girl who worked hard for straight As, flossed daily, set the

4

dining-room table. What Harp doesn't understand is that I *like* my parents—current hiccups in sanity notwithstanding. I like knowing that they like me. That's why I've always been a child they could be proud of. It's why I can't, even now, bring myself to leave their house. Because I don't want to make them unhappy. Because I know if I leave, I'll miss them.

"They're pod people," Harp said, like she was really sorry about the news she was imparting. "There's nothing you can do for them now."

"They're my *parents*," I said, like the word was some kind of talisman.

Now, in the doorway of the mansion, my best friend pulls me close. She is a full head shorter than me, with that messy-sexy hair I've tried and failed to emulate on my own head. Sometimes I feel too big around her, not quite human. But Harp's not quite human herself—she's a tiny, foul-mouthed, mischief-making elf.

"Viv, old bean," she says, "I'd say this hop of mine is turning into a corker!"

"Ritzy as hell, you old so-and-so," I say. "Bee's knees. And how!"

"Okay, let's not push it," says Harp. "There's only one problem, as far as I can see, and it's a dire one."

"What?" I gaze around the living room. This afternoon, Harp and I hung winking white Christmas lights along the ceiling, and everyone—friends and strangers alike—looks soft and happy in their glow.

"It's my friend Vivian," she says, her expression grave.

5

"She's avoiding a good time like it's a new strand of bird flu. Even though she looks straight-up banging this evening, she's standing out in the yard when there are perfectly cute boys she could be in here talking to."

"I'm not going to risk getting Magdalened, thank you," I tell her. While I recognize a few of our Non-Believer classmates milling around, there are plenty of people I don't know, and Harp knows as well as I do you should never talk to boys you don't know. It's rumored that the Church of America regularly sends out its best-looking adolescent males to tempt girls into Falling, confront them into weepy contrition, and then bring them in for full-on conversion.

But Harp won't accept this excuse. "Remember that game we played a couple weeks ago? Let's pretend it's the last normal night of the rest of the world. The four horsemen are en route. Isn't there even one dude in this room you'd want to bone before the locusts start falling?"

To humor her, I look around, bypassing the guys I know to be partnered or jerks or gay. But then the crowd parts, and I see him. He's on the steps in the foyer. I don't know him, but I'm sure he's not a spy. He's around our age—good-looking, but not in the way those Church boys always are, golden-haired and square-jawed. This boy has long fingers and soft, messy brown hair. He wears black-framed glasses and uses the same tricks I do for blending into a crowd—he keeps his red plastic cup close to his mouth, so he can drink from it to keep from talking, and he's found something in this abandoned house to read.

"Who's that?" I ask.

I'm not sure Harp has even registered who I'm talking

about before she takes me by the elbow and steers me into the foyer. We stand in front of him until he looks up, and when he does, I feel a flare of something like excitement, or fear. I might just be a little drunk. But this boy's eyes are the bluest things I have ever seen.

"I'm Harp," my best friend says, business-like. "This is Viv. Personally I think you guys would make really cute babies together."

She's gone before I can groan. The boy looks a little stunned, but he shifts on the step to make room for me. "I'm Peter," he says as I sit.

For a while we gaze in different directions. Peter seems to be watching the dancers, and I'm trying to think of something to say. Something that reveals my charm and my wit, the multitudes I contain. But I've got nothing. Over a minute has passed before I manage to ask, "Do you live in Pittsburgh?"

"I don't," he says.

He doesn't say where he lives. He doesn't say anything. In the Church magazines, they're always trying to convince you that boys who don't talk to you are just shy. That the shyness of boys is a virtue. "*Signs That He Is THE ONE: 1. He doesn't text you back. A boy who doesn't text you is a boy actively trying to resist temptation! A boy destined for paradise! Bind yourself to him in holy matrimony!*"

"So you're dead," I say.

"What?" Peter turns to me—his expression wary, like he's just realized I'm crazy. His eyes are so blue. I worry if I drink too much champagne, I'll start expounding to him on the subject of his eyes and their blueness.

"You said you don't live in Pittsburgh, and yet here you are. The logical conclusion is that you're a ghost. Or!" Peter starts to smile as I continue. "Or, you're a reanimated corpse. That's part of the prophecy of the Rapture, right? The dead will rise and crash our parties?"

He laughs. "Do you really think that's a priority, for the reanimated corpses?"

"Absolutely," I say. "No French onion dip in purgatory."

There's this particular way he laughs, a happy surprise in his features, like it's the last thing he expected to be doing. It feels like an accomplishment, to have made him laugh. I duck my head and see what he's been reading—a page of a newspaper, yellowed at the edges. In the center is the face of Pastor Beaton Frick. The picture's in black and white, so you can't see the twinkling green of his eyes, or how tan his skin is from years of Florida living. But you can see the distinguished gray flecks at his temples, the movie star cleft in his chin, the thick white line of his smile. Sometimes I wonder if the Church would have taken off as quickly as it did if Frick had been some crotchety-looking old guy, with hair coming out of his ears.

"Why do you have that?" I ask.

Peter hands the paper to me. The paper's dated three-and-a-half years ago, and under the picture of Frick is a jokey headline ("*Uh-Oh: The Rapture's A Go!*"), the kind that everyone used at first, before the Church got powerful and its congregants began boycotting the "lamestream" media, claiming religious persecution.

"It was upstairs in one of the bedrooms, framed," Peter

says. "I don't know what that says about the people who used to live here."

I skim the article. It has the usual descriptions of Frick's strong handshake, his toothy grin, the vertical line that forms in his brow whenever he expresses a conviction. I see all the words Frick uses when he's explaining exactly who the unsaved are and how they've incurred Christ's wrath ("gay," "secular," "feminism"). Usually I look at Frick and see a crazy man. But tonight, through the haze of champagne, I see a man who wants to take my parents away.

"I can't wait for this all to blow over," I say.

After a moment, Peter asks, "What do you mean?"

"You know," I shrug. "After nothing happens. After everyone snaps out of it."

"That's kind of . . ." Peter speaks carefully, like he wants to be sure he's saying it right. "I mean, these people really believe what they believe."

"But what they believe is so absurd," I laugh. I wait for Peter to laugh, too, but he doesn't. He's frowning at me.

"What do you believe in?" he asks.

I open my mouth, close it again. I've got no ready-made answer to this question. I have a feeling it would take me time, a long time, to articulate whatever it is I would come up with.

Peter seems to sense my confusion. "Or, okay, let me put it this way—in three years, you've never once considered it possible that the world as we know it is about to end?"

I want to tell him that I have—that not a half an hour ago, for a fraction of a second, I believed. I want to entrust

9

him with this secret. I want to tell him how there was a kind of relief in it, a close and secret sense of safety, like I was falling, yes, but into some kind of a net. But will that sound stupid? Won't these contradictions make me seem blurrier, less defined? I worry that if he can't see me clearly, he'll forget me easily. And, anyway, admitting it feels like tempting fate, like breaking a mirror on purpose.

"No," I say.

"Why not?"

Because. Because if my parents are right, the world will end before I've done anything worth doing. Before I've become a person worth knowing. If the world ends, then I end. And I feel like I've barely started. Is this pathetic? Peter looks at me with a flicker of something unidentifiable behind his eyes. He's invested in this conversation in a way I don't totally understand. I want to trust him, to tell him what I really feel, but all of the sudden I get that magazine voice in my head again. It's saying, *"Your BF has ENOUGH worries without yours to bring him down! A godly woman smiles with the force of a thousand heavenly suns! Brighten your guy's day in this sweet lemonade frock!"* So I muster a dazzling, careless grin, like I'm about to tell him another joke—a really, really good one.

"Because it's a downer," I say.

After a moment, Peter laughs. But it's not the same laugh from before. This one's polite and quick. When it's over, he stands.

"I'm going to get something to drink. The kitchen's that way, right?"

I nod. I think for a second he might ask me what I want,

or suggest that I come with him, but he just says, "Nice talking with you."

It's not the first or worst of the many uncomfortable interactions I've had with the opposite sex, but I have a feeling I won't be able to shake it off quickly. I stand on the step and search for Harp's dark-brown head in the crowd—she is, as ever, at the center of it. I move in her direction, trying to still the sick flutter in my chest. I know I can do better than this. I know I can be more and better of a person. Since today is not, in fact, the start of the end of the world, I might as well treat it like the start of something good. Like it's a new year, after all, a time for making resolutions. As I cross the party, hoping to soak up some of Harp's boundless energy, her endless boldness, I say to myself *Dear God*, and then I scratch that, for obvious reasons. *Dear Universe*, I say. *Make me less meek, make me less afraid. Dear Universe, make me the hero of my own story.*

The next morning, I shake Harp awake before I leave, to see if she wants to come home with me, but she just pulls a pillow over her head, mumbles goodbye. I walk the two blocks alone. No cars pass, nobody walks their dogs or waters their gardens. The street my parents and I live on is peaceful in the late morning sun. At my house, the newspaper's wrapped in blue plastic on the front lawn. I pick it up and slip inside.

I'd expected them to be waiting, to give me a sermon on the sin in which I've no doubt been reveling. But they're not in the living room, the dining room, the kitchen. I sigh in relief. Maybe they never noticed I was gone. I sit on the

11

couch and open the paper, expecting Rapture headlines, but there's no mention on the first page, just stories about all the usual disasters—tsunamis and tornadoes, terrorist attacks, fast-spreading viruses. I can't make myself focus on the words. All I can think about is how empty the house seems. I feel a little nauseous about it.

I stand. "Mom?" I call out. "Dad?"

No answer.

They're out for a walk. They're out to breakfast. It hasn't happened yet, so they're outside somewhere, waiting for it to happen.

I sit on the floor. I lie down. I'm light-headed. I drank too much last night. I should go up to my room, where I can sleep it off. I'll wake in the early evening to find my parents peering down at me in the dark. The cold faith in their eyes will have already started to melt away. They will be looking at me with love.

"Mom?" I say to the ceiling. "Dad?"

The silence is like a weight pressing down on me. If I could just get up and go upstairs.

I should call them. They don't always keep their phones on—their looming salvation has made them weirdly absent-minded—but at the very least, I can leave an ordinary message. "Hi Mom," I say out loud, to practice. "Just seeing what you and Dad are up to today. You guys up for pizza tonight?" I go quiet, like I'm waiting for her response, but all I can hear is the house.

I fish my phone from my pocket and dial my mom's number. I bring the phone to my ear. After a moment, I hear a ring, and then, too soon, another. One is in my right ear, coming through the phone, and the other is somewhere in the house, above me. My parents' bedroom. It's the most obvious place for them to be, and yet I hadn't thought to look there. I walked into the house and thought I could feel its emptiness. But isn't it possible that they're still in bed, the way they are some weekend mornings, poring over their twin Books of Frick, or deep in one of their endless spirals of conversation, their two voices bouncing off each other and conjoining and bouncing again?

I pull myself to my feet and walk up the stairs, the dual rings echoing in my ears. I walk down the hall to their closed bedroom door, not worrying, yet, about the fact that no one is picking up. I am thinking of Harp, asleep on the floor of a mansion—I wish she were here with me. Harp will laugh when I call her tonight, when I tell her what I thought at first, when the house seemed so big and blank. Harp will be hysterical. I am thinking of Harp laughing, so I don't wonder when no voice answers my knock on my parents' door, and I'm not jolted, upon opening it, by the sight of their bed, empty and made. I swear I feel nothing at all, until I happen to glance up at the slanted ceiling above and see the twin holes, rough at the edges but wide enough to fit their slim bodies, opening like perfect portals into the vast cloudless sky. I see the sun streaming down like spotlights beside their bed, illuminating two cylindrical showers of golden dust, and that's when I feel something tear in me, something important.

Chapter Two

I wondered if I should have seen it coming. If I should have been more observant—smarter, more sensitive to subtle emotional shifts. If I had been, maybe I'd have realized that my mother and my father were missing something. That they would find whatever they were missing in God. But the truth is I can't remember anything from our pre-Frick lives that would have indicated how gratefully they'd turn to him. The truth, I'd have to admit once I started asking myself these questions in the weeks immediately following their conversion, was that I hadn't known my parents that well. And once they Believed, I never would, unless their carefully curated masks of piety shifted by accident, to reveal a glimmer of the person underneath.

I know the exact date they officially joined the Church of America, because it was the Sunday after my sixteenth birthday. It was early in March, a little over three months before the end of my sophomore year. I'd invited my few friends over—Lara Cochran, who was my best friend for the pre-Harp years; Corinne Brocklehurst; and a quiet girl from my art class named Avery Caruso. We ate pizza and cake and shared the customary gossip, snippets of rumors we'd heard about parties we hadn't been invited to. They all left promptly at nine, after handing me small gift baskets of lip gloss and body spray from the same place in the mall. We were friends because of the alphabetical closeness of our last names, because of our good grades and our disinclination to draw attention to ourselves. If I was bored at that party, I didn't realize.

When I woke the next morning, my parents were downstairs at the dining-room table. It wasn't late, but I could tell they'd been out of the house and back—they were dressed nicely, and in the center of the table was a platter of bagels, more bagels than the three of us could ever consume in one morning. They sat close together in a conversation they abruptly dropped when I walked in, and immediately I could sense their jumpiness, the uneasiness they sometimes got before imparting bad news. As I sat down and reached for a bagel, I had the sudden thought that maybe someone had died.

"Tell us about your party," Mom said. They'd been home the night before, but had stayed in their bedroom to give me and the girls "privacy." It was the sort of privilege afforded to the parents of a good kid—they had not even the slightest concern that we'd get into anything resembling mischief. The party narrative took about twenty seconds. I was distracted the whole time by the sense they had something they wanted to say. When I mentioned Avery's name, they glanced at each other for a fraction of a second.

"We saw her mother this morning," Dad said.

"At the Bagel Factory?"

"No," Mom replied, very slowly. She looked at my father

15

again. His eyes answered some question she had, and she turned back to me. "We saw her at church, actually. Your father and I, we've decided to join a church."

As far as I knew, my parents had never stepped inside a church before that morning. We were not "church-goers," as my mother referred to the neighbors and friends who got slightly dressed up on Sunday mornings. I remembered the second grade, when Lara had made her first communion. I'd been invited, and sat in the pew behind some of Lara's uncles, watching as she made her way down the aisle, dressed like a tiny bride. She'd looked ethereal, so much prettier than me, and I came home crying to my mother that I wanted to have a first holy communion, too. She sat me down and explained very patiently that only Catholic girls and boys took communion, and that since we weren't Catholic, since we weren't anything, this was one milestone I would not have.

"Why aren't we anything?" I'd asked.

My mother gave me a long look then, chewing the inside of her lip. "That's just not the kind of people we are," she told me. "Some people are that way, and we're just . . . not."

So probably, I should have taken the news that they'd spent that Sunday morning in church a lot less in stride. But at the time, I felt embarrassed. Their going after years of not going struck me as a strange and personal thing, like the sex I'd only recently come to understand they'd at one point had. So I just sat there, aware of the closeness of their gazes, emotionlessly spreading cream cheese on my bagel.

"It would mean a lot to us," my father said, "if you'd come with us next week. You don't have to go as much as us, but you might get something from it. It couldn't hurt, anyway."

I shrugged. "Okay." It didn't occur to me to ask what church they'd joined. I barely understood the differences between them. If they'd said the church they'd chosen was the one founded by Pastor Frick, the white-toothed man whose name I had seen online, whose face I'd glimpsed once or twice in the teasers for the Channel Eleven news, I might have reacted a little differently. I might have understood a little better how drastically my life was about to change.

It must be a while later, because the sun that beamed down through the holes in my parents' ceiling has set, and their bedroom is dark and cold. I sit on the floor at the foot of the bed, my feet tucked under me, my palms flat on my lap. My back aches. I have been sitting like this for hours. I have no memory of time passing, only of the thought I had when I sat down: that if I was very still and very good, if I waited for them patiently, my mother and father would come back from wherever they'd gone.

I didn't fall asleep, exactly, but now I'm awake. I remember things from the hours I've sat here, sounds pouring through the open windows. Shouts, sobs, sirens. The doorbell furiously ringing. My phone vibrating on the floor a yard away. But I stay still. To move would be to break the spell. If I move, it will be like I want them gone, like I want them never to come back.

I hear the front door open.

I hear the creaking of floorboards, the squeaking of steps. A shadowy figure appears at the end of the hallway, and when I see her I let out a sigh, and fall back against the bed, because somehow I know it's over. Harp rushes down the hall towards me.

"Viv." She crouches down and takes my wrist into her hand, like she's checking my pulse. "Are you okay? I called, but . . ." Harp's gaze moves up and beyond me, to the ceiling.

"They're gone," I say to her.

"I know," she says quietly. "Mine, too."

Harp has been very flip about her parents' conversion in the last few months; she shook herself loose from them so easily, I guess I let myself think it didn't bother her that much. But she looks tiny right now, crouched before me in the gathering dusk, her face smooth and hard. I know she must be hurting. How cruel it was of me, not to answer my phone. How pathetic to imagine I was the only one waiting. I lean forward and throw my arms around her neck, knocking her off-balance. When it comes to physical affection, Harp usually runs full-speed in the opposite direction. But tonight she hugs me back, tight. When we pull away she has to help me to my feet, because my legs have fallen asleep.

Harp holds onto my elbow as we walk downstairs. We enter the living room, blue in the twilight, and I gasp at the sight of three figures standing in an awkward clump by the door.

"Viv," one says in a sigh, and Raj, Harp's skinny, gangly

18

older brother, moves towards me and takes me into his arms. Over his shoulder, I can see Dylan, his angel-faced boyfriend, and a scared-looking little girl I take to be Dylan's seven-year-old sister, Molly. Raj lets go.

"Not gonna lie," Dylan says. "I thought you had salvation in the bag, Apple. You're more saintly than most Believers."

"Are you kidding?" Harp says. She sits on the couch and pats the space next to her. Molly, with her long chestnut curls, comes running. "You think I was going to let God beam up my protégée? Not on *my* watch, God. Over my damned body."

The two of them are giggling, partly out of hysterical nerves, I'd imagine, and partly to keep Molly calm. I walk over to the light switch beside the door, but my hand has hardly grazed it before my friends all hiss in warning. "What?"

"It's a little . . . weird out there right now," Raj tells me. "People have gone maybe a tiny bit nuts in the last twelve hours."

I remember my parents' warnings ("Now, this should last you for the six months between the Rapture and the apocalypse," my mother said, stocking our cabinets with cans of soup and tuna, "but the real trouble will be keeping it out of the hands of the looters. And the hell-hounds!"). "Violent?" I say, lowering myself to the floor by Harp's feet.

Raj nods once, curtly. "It's best if we don't draw too much attention to ourselves. It would also be a good idea if you had . . . anything that we could protect ourselves with."

"There might be stuff in the basement," I shrug. "I know

19

my dad has a baseball bat down there." I start to stand but Raj holds his hand up to stop me.

"Hey, Molls, you want to go on a treasure hunt?" His voice is softer and sweeter than I have ever heard it. I see Dylan turn to gaze at Raj, his eyes lit up with love. Molly nods shyly and leaps to her feet to follow him. Raj slips a flashlight out of his backpack, takes Molly's hand, and leads her to the basement door.

We hear their voices echoing down the staircase, and Dylan sinks to the floor and sprawls his lanky body across it. Dylan is probably the handsomest boy I know, and every move he makes lets you know he knows it. He's constantly trying to be the center of everyone's attention; it might explain why he and Harp don't always get along. "We walked here; did Harp tell you that? We walked from Lawrenceville to Highland Park to pick up Molly at my parents' house. They're gone, but there's this big Believer compound next door—they knocked down a few houses last year to build it. Big ugly stone building with an electric fence around it. There are always Believers wandering around the yard, calling out offensive shit. Today, the place was . . ."

"Empty," I supply.

But Dylan shakes his head. "Not empty. Quiet, but not empty. No one was out in the yard, but we could hear voices coming from inside. We heard a kid crying." He pauses and finds my eyes in the dark. "As we were leaving, we stood by the fence for a while, trying to make out something distinct. And then we heard a gunshot."

"What?"

"Yep." Dylan taps his fingers on the coffee table. "Vivian, do you mind if I smoke?"

My parents have rules against smoking—on the few occasions that my maternal grandparents have visited, my mother has always made them smoke on the front stoop. I'm about to say yes, apologetically, but then I remember the holes in the ceiling and my throat goes dry. I shake my head. Dylan snakes a package out of his pocket and taps it on the table. He pulls out a cigarette and lights it, and for a moment his face is the only lit object in the room— golden, unshaven, gaunt-eyed. The tension in it melts as soon as he takes a drag.

"Anyway," Dylan continues, "it seems like not all the Believers were saved. At least not based on what Harp was telling us."

I tip my head back to look at my best friend's upside-down face. She holds out her hand to Dylan and doesn't speak until he hands her a cigarette. "I didn't wake up until two," she says. "When I did, I had like fifteen hundred missed calls from Raj. I didn't know what they were about, but I figured they would be nagging in some way. So I didn't call him back. I cleaned up the mansion a little and when I got tired of doing that, I turned on the TV. All the networks were taking the same line. 'Mysterious Mass Disappearances.' All of them were dancing around the word 'Rapture.' The thing is, it's a lot less people than Frick said it would be. There were how many Believers? Hundreds of thousands, probably? And they don't think even five thousand are gone. Frick's nowhere to be found, and Adam Taggart, the official Church spokesman, is gone too. But the celebrity Believers are still present and accounted for. Including," Harp says, as if anticipating my next question, "the President."

"People are freaked out," Dylan says. "We only saw five cars on our whole walk here, and the people in them had shotguns across their laps. We saw an abandoned bus on Liberty Avenue. Like—just sitting there in the middle of the street. And when we got into Shadyside, we came probably *this* close to getting mugged. A group of kids came towards us, and one of them had a knife out, but they saw Molly and backed off." Dylan exhales a ragged line of smoke. "Never in my life did I anticipate using my baby sister as a human shield."

The three of us sit in silence, until Raj and Molly come tromping back up the steps. Raj has made our self-defense a quest, a mission, and Molly dutifully carries a jumble of items in the basket she's made of her skirt: duct tape, a ball of twine, a hammer, a tennis racket. Raj has the baseball bat and another hammer. To me he hands a sledgehammer. It has the remains of a white sale sticker on the handle, still tacky to the touch, and when I run my finger across the heavy black head of it, I come away with a small pile of white dust. Even in the dark living room, surrounded by my hushed and fearful friends, I can see it.

We set up camp in the living room that night, and light candles. I can't blame Raj or Dylan for their fears—they've actually stepped foot into the post-Rapture world—but from our vantage point on the living-room floor, it's hard to sense any particular dangers lurking on my suburban street. In

22

the hours since my friends got here, I haven't heard a dog bark; I haven't heard a car door slam. For all I know, all my Left Behind neighbors are doing exactly what we are— hiding. But I'm so relieved not to have to spend the night by myself. I treat it like a slumber party. I help make Molly a fort out of couch cushions and pillows; I throw open the kitchen cabinets and laugh when my friends' mouths fall open at my horde. The food is all Church of America brand; in addition to the founding the Church itself, Frick was the CEO of its accompanying multi-million dollar corporation. They publish the magazines and run the Church television networks, and they produce end-of-the-world provisions like these—bottles of Holy Spring Water, bland Spaghetti-Os knock-offs called Christ Loops. For a long time I took a moral stand by not consuming them, but now the Rapture has come and I'm starving. We eat cold Christ Loops out of the can, even though the electricity still works, for now. When Molly falls asleep, Dylan and Raj speak in hushed voices about what comes next—Dylan has a plan to bring Molly to an aunt's house in New Jersey. Raj will go, too, though the aunt hasn't spoken to Dylan since he came out. It's odd now to remember the old ways in which families used to fracture. Raj and Dylan study a map they took from Dylan's parents' car, trying to determine which roads will be used less.

"My fear," says Raj, "is that we're not going to be able to make this trip in six months."

"What are you talking about?" Dylan says. "Of course we can. New Jersey's not that far."

"It's farther than you think," Raj replies. "On foot? With

23

supplies we don't even have yet? A tent? Food? I'm wondering if it's worth it, if we shouldn't just stay here with Molly and wait it out."

"Maybe you're right," Dylan sighs. He folds up the map. "Probably we'll want to be inland in six months anyway."

I'm about to ask him what he means—what's happening in six months?—when I remember. "You're not serious," I say. Raj and Dylan stare. Beside me, Harp laughs a strained, chirpy laugh. "You don't really think the apocalypse is coming in six months, do you?"

"Look, Not Believing was all well and good when there was nothing to believe in," Dylan says, a little snippily. "But now it's happened. Our parents have shot through the ceiling and embraced the eternal kingdom, so I'm not going to operate like the world's *not* about to end. I've got a kid to take care of; I can't afford to be skeptical."

Raj leans over and puts his hand on my forearm, and I'm reminded of the crush I had on him when we were younger, when he was the tall, sharp-cheekboned boy at the bus stop. Always he seemed so much nicer than the boys in my class, so much calmer. He squeezes gently. "It's okay, Viv. It's scary, but it's okay. It's just a case of admitting we were wrong."

I say nothing. Harp stands up suddenly, her empty can of Christ Loops hitting the hardwood floor with a dull clatter. "It's stuffy in here," she says. "I'm going to get some air."

"You can't," Dylan hisses.

"I'll go on the back porch," Harp snaps. "I'll be quiet,

24

promise. And I'll take this." She picks up the sledgehammer lying across my lap. "Viv?"

I don't particularly want to leave the safety of the house, but I follow Harp onto the back porch, presuming little to no harm can come to me so long as I'm with her. As soon as she pushes open the screen door leading to the deck, though, all other thought leaves my mind. It's freakishly hot out. It's only the end of March. Walking home this morning I'd had to pull on a cardigan, but right now, deep into the evening, it feels like July—the air is thick and humid, practically unbreathable.

Harp senses my surprise. "Oh," she says. "I forgot that part. Alarmingly unseasonable weather. We'd better get used to the heat. Hellfire and damnation and all that."

She wanders off the edge of my parents' deck, resting the sledgehammer on one shoulder. I stand beside her. Harp stares into the dark, where her parents' house stands empty. I know I should say something. But it's still hard to get serious with Harp. It's hard to say, "How are you doing?" in that gentle way that indicates you're expecting a sad answer. I know she'll flip her hair and crack a joke—I know if she didn't, I'd have no idea how to handle it.

"My parents didn't go through the ceiling," she says.

I don't know what to say to this. "Oh."

"There aren't any holes in the ceiling; there aren't any broken branches in the backyard." Harp focuses her stare straight ahead; her voice is flinty, almost sarcastic. "There's food in the fridge. They're the only things gone."

I'm so tired. I sit and pull my knees up to my chin.

"But there are holes in your ceiling," she says. "That's

25

hard to ignore. It's hard to pretend that's something other than what it is." She sits beside me. I feel her razor-sharp gaze. "What do you think happened? What do you think is going on?"

I can tell the questions aren't just desperate ones she's throwing out to the universe. Harp's not trying to make sense of it. As always, she knows her own mind perfectly—she knows exactly what she believes. There's a note of suspicion in her voice. She's testing me now, the new post-Rapture me, to see if I've gone belatedly Believer on her.

"I don't know," I say. "I can't wrap my mind around the world legitimately ending, you know? But I don't know where my parents are. And if they're actually in"—I cringe just thinking the word; it sounds so ridiculous—"*Heaven*, then why aren't all the Believers there? I wish there was somebody who could explain this to us."

"Don't hold your breath."

"I won't." We sit together in silence for a moment, listening to the crickets chirping. "Mostly I wish I knew what we're supposed to do now."

When Harp begins to speak, I can hear the quiver in her voice—I don't know if she's trying to keep herself from crying or laughing or screaming, but she's quieter than I've ever heard her. "Raj and Dylan, they made that plan without even telling me. They've been planning for the end of the world for months, probably. And I just play no part in it."

I know exactly how she feels. It's how I've felt for a year now, watching my parents pray and preach and stock the cabinets with canned goods. But Harp—I can only ever imagine her in the middle of a crowd. It must feel so new and so bad to be so alone. I reach out in the dark and take her hand into mine. She doesn't squirm away. My best friend holds onto my hand tightly, and together we drink in the new world.

Chapter Three

In the morning, the sunlight slants on the living room ceiling and I realize I'm not in my bed. I hear four other bodies, close and breathing, and I remember what we're doing there, what's happened. My parents are gone. I know then it will always hurt—I realize that if I let it, their absence will turn into something I'm constantly remembering and forgetting and remembering. A new flash of pain every time, like pressing down on a bruise. I get up quietly and walk upstairs to my parents' bedroom. It looks exactly as it did when I entered yesterday, except for a single green leaf that has fallen through one of the holes in the ceiling. I check the drawers of their bedside tables—empty now, except for the Books of Frick they'd kept there. I examine my father's dresser—bare but for a comb, a stick of deodorant, and my kindergarten school picture, in which I am close-lipped in a pageboy haircut. He loves this picture of me. He *loved* it. Time to start thinking about them in the past tense. If I have any resentment over the fact that the version of myself my father thought of each morning is one from twelve years ago, it's easy to let go of once I examine the mirror of my mother's vanity. It's so covered in pictures, you can't see your own face in it. And all of the pictures are of the two of them. I am nowhere to be found.

"They're gone," I say out loud to myself. A little shakily, because I don't want my friends to hear me downstairs. But then I say it louder, and more firmly. "They're gone."

I go into my bedroom to find my diary. Actually, it's more of a mess than a diary. I've kept records of the last few years on loose-leaf paper which I've stuck in any number of hiding spaces—between my mattress and my bedspring, in the lining of my winter coats, in the pages of the Book of Frick my parents gave but never expected me to read. I collect them now and staple them together. Then, on a fresh piece of loose-leaf, I start writing.

"My Parents," I begin. Then as a sub-heading, "Mom."

- Mara Apple, née Pederson, DOB: June 28, 1968.
- Hair blondish red; long.
- Favorite food lasagna.
- Once in the second grade, I told her I had a crush on a boy and wanted to send him a secret admirer note. She helped me write it; even drew a sketch of him and me to include in it, then at the end of the night she took it away, saying she wanted to check it for spelling errors, and never gave it back. Thus saving me mortal embarrassment, probably.
- One summer at the beach. I was eleven, maybe. She lay in the sun, one arm thrown over her eyes, while Dad and I sat under the umbrella and read. Dad looked up, nudged me. She wore a purple and

white one-piece bathing suit. She looked like a teenager. Dad said, "Your mother is the most beautiful woman in the world," and I saw her smile, so I know she heard him.

"Dad"

- Edward "Ned" Apple, DOB: February 14, 1969.
- Short, dark brown hair, thinning slightly. Brown eyes. Once he looked at me and said, "I'm afraid you've got the Apple body," but I didn't know what that means.
- Used to look at stars through his telescope. Used to track meteorites and comets.
- He signed me up for soccer in kindergarten and on the first day cheered me on louder than any other dad as I ran the length of the field during a scrimmage. Afterwards in the car, I cried and said, "I hate it," and he never made me go again.
- Last year, he said, "No daughter of mine will go to hell," and I said, "Don't be an idiot." He lifted his hand like he was going to hit me, but didn't. He walked out and Mom said, "Never speak to my husband like that again."
- Once in the car (how old was I?), Mom said, "You know your dad saved my life, right?" and I said, "Yes," but she didn't elaborate and I didn't ask questions.

I stare at my notes. What does any of this add up to? Who are these people I'm describing? My parents loved each other. They protected me from harm. But they're like stick figures in my memory, with no substance. Who were they, actually? Now that I'm an orphan, I guess I'll never know.

What I need is an adult, someone who cares about my well-being. I do still have some living—and, as far as I know, Non-Believing—family out there. There are my grandparents in New York, my mother's parents, whom I hardly know and haven't seen since I was nine. There's Aunt Leah, my father's sister, whom I've never met, who lives all the way out in Salt Lake City. I consider calling one of these people, though my parents have long been estranged from all of them. But then my eyes fall on my backpack, and I think of Wambaugh—my old history teacher, and one of my favorite people on Earth. If anyone could point me in the right direction today, it's her.

I slip on my shoes and go downstairs. Raj and Dylan spoon on a mess of couch cushions. Molly is awake, sitting primly on an armchair, leafing through a book she's brought with her. I wave at her, and shake Harp gently. She rouses slightly, half-opening bleary eyes.

"Viv?" she mutters. "Is it locusts?"

"What? No. I'm going to school; you want to come with?"

"School? Are you fucking kidding me?" Harp pulls her pillow over her head and her voice becomes muffled. "No, thank you, crazy. I'll just stay here and nap it out."

"Okay," I say. "But I'm taking the sledgehammer."

I slip it out from between Harp's sleeping bag and mine, and head for the door. It's still hot out, but a nice, dry heat now; it reminds me of a few beautiful days last June, when the end of the world still seemed pretty hypothetical. Lara

31

had just converted, the last of my friends to do so, and it was still a month before Harp and I started hanging out. On those sparkling late mornings, I'd pack a lunch and a bunch of books and trudge up to Schenley Plaza, to lie in the grass, considering my options. I thought about running away, or even converting, but only a little and never seriously. And then one day in July, Harp called me over to her front yard, where she was sunning in a bikini to the shock and consternation of the newly converted Harrises across the street, and said, "Please tell me you've still got all your marbles, Vivian?"

There was something innocent about those lazy days, sitting in the sun until my skin went pink. I felt like I had choices then. Right now I feel like I'm surrounded by blank space. Like I could go in any direction I choose, but not a single one would yield anything.

It takes me half an hour to walk the mile to my high school. I'm slowed down by the weight of the sledgehammer on my shoulder, but I don't see a single looter. In fact, Pittsburgh seems relatively normal, nothing like the nightmarish hellscape Raj and Dylan led me to expect. A few cars pass as I walk, and their drivers wave with manic smiles plastered to their faces. I know we're all putting on some kind of a show for one another. A we-will-form-a-stronger-community-in-the-wake-of-this-loss show. A life-can-go-on-after-tragedy-no-really-we-swear show. It's not convincing; in a way, it makes everything worse.

I pull open the doors. For my first two years of high school, there was always an ineffective security guard sitting at a folding table in the entrance hall, but when attendance dropped as low as it did last fall, that guy disappeared, as did many of the teachers. I want to call out, hear my voice bouncing off the walls; I want to hear someone call out in return. This is how it felt at the end. I was one of the few who even showed up at the start of junior year. Between the tornadoes and bomb threats and distrust sneaking its way into everybody's view of the world, plus the Church of America's well-known stance on public schools ("harbingers of secularist terrorism," announced Adam Taggart), everyone sort of fell out of the habit of showing up. Life took on the dreamy, structure-less quality of an eternal snow day. When I stopped bothering to attend, right after Christmas, I missed it—ringing bells, pedestrian gossip, cheesy breadstix in the cafeteria. I missed the sense that we were all working, however inefficiently, towards something. Most of all, though, I missed Wambaugh.

She was my freshman year World History teacher, the woman standing by the blackboard in the first high school classroom I walked into. All the usual nerves about what high school would be like had been compounded by the recent calamities—I saw many kids, that first month, bursting into loud tears in the middle of the hallway, or pulling out clumps of hair in their stress. Wambaugh did everything she could to calm us. She led breathing exercises; she played loud music and made us get up and dance the fear away; she drew a timeline of all the varied doomsday predictions in the whole of human history, and assured us that our world would keep turning. Somewhere along the way, we dropped the "Ms." from the front of her name. She was more than that, more than some average teacher. She's the adult I wish I had the moxie to become.

Now, walking through the deserted hallways, I wonder if this trip wasn't a waste of time. The schools have been empty since the fall, and surely Wambaugh has found some better place to lend a hand. I imagine her in one of the hospitals, draping a blanket over a shock victim, handing them juice. But when I'm within a yard of Wambaugh's classroom door, it opens, and her familiar blonde head pops out.

"Vivian Apple," says Wambaugh, a grin spreading over her face as she sees me. She opens her arms and without even thinking, I rush in for a hug. "I never took you for one of the damned. Your grades are too good."

I laugh weakly. I'm trying not to cry. Wambaugh lets go and brings me into the classroom, which turns out to be full. There are people from my class, plus sophomores, freshmen, and seniors; there are even, scattered throughout the room looking a little embarrassed, kids I know to have graduated last spring. They sit two to a chair, they line the shelf by the window; some have pillows and sleeping bags and baby brothers; some have baked goods and twenty-four packs of plastic water bottles. Everyone chatters nervously and no one seems surprised to see me. I see one or two nods of welcome. Cheerleaders talk to chess club members; chess club members talk to lacrosse players; lacrosse players talk to stoners—the Rapture has shaken us out of our cliques and brought us together here, helpless, to the only sane adult any of us know.

"Okay," says Wambaugh. She claps her hands together and conversations break off; everyone sits up straight. There are no empty desks, so I sit at the feet of Melodie Hopkirk, a girl who has never before acknowledged my existence on this plane, but who now smiles warmly at me—a fellow survivor. "What were we talking about before Viv came in?"

"Nuclear disarmament?" B.J. Winters offers.

"Right," Wambaugh frowns. "That was getting grim. What else?"

She picks up a piece of chalk and I take in what has been evolving all morning. At the top of the board, Wambaugh has written I BELIEVE THAT CHILDREN ARE THE FUTURE in chalk letters, and now, ballooning below it, is an apparent list of ways we can save the world. It's like a crash course in liberal do-goodism: recycle, conserve water, charity, etc. Maybe I'm missing some key element—specifically, what does this have to do with anything? Wambaugh points at a raised hand behind me.

"I think one important thing is, like, not making assumptions about people based on what they look like and who they hang out with?" Melodie says tentatively.

Wambaugh nods. "End prejudice."

"For sure," says Melodie. "And that goes for, like, racism, too."

Wambaugh finds an inch of empty space between "Support unions" and "Carpool" to write down this new entry. When she turns back, she catches my eye.

"Viv? Anything to add?"

"What is this?" I say. I realize I sound angry. If Wambaugh is surprised, she doesn't show. I know *I'm* surprised—questioning a teacher's lesson plan, even when I'm not enrolled, even when the school is not technically functioning, constitutes full-on anarchy for me. Wambaugh just leans on her desk, arms folded, waiting for me to continue.

"What I mean," I say, "is what does any of this have to do with anything? How are we"—I wave my arms around a little to represent something or other, the huge and impenetrable world—"How are we supposed to . . . ?"

"We went over this before you got here," Wambaugh explains. "Does anyone want to explain to Viv what we were talking about? About compiling this list?"

She points to a hand raised in the crowd behind me. Grayson Wagner, who probably would have been valedictorian had he been given the chance, stands. "Ms. Wambaugh led a discussion on the futility of spending the coming months anticipating catastrophe," he explains. "Instead, we should consider this a time to start re-shaping the world in our own image."

"Exactly," says Wambaugh. "And I want to stress, I'm not saying that's easy—we just went through something traumatic. Each of us has lost somebody; some of us have lost just about everybody." She looks at me searchingly, and I nod to answer her unasked question—they're gone. She gives me a quick, sad look. "All I'm saying is, we need to move forward in the spirit of rebuilding. Because your world's not going to end. No way. Not any time soon."

"But that's the thing I don't get," says Melodie. She sounds as frustrated as I feel—much as I love Wambaugh, I'm skeptical of the certainty in her bright smile, the perky way she bobs up and down on her heels. "Before it was, like, what evidence does anyone have that the world is *going* to end? And now it's like, what evidence do we have that it *won't*? My grandmother"—her voice gets shaky, and I remember that Melodie's grandmother was a vocal

Believer, infamous for walking the length of Murray Avenue in blistering heat or freezing cold to knock on doors and hand out literature she'd typed herself on an ancient word processor—"she's gone. She told us she'd be gone, and she is. So she was right, wasn't she? She was the one who was right."

I hear an uneasy shift as everyone nods and murmurs their begrudging assent. "Plus," someone cries out, "it's so hot out!"

From the back, it sounds like someone has started crying. Someone else adds, "And it's *March*!" like that seals the thing, and now there are a handful of people talking, about missing friends and last month's blizzards, the antibiotic-resistant strains of flesh-eating bacteria ravaging South America.

Wambaugh holds up a hand. "It's been hot in March before," she says.

Everyone starts shouting at her at once and I can hear my own voice among them. "Come on, Wambaugh!" I yell. All I want is for someone to tell me the truth.

Wambaugh holds up a silencing hand. "Listen," she says. "The world is ending. Not in your lifetime, not in your children's lifetime, not in their children's lifetime . . . *Maybe* in their children's lifetime, though, let's face it. And it's our fault. The way we live our lives is not sustainable. I don't just mean recycling and turning off the faucet while brushing your teeth. I mean the way we treat each other. The way we pick and choose whose lives are important, who we actually treat as human. There is nobody on this Earth whose life is not of value. And that includes those of us who have been Left Behind. I don't know where all those people went. Maybe they did go to some Christian heaven. But what I'm saying is, we're good people, too. We're worthwhile people. I'd vouch for every last one of you. So what I don't want is for you to lie down now and wait for it to happen. I don't want you to write off the rest of your lives, just because someone else's God didn't try to save you. Because you know what? The fact that he didn't means that he's a bad God."

Her voice trembles on the last note, but Wambaugh stares down at us, a pillar of blonde fury, righteous in her convictions. Maybe she's waiting for someone to question her, but no one does. Melodie sniffles behind me. I reach behind me, without turning around, and take her hand. Wambaugh picks up her chalk and finds a small space of empty green on the chalkboard. She turns to face us.

"What else?"

I'm trying to stay positive. I'm trying to be more like Wambaugh's dimples. *I believe that children are the future*, I sing to myself on my walk home. I guess it's encouraging, how seriously Wambaugh takes the idea. That she showed up at school the Monday after the Rapture, ready to teach all these motherless kids, an undaunted ball of energy. But that's not me. It never was. At the end of my block, I can see my house shimmering in the heat, and I think of my best friends inside it. When I get home, I'll assign rooms to each of us, and I'll make us lunch, because the world is still turning hotly on its axis and the grocery stores are still open and there's nothing for us to do now, really, but live.

It's like Wambaugh said: we're good people, too. It was the main thing my parents failed entirely to convince me of, as they worked to convert me—that I was not good, that I needed to change to be good. Because good is all I've ever been.

When I open the front door, I see the sleeping bags abandoned, the sheets in tangled disarray. Harp's not in sight, so I open my mouth to call for her—she'll roll her eyes when I tell her what Wambaugh said, but she'll appreciate hearing it just the same. But my voice dies in my throat. A man has stepped out of the kitchen and into the dining room, into my line of sight. He's tall and imposing, with gray at his temples and a white toothy smile he smiles at me. The man comes towards me with his arms outstretched and I flatten myself against the wall, because I don't know what this is. My parents warned me of ghosts and zombies, of pestilence, of darkness—but they didn't tell me what to do, how to protect myself, from a living, breathing adult male, standing in our living room like he wants something from me. My only thought is that he's from the Church—they've taken my parents and now, for some reason, they've come for me.

"Vivian," he says. "We've been looking all over for you."

Chapter Four

If it were Harp in my place, she would run or fight, but I still have that yearning to be good, and it's stronger than fear or the instinct for self-preservation. "What do you want?" I whisper. "Just tell me what you want."

The man's face falls in disappointment and his arms drop half an inch. "Vivian?" he says again, blinking his brown eyes in worry. "Are you all right, dear?"

Something in his voice triggers my memory and my shoulders relax as I realize. "Grandpa," I say. I take a step forward and let myself be hugged. "What are you doing here? Why aren't you in New York?"

"We were worried about you," Grandpa Grant, my mother's father, speaks to me very slowly, like I'm a much younger child, and I realize this is the only way he knows to sound gentle. "We were worried about you and your mom and your dad."

I don't know what to say, how much they know. I don't know how to speak to him at all, really. I hear the sound of footsteps on the stairway, and I'm not surprised when my grandmother appears, looking red-eyed and tired.

"Vivian," she says. In the few times I've met her, my mother's mother has always struck me as extremely

40

foreboding—tall and stylish, with long silver hair she keeps swept into a neat bun. She's never spoken to me like I was a child, not even when I was one. But to see her now, her hair loose and messy, her eyes glazed from hours of crying, I can't hold myself back. I put my arms around her waist.

"Grandma," I say. The word sounds weird in my mouth. "They're gone."

"We didn't know," she whimpers into my shoulder. "We didn't even know she Believed."

I knew my mother had been estranged from my grandparents, but somehow it hadn't occurred to me that they wouldn't know my parents converted. Their conversion had reshaped my entire life—didn't the effects of that reverberate across state lines and bloodlines?

"I don't know how they pulled this one off," says Grandpa Grant. He walks to the mantelpiece and picks up a two-picture frame. In it are pictures of my parents on the day they were baptized last year in Carnegie Lake. As a Non-Believer, I wasn't allowed to attend, so all I know of that day is what I see in these pictures—my mother and father looking sun-dappled and devout, drenched, so happy. "I really can't figure out how they managed it. I mean, a couple of people—you can hide a couple of people. But the news says a few thousand. And how could they do a few thousand?"

"We raised her right; we did everything we were supposed to," my grandmother murmurs in my ear. "I don't know how it all went so wrong."

"What are you doing here?" I ask again. My grandparents look at each other.

"Well," says Grandma Clarissa. "When we started hearing about the . . . *disappearances* late yesterday morning, we called but no one picked up. At first I didn't think much of it, but then as the day went on—"

"I've said from the beginning it's a scam," my grandfather interjects. "And if Ned and Mara got themselves dragged into it, well, I'm not happy about it. But you make choices in this life. That's what we always taught her. You make choices, and there are consequences."

"We didn't know if you'd be here," my grandmother says, wiping her eyes with the backs of her hands. "We didn't know what to expect."

Grandpa Grant launches into a description of the complicated avenues they had to take in order to get here—they had to rent a car, and since the man who ran the closest car rental had been Raptured earlier that day, my grandfather paid a Left Behind widow a sizable fee to buy her old sedan to drive the seven hours to Pittsburgh. They would have gotten here a lot sooner, too, he says, but the outgoing traffic on I-78 was unbelievable. People were fleeing the city in droves, with all their belongings piled in their backseats. "No one wants to be in New York when the nukes drop," Grandpa Grant explains, chuckling. It's clear he finds these people foolish, and he isn't persuaded by their panic. Mostly he seems annoyed that the traffic kept him sitting upright in the driver's seat all night; he keeps rubbing at a painful kink in his neck.

"I really appreciate you coming all this way," I tell them, "but I'm doing okay. They left me canned goods and water

42

and stuff. And I'm not alone—my friends came to stay with me. They were here this morning. Are they still here?"

Grandma Clarissa shakes her head. "Nobody was here, Vivian."

"Well, maybe they're taking a walk or something. But I'm doing fine. I'm sorry you had such a rough trip. You should stay for a couple days, if you don't have to go back to work right away. We could maybe see if the Warhol Museum's open."

They don't have to look at each other for me to feel their telepathic communication in the vibrations in the air. I can tell what they're thinking by the slight frown in their foreheads, the curious glance you give an animal or an extremely dumb child, when they're doing something that absolutely confounds you.

"What?" I say.

"Vivian," my grandmother says. "Don't you see? We're your legal guardians. We're taking you with us."

When I was little—when all I knew of them were the hundred-dollar checks they sent on birthdays—I used to dream my parents would die and I'd be sent to live with Grandpa Grant and Grandma Clarissa. This was always happening in books: feisty heroines left their dull surroundings, snatched up by rich relatives who took them in and fed them lavish meals and dressed them like princesses. I don't know when this dream began to die. When I was eight, the birthday check came in a card identical to the one they'd sent the year before. "*For a very special granddaughter.*" They hadn't signed the inside, hadn't even dated it. My mother made an angry sound at the back of her throat when she saw it. I began to understand that we never saw them because they were cold. And life with Mom and Dad, until recently, was such a warm one that I no longer thought of my grandparents as would-be guardians, as the people who would remove me from my life to a more glamorous one.

But when my grandmother tells me they're plucking me out of my orphan-hood and bringing me to live in New York City, I feel immediately relieved. I realize I've been holding myself upright for the past twenty-four hours under the assumption that there were things to be done, that I would now be the person who'd have to do them. I'd have to feed myself, mow the lawn, pay the internet bill with money I'd have to figure out how to make. I'd have to turn into an adult. My grandparents' offer—which isn't presented as an offer, so much as the way we'll be doing things now—turns me instantly back into a teenager. I didn't realize how badly I wanted to be one until they showed up.

It all goes very quickly. In an hour my bag is packed, and Grandpa Grant has secured a packet of documents—tax returns, my birth certificate, a slip of paper with all my parents' bank account information. "We'll take you in, kiddo, but we're not paying for college," he tells me. I don't tell him what I know, which is that my parents were broke when they were Raptured; it was my father's losing his job that started his downward spiral into Belief, and all their savings were funneled into the Church. If the Rapture hadn't happened, we likely would have had to move into an apartment. We step onto the stoop and the door closes behind me. My grandmother says, "Make sure to lock it, Vivian; we want to sell it later this year." But I can't just lock the house and leave it, not this quickly. I have a childish fear that if I lock the door, I'll never be able to go back inside. That if I lock the door, my parents will never be able to come home.

"Why don't I give a key to the neighbors, so they can keep an eye on it?" I say. Grandpa Grant looks dubious, distrustful of anyone in a neighborhood so thoroughly Raptured, but I keep my face positive. "If looters break in, you'll want someone around to let you know the damage."

He sighs. "Okay, but keep it quick."

I hold tight to my house key and run to the Jandas', saying a silent prayer that this is where Harp, Raj, Dylan, and Molly have been these last hours, that they'll be here now. I knock on the door and wait. After a minute, it opens a crack.

"Did you lose them?" says Harp's voice from within. "Just shake your head once if you didn't; we've got the baseball bat."

"What?"

"Those people. The Church Elders. Did you lose them?"

"Oh!" It's sadder than it is funny, but I laugh. "Those aren't church elders; they're my grandparents. They're also pretty much the staunchest atheists in the world."

I hear the scraping of the chain-lock and then Harp opens the door. She looks worried, and she holds a metal baseball bat in her left hand. "Your grandparents?"

"Hand to Frick," I say, raising my right one. "I had no idea they were coming; I would've warned you."

She relaxes in the doorway. "Holy shit, Viv. We had no idea what was happening. We were just laying around the living room, eating soup, when suddenly this black car pulls into the drive. We flipped out and ran. I've been watching through the window the whole time—I wanted to warn you before you walked in, but I didn't know how. We thought they were Left Behind Believers, you know? Like maybe they were shaking Non-Believers down for info? Don't laugh," she says, because I'm laughing.

"Sorry. It's just, if you met them—they would find nothing more insulting."

Harp smiles. "Good. I like them already. I'll tell Raj and Dylan to stop cowering in the basement. Dinner at your place? We can ·bring over everything that's left in our kitchen, but I warn you—it's more Church of America brand."

"Oh," I say, "no, actually." I hold out my hand with the key but Harp just stares. All of the sudden I feel my heart pounding uncomfortably in my throat. "I'm leaving, actually. They're taking me with them. To New York. Where they live."

"What?" Harp's gaze immediately turns steely.

"I'm—I'm sorry. They're my legal guardians and they want to take me with them. You know I have to go."

"Why would you have to go? You're seventeen years old; you can decide for yourself where you want to live. You think in the six months before the apocalypse, the cops are going to be knocking on our doors, asking where our legal guardians are?"

"No," I say.

46

"Then why are you going?"

I shake my head. I don't know how to answer.

"Because you want to," Harp supplies. "Because it's easier."

I don't have to say anything. Harp knows she's right. She plucks the key from my hand and pockets it. "Understood," she says. "I hope your last months on Earth are really *stress-free*."

She slams the door in my face. I hear the lock turn. I don't blame her for being angry with me. I would be angry with me, too. I *am* angry with me: I'm angry that I don't have the strength or energy to do things the hard way. To huddle in a house with my friends and no money and wait out the end of the world. I'm angry that I'm doing exactly what the adults in my life would have me do. I want to bang on the door and demand she give me a proper goodbye, that she forgive me for being me. I want to say goodbye to Raj and Dylan and Molly; I don't want them to hear Harp's distorted version of the story. But I can't bring myself to do it. I stand on the stoop for a moment, and when the door stays shut, I turn and trudge across the lawn and into my grandparents' idling car. As Grandpa Grant pulls out of the driveway and down Howe Street, I watch Harp's windows to see if anyone's watching me. But there's nobody there.

It's dusk when we leave Pittsburgh, and Grandpa Grant was right: we're heading in the unpopular direction. The roads leading back to New York are all but empty; excited, my grandfather leaves the speed limit in the dust. But the other side of the highway, the one heading west, is jammed.

As night falls, I can see the trail of headlights leading far into the distance.

My grandmother turns on the radio an hour into our drive, and I realize it's the first time in the last two days I've heard news accounts of the Rapture firsthand. They play snippets from a Presidential press conference made earlier in the evening ("It's about time," says Grandpa Grant, "I thought they'd locked him in a bunker somewhere"), in which he encourages us to stay calm, use caution, and pray for one another's mortal souls. The reporters try to get him to state definitively whether and how he'll prepare for the apocalypse, but he dodges the question. "The best we can do now is carry on," the President says. "Trust in God and trust in Frick and pray they'll show us mercy." The ongoing federal state of emergency that was declared sometime around the last deadly flu pandemic has been, obviously, extended.

From the reports, it sounds like every state, city, and town is in disarray. The newscasters discuss riots in Cleveland, Orlando, Detroit, Kansas City; reporters interview distraught Believers left behind in Philadelphia, Nashville, Seattle, Duluth. "It isn't fair!" one woman cries so loudly that the car speakers crackle. "We're godly people; we followed the Book of Frick to the letter! What have we done to deserve this?" The one subject everyone seems to avoid is what we're going to do now.

"That's enough of that," Grandma Clarissa says, after the station we're listening to cuts to a commercial for Church of America brand car insurance. "I've heard enough about Beaton Frick to last me a lifetime."

"How many Believers were *actually* Raptured, though?" I ask. "I was hoping they'd have an exact number by now."

"I can give you the exact number," says Grandpa Grant. "It's a big, fat zero. Nobody was *Raptured*, Vivian. There's no such thing as a *Rapture*."

"I meant, you know, how many people disappeared," I say quietly, cowed by the disdain in my grandfather's voice.

"I'm sure they'll have a number at some point," my grandmother says dismissively. "For now, why don't you get some rest? We still have a ways to go before New York."

I lean back and shut up. I wonder what Harp and the others are doing right now, how angry they are with me. Outside my window, Church of America billboards flick past. "*For God so loved the United States that he gave it a way to survive the destruction (The Book of Frick, 4:18).*" "*FORNICATION: Is It Worth the Millennium of Torment?*" Right before I fall asleep, somewhere outside Reading, there's one with a picture of a scantily dressed woman cowering in the shadow of a cartoonishly buff Adam Taggart. "*Have you OBEYED today?*"

Yes, I think. *Of course I have. I've done nothing but.*

When I wake up, we're driving through the streets of New York City, a place I've never been before. I press my face to the window, but I can barely see anything—no light shines from the apartment windows and none of the lampposts are lit. Grandpa Grant is creeping through the intersections because all the stoplights are dark. The city, it would seem, has no power.

My grandparents are appalled to enter their apartment

building on Central Park West and find no doorman on duty. "It's Carlos's night, isn't it?" my grandfather says. "You better believe I'm calling the super in the morning." Since the electricity is out, we have to take the stairs to their apartment on the tenth floor. Grandpa Grant leads, using a small flashlight that hangs from his keychain, and Grandma Clarissa wheezes behind him. I follow, dragging my suitcase, trying not to get too spooked by the cold, concrete stairwell, the echo of our shoes on the steps, the black nothingness below.

Finally we make it to their floor and enter their quiet, pristine apartment. My grandfather goes from room to room, flicking the useless light switches and cursing the electric company under his breath. My grandmother leads me down a thin dark hallway with no pictures on the walls, and deposits my suitcase at the foot of the bed in a guest bedroom. The room has had all its character carefully interior decorated out of it: it is a plain blue bedroom that could easily be in a hotel. I fall onto the bed without taking my shoes off, without getting under the covers. I expect Grandma Clarissa to scold but she just stands there for a minute in the dark.

"This used to be your mother's room," she says, and she closes the door behind her.

Chapter Five

The power is still off when I wake up the next morning. I begin to feel a creeping anxiety—this is how it starts; this is how everything begins to fall apart. If my grandparents feel it, too, they don't immediately show. Grandma Clarissa sits very straight at the kitchen table, eating a grapefruit, flipping through the Arts section from a paper delivered two weeks ago. Grandpa Grant mutters darkly about the government, the electric company, Beaton Frick—all the forces that have come together to form this inconvenience. He goes out late in the morning, saying he has to teach a class at the university this afternoon, and returns only an hour later, appalled that the school is closed until further notice. My grandmother begins to get edgy. She sees me sitting by a window and makes me moves away—"If a riot breaks out," she explains, "you could get hit by a stray bullet." She serves a small dinner of lukewarm canned soup. When my grandfather complains, she finally loses her temper. "For God's sake, Grant, we might have to ration!" she cries at him, and he slurps the rest in silence, his eyes wide.

In the middle of the night, I wake to the hum of an electric surge. The clock radio beside me blinks "12:00" and my window is yellow with light from a lamppost outside.

I'm not comforted by it—like the grinning drivers in Pittsburgh, this bit of normalcy feels surreal, unearned. It makes me think things are even worse than I imagine.

When I get up a few hours later, I enter the living room to find both my grandparents in front of the television. They're watching a press conference led by a pudgy, balding man in a dark gray suit. The caption under his name says *"Ted Blackmore: Deputy Church Spokesman."*

"Of course it's concerning," he's saying, his voice calm and commanding. "We're all concerned. But my predecessor, the blessed Adam Taggart, left very clear instructions: the only thing we can do now is continue to act in accordance with the Book of Frick. You really think God would have us shut our economy down? When our capitalist foundation is part of what God so loves about America? If you believe that, folks, I'm sorry, but I have to question how devout you were in the first place. All is not lost. Go to work; go to church; do *better*. Book of Frick, Verse 9, Line 9. That's all I'm saying, folks."

"What a nut," Grandpa Grant says, turning off the television.

"Verse 9, Line 9 . . ." I echo. I've flipped through the Book before, mostly for laughs with Harp, but I can't imagine what this verse says. "Do you keep a Book of Frick in the house?"

It's well past lunch before they finally manage to stop laughing.

Weeks go by. At the beginning, I'm content to do exactly as my grandparents instruct. I take the vitamins Grandma

Clarissa sets by my plate every morning; I watch what Grandpa Grant wants to watch on TV at night. He likes reruns of old crime dramas, reality shows about hoarders. He only flips to the news by accident, and when he does he lingers a moment to scoff at whatever they're telling him. "Some secular experts wonder whether subtle shifts in atmospheric pressure are responsible for last month's disappearances," the newscaster reports, and Grant snorts. On the Church of America channel, sullen-looking Left Behinds stare into the camera and pray. Sometimes Grant turns it on out of morbid curiosity, but I can't bear to watch. They look miserable, lost. I think the Left Behinds must feel more alone than anyone.

I have nothing to do but be lazy. The schools are shut down indefinitely, and my grandparents are wary of letting me leave the apartment alone, so I lie around, eating their food and leaving their books open on couches, sleeping until noon and then napping in the early evenings. I spend long hours staring at my phone, watching the battery die—I've left my charger in Pittsburgh, and no one's paying the bill anymore, anyway. I keep waiting for some sign of life from Harp, but none ever comes. It's starting to seem impossible that I would have ever had the energy to be friends with her. Because sometimes I wonder if the news is right, and the atmosphere has changed ever so slightly. Something feels different in my body. Gravity: I'm sure I have more of it. I move slower and less each day, and only get more tired. In my head I picture a calendar of all the days I have left to live. Sometimes I see years' worth, and sometimes only a few more months. The second option begins to feel sweeter. Less hours to fill. Fewer expectations. Just a handful of weeks, and maybe some pain, but after that nothing but darkness.

The weather gets strange. The intense heat that immediately followed the Rapture burns off, and for a while it's cool and rainy, typical early spring. Every day, the city is shrouded by fog, and a light rain falls, morning into night, until its quiet tapping on the windows no longer seems noticeable. The weather matches my mood so perfectly that I don't think much about how very long it's been going on, until one evening at the beginning of May, Grandpa Grant stops on the weather report in his round through the channels. I'm sitting beside him, flipping through a family photo album on my lap—I've reached my mother's middle school years, her saddle shoes and braces—when the voices of the newscasters make me look up.

"Well, Sam, any relief from this *gloomy* weather?" the newscaster chuckles.

"No, Bob," Sam the weathercaster replies, and when they cut to him he looks tense and pale, clutching some papers in front of a swirling green screen. "In fact, I have a report here that says the warm, humid conditions currently coming in from the north Atlantic could cause a hurricane-level storm in the next few weeks. Remember folks, that will be late April, early May—usually not what we think of as hurricane-level storm months."

"What's a hurricane-level storm?" Grandpa Grant asks the TV. "Is that just a hurricane?"

"We better batten down the hatches, then, eh, Sam?"

The newscaster is still chuckling but now that I'm looking at him I think it might just be a nervous reflex—he looks worried, too, and too skinny in his suit, like he's lost a lot of weight recently and not on purpose. The channel flicks abruptly to a singing competition.

"Yikes," I say.

"Oh, please," scoffs Grandpa Grant. "These meteorologists, they don't know a thing. They always get it wrong. Always! Hurricanes in May? I don't think so."

My grandmother sits beside us, leafing through an old issue of *Vogue*, from before it was bought by the Church of America Corporation. I glance to see her reaction to the forecast, but she seems serene, trusting in Grandpa Grant's judgment. I try to ignore the panicky feeling in my chest. I focus back on the photo album. It reveals my mother to have been very much like me, I think. She's always primly dressed and smiling at the camera, at whichever parent is holding it. She holds up good report cards and stands gawkily by the Christmas tree. All of the sudden, though, around the time she would have started high school, the pictures of her abruptly stop. Instead there are more of my grandparents together—dancing at some fundraiser, vacationing in Bermuda, out with other middle-aged friends in horrible 1980s fashions. I come across a photo of my mother's extended family, at what my grandmother's handwriting on the back of the picture identifies to be "Cousin Judy's wedding, 1985." Cousin Judy wears a white cupcake of a dress; her mustachioed groom grins alongside her. I find my grandparents in the back row, looking uncomfortable. But I scan the faces of the younger guests and I can't find my mother. Why wouldn't she have been at Cousin Judy's wedding—whoever Cousin Judy was? My eyes skip along the line of teenagers again, and suddenly I'm drawn to one face in particular. It's stuck in the middle, partially in the shadow of a broad-shouldered quarterback-looking cousin. The face is lovely, high-cheekboned, with a smattering of freckles, but the girl whose face it is has covered her eyes in black liner, cut her hair on a short, sharp asymmetrical angle, dyed it blue. She scowls. She appears to have a small glittering dot on the side of one nostril. The girl looks nothing like any version of Mom I have ever seen before. And yet.

"Is this my mother?" I ask my grandmother, turning the photo so that she can see and tapping the face with my finger.

She looks up from her magazine without interest, and squints at the picture I'm showing her. All of the sudden her eyes narrow, and she yanks it from my hand. "For heaven's sake," she grumbles, "I thought we got rid of all these. Your mother ruined more pictures that year . . ."

"That's her?" I reach for the picture but Grandma Clarissa holds onto it. "That's what she looked like in 1985?"

"That's what she looked like for *years*, dear," Grandma Clarissa moans. "From her freshman year of high school until long after. I'd always say, 'Are you *trying* to make yourself as unappealing to men as possible?' It was her difficult phase."

"It's been her difficult phase ever since," Grandpa Grant mutters from his armchair. His eyes are trained on the girl on the television singing "Jesus (Thank You for Making Me American)" in front of a panel of misty-eyed judges.

56

I flip through the next few pages of the photo album, but there's no other record of my mother's punk years. In fact, the pictures skip her adolescence entirely: the next one is of my parents together, well past their wedding day—I know this because I'm in it, a smiling baby with a full head of brown hair, bouncing on my father's knee.

"Are there no other pictures of her when she was my age?" I ask.

My grandmother shakes her head like she's trying to shake the memory loose. "Oh, I don't want to think about her at that age."

"She was a monster," Grandpa Grant says with some affection, though it feels like affection it's taken a long time for him to develop. "Just horrible. Mouthed off with every sentence, took off in the middle of the night for God knows where, to do God knows what . . ."

Grandma Clarissa stares at the photograph in her hand, at my teenage mother's frowning face. "It was very hard," she says quietly. I have a feeling she's looking down so I won't be able to see the emotion on her face. "It felt like she did just about everything she could to hurt us."

"Everything," my grandfather agrees. "And no good reason for it. You never saw a more privileged girl in your life. She finally straightened out when she met your dad. At least," he says darkly, "that's what we thought."

On the television, the judges praise the young girl's performance. "Extraordinary!" "I can't believe a girl as gifted as you would get Left Behind." The studio audience roars with approval but the girl immediately starts weeping. What would my teenage mother say if she could see me sitting here? If she'd known that for the last month and a half, I've let myself go soft and lazy in a home she used to escape from in the middle of the night?

"You're not like her, Vivian," my grandmother says, guessing my thoughts. "You couldn't be less like her at this age if you tried."

She means it as a compliment, I know. I try to smile. I reach out for Cousin Judy's wedding picture again, but Grandma Clarissa just stands up like she doesn't notice, and leaves the room with it, taking it down the hallway to someplace I can't see.

A few mornings after I find the picture of my mom as a young punk, I wake up in her old bed late in the morning and stare out the window a long time. The weather hasn't changed, and all I can see is gray, the little beads of moisture that run down the glass. I'm thinking about the specific shade of blue of my adolescent mother's hair. I'm thinking about the gleam Harp gets in her eye when she's scheming. I pull on my jeans and my shoes and my coat, and I leave the bedroom and walk down the hallway. Since I don't run into Grant or Clarissa on the way, I go out of the apartment, into the elevator, down to the lobby, and out the front door.

It's the first time I've been out of my grandparents' apartment alone. They're staunchly skeptical that the apocalypse is anything more than a temporary situation, but they also see enough of the news each night to know that it's dangerous out here. There have been deadly riots in nearly all the major cities, a huge spike in violent crime. I've seen the reports, too, but it still feels so wonderful to stand out here in the cold heavy mist. I don't have any destination in mind. I turn so that Central Park is on my left, and I start walking.

It feels good to move even as it hurts—my body had gotten used to the supine position. I left without eating breakfast and my stomach begins to cramp, and I left without money in my pockets so I can't buy anything to eat. Not that I'd be able to. The city seems deserted. Many of the shops I pass are dark or boarded up. The New York I've seen in movies—so brimming with energy and light and people—is gone. I have to curl my hands into fists to keep my fingers from freezing. At the corner of the park, I hit Broadway, what I take to be Columbus Circle. Finally, I begin to see people, but they are shivering in the fog that envelops the fountain. They're lying on the sidewalk, strung out or starving. They're walking slowly, and stopping periodically to shout nonsense up at the clouds or to fall down and weep. They're wearing sandwich boards that say THE END IS NEAR. THE END IS NEAR. THE END IS NEAR.

As I head down Broadway, things begin to change. The fog here is lighter, and the sun periodically peeks through. There are expensive-looking shops open, though you have to ring a buzzer to be admitted, and there are men and women running around in suits and skirts, yammering into cell phones, hailing cabs. Here in Midtown, the world is still turning, and it feels as though these are the people turning it. I want to stop them and ask them what makes it so easy for them to keep going. How do my grandparents, for instance, get up every day and pretend everything is how it should be? What does it take to live in comfort these days—not just physical comfort, but spiritual, emotional comfort? How are they not afraid? Do they have some force of character I lack? Or just a lot of money?

Abruptly, the buildings before me clear out and the noise increases. I look up and realize I'm in Times Square—the New Year's ball shimmers on its pole at one end. There are ads flashing blindingly from every direction: *Lot's Wife Jeans: Go Ahead, Turn Around. Church of America Brand Vitamin Water: Don't Be Stressed . . . Be Blessed!* There are, even now, a lot of tourists. "I had to see the Big Apple while I still had the chance!" gushes a woman with a slight southern twang to a Japanese man with a camera held up to his eye. There are cars honking and on one giant screen, the emotional performance of "Jesus (Thank You for Making Me American)" from the other night plays on an unending loop. In the center of the square, there are voices shouting. I push my way towards the crowd of people gathered there, and try to hear what they're saying. In the center, a young, black-haired woman with thick-framed glasses stands on an overturned crate and screams into a bullhorn.

"HAS THE WORLD ENDED YET?"

"NO!" the crowd screams back.

"ARE WE GOING TO LET IT?"

"NO!"

"BECAUSE WHOSE WORLD IS IT?"

"OURS!" The people pump their fists in the air as they say it, in one gloriously synchronized moment. The crowd is my age or a little older, and they are so fashionably dressed and have such beautiful faces and all look so hopeful that I wonder for a second if I have stumbled not on a real protest, but an ad depicting a protest for a hooded sweat-shirt catalogue. Then someone pushes a small orange flyer in my hands.

WE ARE
   The New Orphans
WE BELIEVE
   The older generation has seriously fucked it up for the rest of us
WE WILL
   Take back this country

The girl on the crate is screaming, "ARE WE ALONE?" and the crowd screams, "NO!"

"ARE WE ALONE?" she screams.

"NO!"

"ARE WE ALONE?"

"No," I say.

I stand there for a while, listening to the New Orphans chant. I want to talk to the girl with the bullhorn, and ask her what to do, how to help, how to join. But I can't work up the nerve. Even here, I don't have Harp's extroversion or my teenage mother's tough exterior. The only thing I have is this tiny seed of energy, willing me to change while I still can.

I think of the Rapture's Eve party, my interaction with that extremely cute boy. He wanted to have a conversation with me, the real me, the one behind all the confusion and awkwardness and terrible advice from magazines. He'd asked, "What do you believe in?" and I couldn't answer, didn't want to tell him the truth because I didn't want to try and figure it out for myself. Even now, I think I could only list to him the various things I *don't* believe in. But still I wish I could. Because I'm starting to narrow it down. I don't believe in hate. I don't believe in money. I don't believe in God. I don't believe it's too late.

Chapter Six

My grandparents are watching television when I get home. It's a little after six. I stand in the doorway, waiting for them to look at me, bracing myself for an explosion—I've defied them for the first time, and for hours now they haven't had any idea where I was or what I was up to. But they don't even turn around. They're watching a show in which two men sit across the table from each other in front of a black background, discussing something extremely seriously.

"Would you mind reading the verse in question aloud to us?" the host says to the guest.

"Not at all, Charlie," the other man replies. He's wearing a black turtleneck and has a high forehead and eyes so light they're nearly translucent. "But I don't have to read it; I have it memorized. It's in the Book of Frick, Verse 9, Line 9: *'Thou canst be ransomed from thy wicked ways; thou can embrace thy Savior as thy Founding Fathers would have wanted. Never forget this: the island of heaven lies across a deep ocean, but the boat makes more than one trip.'*"

"And some are calling this the verse that will change everything for the Left Behind population. Why is that?"

"Well, it's right there in the text, Charlie. *The boat to*

heaven makes two trips. If I'm interpreting that correctly—and I've only been a Professor of Frickian Theology at Harvard for the last three *years*, so that should tell you something—then March's Rapture was only the first of two. Now, Frick didn't leave us any specifications as to the date of the second Rapture, but it's clear he anticipated that not everyone would be saved on the first go-round. It's thrilling news for Believers across the country, and for scholars, too."

"Hi," I say, over the host's response.

Grandpa Grant and Grandma Clarissa don't answer. After a moment, both of them give an almost imperceptible nod of acknowledgement. There is a space on the couch next to my grandmother, where for over a month I have dutifully sat each evening, not speaking unless I was spoken to, going to bed when they told me it was time. But tonight I don't sit in it. I walk down the hall into my mother's old bedroom, and I shut the door behind me.

The weather forecast is getting increasingly dire. Sam the weatherman commissions a short animated video to demonstrate the toll the upcoming storm—what he calls "Prospective Hurricane Ruth"—could take on the city. Buildings sway in heavy winds; cabs are submerged under water; little uncanny valley people cling to the tops of the trees in a flooded Central Park, crying out for help. Bob the newscaster is no longer chuckling. The mayor has declared a state of emergency. He's evacuated the parts of the city below sea level.

My grandparents don't seem concerned. They've got non-perishable food and plenty of double-A batteries.

They've lived through any number of deadly hurricanes at this point, and see no reason to move inland. But I have a sick feeling in the pit of my stomach every time I watch Sam on their TV screen, waving his arms in front of an ominous graphic in which a mighty swirl of wind batters down on the Eastern seaboard. I watch it and wonder if this is how I'm going to die.

In the days that follow, I try repeatedly to reach Harp. I sneak into the study late at night, and tie up the phone lines for hours, calling every number I can remember from back home. She doesn't pick up her cell, and no one answers at my house or the Jandas'. I try to reach the high school, thinking I can leave a message for Wambaugh, but when I dial the number I find online, I immediately get a recorded voice. "The call cannot be completed as dialed," it says. "Please hang up and try again." From midnight until dawn, I sit by the phone, dozing, waiting for it to ring. I e-mail Harp the words, "I'm coming home," but she doesn't respond.

One morning while she's showering, I sneak my grandmother's cell off her nightstand, and text both Harp and Raj. *It's Viv. Call me late tonight. Don't text back.* I give my grandparents' home number and then delete the texts from the phone history. The secrecy is a precaution, maybe an unnecessary one: it's possible that if my grandparents found out I was planning to bolt, they'd do nothing to stop me. Since I walked out that morning last week, they've barely spoken to me. I don't believe they'll worry much when they discover I'm gone. They'll write me off as my mother's daughter, and they'll take the baby picture out of the album.

Still, I can't bring myself to sit them down and tell them I'm going. If I told them, that would make it real. It would mean I couldn't change my mind.

The storm is expected to hit late in the evening on Friday. I am running out of time to run. Ruth is also complicating my plans to leave my grandparents behind. It doesn't seem right, to leave them alone during an apocalyptic storm. On Thursday, at dinner, I say, "Do you think we should maybe get out of town for a few days?"

Grandma Clarissa passes me a serving dish of green beans like she hasn't heard me. Grandpa Grant doesn't look up from his mashed potatoes.

"It's just," I continue, "this storm's starting to look pretty serious." I nod towards the window behind them, through which we can see dark clouds, rain battering down on the panes.

"It's just a little rain," Grandma Clarissa says. "Eat your potatoes, Vivian."

"It's just a little rain right now, but they seem to think it's going to be a lot more than that. I know we're not below sea level in this area, but it doesn't seem worth the risk—"

"There's not going to be a hurricane at the beginning of May," Grandpa Grant says. "That's scientifically ridiculous."

"I know that," I say, "but science can't explain everything."

He laughs. "So what's your explanation for this supposed hurricane? Is it *God*?"

"I don't know what it is. But weird things are happening. They're real, and they're happening, and you can't pretend they're not just because you haven't seen them before. I think we should get out of the city. Now, while we still have the chance."

"Clarissa and I aren't leaving," my grandfather says. "You want to feed into the mass hysteria? Go ahead. Take the car and go. It's no skin off my nose."

"This whole country," says my grandmother evenly, "supports a culture of ignorance and anti-intellectualism, which posits that *not* understanding a phenomenon is just as valid as understanding one, and I'm frankly sick of it."

"What is the matter with you?" I nearly shout. It's out of my mouth before I realize I'd planned to say it, and my grandparents stare at me, stunned. I feel my face go hot but I can't stop now. "My parents are gone! My parents were here and now they're gone. Where are they? Where did they go? Do you understand that? Explain that to me."

"Your parents got caught up in a cult," Grandpa Grant says. "They're probably all out in hiding, somewhere in the desert. It's a big stunt to breed new Believers. That's all. They didn't get plucked up into heaven."

"Even if they didn't!" I say. "Let's say they didn't! Let's say they chose to hide in the desert instead. That still means they left me. My parents left me and chose a church instead. Can you explain *that*, please? Because I don't understand."

Grandpa Grant says nothing. My grandmother puts down

her fork and folds her hands in front of her. It feels like she is about to explain something to me, something about adulthood or parenthood that will make everything, finally, clear. But when she opens her mouth, she says nothing. She just looks at me, sadly and silently, with her mouth open.

At midnight, I open my door a crack. No light spills out from under my grandparents' door, so I pick up my packed suitcase and tread softly down the hall. When I reach the study, I stop. My grandfather took my birth certificate when we left Pittsburgh, and now I want it back. It has my parents' signatures at the bottom of it, their names and mine. It says that legally we were once a family. I sneak in, making my way to the desk by the moonlight pouring in through the windows, and turn on the lamp. Grandpa Grant's desk is covered in notebooks open to lectures in progress, notes, future syllabi. The rain slams against the windows and I have a ball of panic in my chest that grows larger and larger—I don't have much time. I open all the drawers on the left side of the desk and find envelopes, sharpened pencils, student files. Then I open the top drawer on the right side. It's empty except for two photographs. The first is the picture from Cousin Judy's wedding, stolen away by Clarissa a week ago. I hadn't expected to find it again, but now that I have, I'm keeping it. I stick it in the inner pocket of my coat.

The second photo is harder to figure out. It's an old picture of a baby—a newborn wrapped in a white cotton blanket, his or her eyes shut tight. I flip to the back of the picture, but all that's written there is a year: 1986. So it isn't a picture of my mother, and it isn't a picture of me either. I stare at the picture for the longest time. This could be almost anybody in the world. But for some reason the hair on the back of my neck is standing up.

The phone rings then. I grab for it and as I do, I notice the caller ID. The caller is unknown, but the area code is '412'—Pittsburgh. My heart leaps, thinking of Harp. But as I pull the phone towards me, I realize that it actually says '415'. I have no idea where that is.

I take a breath. "Hello?"

Silence.

"Hello?" I say again.

Nobody responds. I think it's a mistake, a wrong number or a robot, but then I hear the faintest, most distant street noise.

"Who is this?" I say. I'm still holding the baby picture in my other hand and all of the sudden the two things seem connected. I know that's silly. I know it's late and I'm scared and my mind is playing weird tricks on me. But I have this sense, this knowledge I can feel all over my body, deep in my bones, that I'm right. That this phone call *means* something. That the silent person at the end of the line is trying to tell me something by not saying anything at all.

"Mom?" I whisper.

Whoever it is hangs up.

I leave. Before I button my coat I slip the baby picture back into the drawer. I don't know what these things mean. I don't know if I'll find out. All I know is that I can't stay in this place any longer. I grab my suitcase and slip a ring of keys off the hook right by the apartment's front door. I take the elevator into the basement, where the car Grandpa Grant bought off the grieving woman is parked. This is car theft. This is running away. This is some punk rock New Orphans shit. This is not like any Vivian Apple I have ever been before. But this is Vivian Apple at the end of the world.

Part Two

Chapter Seven

I told my parents I wasn't a Believer over dinner on my mother's birthday, last June.

I hadn't planned to do it that way. To be honest, I'd been thinking about never doing it at all. I was thinking it would be relatively painless to fake Belief for the year that followed, until Rapture Day came and went and everything went back to normal. What sort of challenges could it entail, besides attending Church services with my parents and feigning enthusiasm?

For her past birthday dinners, we'd gone to my mother's favorite restaurant, a Thai place in Bloomfield with the best panang curry. But my father had been out of work for nearly half a year at that point, and our only income came from the part-time administrative work my mother did at the local Church. Instead of going out, Mom made a three-bean casserole. I offered that Dad and I would make dinner for her, but both she and my father turned me down—the Church advocated very traditional gender roles, and my parents were starting to comply.

After they'd said an elaborate grace and I'd moved my

lips along, my father said, "Vivian, honey, have you given any thought to when you want to be baptized?"

I nearly choked on a mouthful of hot beans. "Uh . . . not really. What would I have to do?"

"It's real easy, Viv," my mom said. "And such a beautiful ceremony! They bring you to Carnegie Lake, in Highland Park, and it's *so* spiritual."

"Well, and also," said Dad casually, "it might involve some tiny changes to the way you live your life."

"What does that mean?"

"The Church has very specific standards for its members," he said. "You know that. We've been trying to be lenient about easing you in, letting you fall away gradually from the secular world, but it's hard to watch you make choices we know to be damaging ones."

"Damaging?" I echoed. I raced through my memory to determine which choices he was alluding to, but I had nothing—I'd never skipped a day of school, had even a sip of alcohol. I'd never kissed a boy (though that was not so much a matter of my being good as it was one of my being incompetent). Even the people at the Church were always telling my parents what a "nice" girl I was. So what was I doing wrong?

"Our main concern is about your friends," Mom said, gently.

"I don't have friends," I replied. This was true—Lara and Corinne had converted within a month of my parents; Corinne was already two months pregnant. Avery had disappeared.

"We know," Dad said. "But you used to see so much of Lara, who is *such* a nice girl, and *such* a good spiritual role

74

model. What happened to you girls? You didn't have a fight, did you?"

"No," I said slowly. "But she left school, so I don't see her around anymore." This wasn't totally true. After she dropped out of school, Lara came every morning to stand outside it with a small group of virulent young Believers, all brandishing signs that said, GO TO HELL, SECULARISTS—LITERALLY! or extremely clunky slogans such as, FAGS, WHORES, AND EVOLUTIONISTS—IS THIS SODOM? NO, IT'S JUST AN AMERICAN PUBLIC SCHOOL. Some mornings they'd shout at you about your sin as you were walking in, and others they'd just say a brief murmuring Hail Frick for you, as if to guard your soul from the dangers lurking within. I didn't explain this to my parents because I had a sick feeling that if I did, they'd approve of what Lara was doing; they'd wonder why I was not doing it as well.

"Well," said my father, glancing at my mother, "that's another issue."

"If you were baptized," said Mom, "you know you would have to leave school, right?"

Surely I must have known this at some level, but it never occurred to me that my parents would actually expect me to. I shook my head.

"Nearly everything they teach you there is completely contradictory to the Church's position," Dad explained. "It's been hard enough as it is these last few months to let you go, but we felt too much change too abruptly could take its toll on your faith."

I thought of Wambaugh. I thought of what she would

think of me if I didn't come back. I thought of myself, standing beside Lara, screaming at our former classmates—people I didn't necessarily like, some whom I actively disliked. But all of them people.

"Don't you think if I drop out of high school after my sophomore year it could have serious repercussions for my future?"

"Vivian," my mother said. "If you don't drop out, you won't *have* a future."

It was then that I realized: the scope of my parents' vision of me had narrowed dramatically. Where once they must've stood over my crib and wondered what sort of woman I'd grow up to be, now they saw only a thin line between glory and damnation. And at the rate I was going, I was doomed. They loved me, still. I could see all the fear and hope in their eyes as they waited for my response; I could see that they stood just on the precipice of heartbreak. But they no longer believed in me. And it hurt. And I knew it would hurt them, too, as I took a deep breath, looked into their eyes, and told them no.

That act of insurgence, that personal declaration of independence, has nothing on this moment: driving across the state of Pennsylvania in the early hours of Friday morning in a car stolen from my grandparents, constantly glancing in the rearview mirror for the blue-and-red flash of police lights, as though the police have nothing better to do than track down teenage runaways. I was very awake as I left New York, aware that Hurricane Ruth was right at my heels; the anticipatory rain that pounded down on my windshield made it impossible to see more than a foot in front of me. I kept my eyes wide and gripped the steering wheel so hard I thought my fingers would break. But I'd slipped out from under the storm about midway through Pennsylvania, and since then it's been a struggle to stay awake. I'm so tired. I just want to go home; I want to sleep in my bed. I want to see Harp's face when I walk in. What I've accomplished tonight has been a rebellion of Harp-ian proportions.

The sun has risen by the time I'm driving into Pittsburgh, and my heart swells to see the familiar exits. I get off the highway in Squirrel Hill and search for the pizza places in which I've eaten, the movie theaters in which I've sat. They're still there, but Pittsburgh looks different. I'm struck by how clean everything looks, sparkling in the early morning sunlight, by how peaceful and calm the city seems. There is a surprising amount of people out on the streets for so early on a weekday morning. They're all walking up Murray, towards Wilkins Avenue, stopping here and there to congregate in little chatty circles. I'm very briefly, in my exhausted state, overcome with love for my hometown.

But then I look a little more closely at the people. I look at what they're wearing. The women are in long skirts, their heads covered in small hats, or even what appear to be old-timey white starch bonnets. They don't interact with each other, but they hold the hands of children and walk a step or two behind the men, who all wear suits and ties.

Everyone on the street looks like this, and I don't know why until I follow the crowd all the way to the corner of Shady and Fifth.

They're streaming through the open chain-link fence that surrounds one of the old Believer compounds, which I would have thought long abandoned. It's just about seven a.m.: time for the daily Church of America services. I roll my windows down and hear the church bell ringing, the crowd singing spooky Believer hymns. All these people. Everyone within my line of sight. They comprise a whole new crop of Believers.

Suddenly that glow I felt upon entering Pittsburgh, that sense of safety and security, is gone. Driving into my neighborhood, I realize I'll have to adjust to a new version of my old city. The first wave of Believers came on so gradually: Frick said the world was going to end, and over the next three years, things changed little by little. Families reoriented themselves, friend groups broke apart, old apartment buildings and museums and libraries were bought up by the Church and converted into compounds. The secular radio stations and magazines began to fade into memory. Television shows without a Believer element became rarer—soon they were so hard to find, sprinkled across obscure channels at odd hours, that you just stopped looking for them. Still—maybe just because of Wambaugh and later Harp—it never felt like the fabric of the world had quite changed. We were still Us; the Believers were Them. Now it feels different. Now, maybe just because I've been away, it feels like I am the outsider. Suddenly I'm worried that Harp never responded to my calls, my texts. Did the Church gobble her up, too?

I pull into my empty driveway and step out of the car. My legs feel wobbly and my head is pounding. I'm stressed, exhausted, thirsty. I've started for the front door before I realize it's wide open.

This is wrong. Harp would not leave my house in this state, even if she genuinely believed I wouldn't be coming back. There are broken windows on both floors; the grass is long and dying. I glance over at Harp's house and see that it's in a similar state, except her windows are boarded up with plywood and—sickeningly—there's a message scrawled in black spray paint over the padlocked front door: "SIN."

I pick up a branch that's fallen in my yard. It's not huge, but I have no other weapon, and if there are squatters in the house I have no doubt they'll be armed. I step into the doorway.

"Hello?" I call out. I wish my voice would not tremble now. "Is there anybody here?"

I hear only my own echo. I take a step inside and realize how thoroughly the place has been looted. There are stray bits of furniture in the living room—the couch, which looks recently slept on, a few of the dining-room chairs. The floor is littered with empty granola bar wrappers, torn bed sheets, waterlogged back issues of Church of America magazines. I take a deep breath and nearly gag—there's a sharp, pungent urine smell rising up from the couch fabric.

"I live here," I shout, with more confidence. "I live in this house, so if you're here you better leave before I fuck you up."

I swing the branch a few times for emphasis, but the house is empty. There wasn't enough to take. Someone would have nabbed the electronics early on (the computer and the big-screen TV, ordered specially blessed through the Church website—all other brands being "gateways to filth and spiritual atrophy," according to Adam Taggart), and whoever stayed in the weeks between my leaving and my return apparently had no interested in my parents' baptism pictures or the framed photograph of Beaton Frick superimposed over a bald eagle hanging over the mantle. The most damage has been done to the kitchen, which has been completely emptied. I can't blame them. For over a month now I've been living on Central Park West, sleeping in a real bed, being fed real food, in exchange for nothing but my own quiet compliance. If I'd been here, in a city so quickly converted to Believer, turned out of my home and on the run, I'd have been emptying all the abandoned kitchen shelves I could find.

There's nothing to stay here for, and hardly anything to take with me. But before I leave, I snap open the frame on the mantle and pull out the pictures of my parents' baptisms; I tuck them in my coat pocket.

There are only so many places my friends could be. The most obvious would be the apartment in Lawrenceville. Assuming that when Raj and Dylan left it on Rapture

Morning, no surly squatters immediately took up residence, they might have felt safer there, less exposed than they'd be in these big Shadyside houses. I tell myself that's where they're staying, because I can't accept the possibility that they've left Pittsburgh entirely, and are now tucked away somewhere I can't find them.

I don't bother to shut the front door behind me. I've reached the driver's side door of the stolen car when I hear a faint tune growing louder and louder. Someone is on a bike, a block away, still out of my line of sight, whistling a jaunty version of "Jesus (Thank You for Making Me American)." I can see them vaguely through the branches of the tree on the corner of the Jandas' property. The girl on the bike slows down to take in the sight of Harp's abandoned house as she whistles, and I recognize her expression a split second before I recognize her face. She looks at Harp's house with what I take to be unmitigated delight.

"Lara!" I call out to my former best friend.

This startles her, but she quickly composes her expression into one of sublime pleasure. She dismounts, smoothing her long skirt as she does. I had no idea that Lara had not been Raptured with the rest. I'd have expected Lara to be a sure thing—she was so serious about the Church, so judgmental, and all her life, so good. In retrospect, she'd always been prime Believer material. You couldn't get Lara to admit to having a crush, to eating a soft pretzel in the food court if it would mean spoiling her dinner. Towards the end of our friendship I'd started to wonder if there wasn't a competitive streak in her goodness, if she wasn't being good for the select purpose of making everyone else look bad in comparison. She could get a mean glint in her eye sometimes, watching me try on a shade of lip gloss she deemed "too slutty." A gleam of triumph not unlike the one I just saw.

"Vivian!" Lara walks her bike up to a spot three yards from where I'm standing; it's clear she doesn't want to get any closer. I'm still a spiritual threat, a hardened Non-Believer; plus my hours in the car, and the shock and anger still coursing through my system, must give me a rattled, crazy-eyed demeanor. "It's nice to see you. I'd heard you'd gone to live in New York."

She wrinkles her nose in distaste as she says the name of the city. Suddenly I feel complete vindictive pleasure in her continued presence on the slowly deteriorating Earth.

"Yep," I say, folding my arms. "That's right. With my grandparents. They're not just Non-Believers, you know. They're straight-up atheists."

Lara flinches, as I expected she would. "You must have felt right at home then." She moves her gaze beyond my face, taking in my ransacked house with a peaceful smile still fixed in place. She makes a *tsk*-ing sound. "Gosh, what a mess. Well, it's no surprise the lengths to which the divinely bankrupt will go. The only odd thing, really, is that they don't find themselves so desperate that they embrace Frick's wisdom and come to Believe."

"Yeah," I drawl. "Very mysterious."

Lara stares at me hard. "You know, Vivian, you might find that things have changed around here, since you've been gone. So many of us thought being Left Behind meant we'd failed, that we were damned in some way. But it isn't like that at all! He kept us here because there's still work to be done. Your friend Harp Janda learned that firsthand."

I take a step towards Lara, and am satisfied to see that she takes a frightened step backwards. I have just the littlest bit of power over her, because I am wild to her, unknown. But I can't enjoy it too much; I'm so worried.

"Harp," I echo. "What did you do to Harp?"

Lara swallows. "I'd do nothing to hurt any of God's children, even the damned ones," she says in a hushed voice. "But there are plenty of the Left Behind who see people like Harpreet and her group as roadblocks on the path to salvation. I'm not saying it's right!" Lara continues to shrink away as I continue to move towards her. "I'm just telling you because you asked."

"Where is she? What happened?"

Lara takes another giant step out of reach before she blesses herself. "It was her brother, the sodomite. The poor lamb got himself killed."

I feel the ground slipping away from me. I feel the blood drain from my face. My fingers. Raj. I should have known from Lara's face as she rode her bike past the Jandas' house. It was so twisted with satisfaction. I should have known from her face.

"Where is Harp?"

Lara shakes her head at me. She doesn't know. In spite of everything, she looks a little sorry for me. I turn my back on her and get into my grandparents' car. As I start the ignition, Lara rolls her bike into my driveway, and stands astride it beside my open window.

"It doesn't have to be like this, Viv!" Lara calls to me. "Now is the perfect time to make a fresh start. Think about your blessed parents! They would've seen this as a sign: it's time to accept Frick into your heart and beg for forgiveness. Let yourself be *saved*, Vivian!"

Dear Universe, I think as I drive to Lawrenceville, *let her be there. Let them all be there.* I'm barely aware of my surroundings. I know only that the sun beams down from higher in the sky and the only people on the sidewalks appear to be Believers. The bars are all closed down. The only buses I see are Church of America shuttles— "Sacramental Rides." If I can get to Harp right now, if she is in her apartment and not somewhere else, somewhere secret and out of my reach, then . . . I don't know. Raj won't be dead. He'll be injured, maybe badly injured, but he'll be alive, lying on the couch with some appendage or another in a cast, while Dylan brings him sandwiches and Harp reads aloud from the Church magazines and Molly draws pictures on the coffee table. But only if I get there quickly. Only if Harp is there.

I park a block away and am careful to lock the door—the car may be where I live from now on. I race to Harp's building and press her buzzer. The label with their last names ("Janda/Marx") is gone. My heart sinks, but I keep pressing. Eventually, I hear a crackle of air. Someone inside has turned on the intercom. Whoever they are, they can hear me now.

"Harp?" I shout. "Harp, it's me."

Nobody answers.

"Harp. It's Vivian. I'm sorry I left. Please let me in."

Silence.

"Whoever you are, can you tell me what happened to the people who lived in this apartment? If you know, can you please tell me? Please." I start to cry a little in my panic. "Please tell me where they are."

The door buzzes and I jump. I push it open. I don't know who is letting me inside. I wipe my eyes with the back of my hand. I should be afraid. This is the part where Vivian Apple is usually afraid. The foyer is empty except for a pile of unopened mail accumulating dust in one corner. It comes up to a little above my knees. The stairs are covered in garbage and stray items of clothing that might have fallen out of somebody's unzipped suitcase on their hasty trip out.

I don't know what's waiting for me up the stairs, but I trudge up the five flights, repeating a new version of my silent prayer over and over with each step. *Let it be her. Let it be her. Let it be her.* If it isn't her, I might be in trouble.

With one flight to go, I can just glimpse 5E and I see the door is open. My palms are slick with sweat. I trudge up the last few stairs and step into the doorway.

She leans exhaustedly against the arm that holds the door open. She wears a pair of plaid pajama pants and what I think must be one of Raj's old sweaters. She is smaller than I remember, but I think some of this smallness must be new. She is so skinny. Her hair is limp and unwashed;

she has deep shadows under her closed eyes. Even as I stand there, they don't open. I wonder if she's fallen asleep. I can smell a dank alcohol smell emanating from the apartment.

"Harp?" I whisper.

Her eyes flutter open and she gazes at me for a moment, her eyes slowly focusing. The last time I saw her, we stood like this, on either side of a door. For a moment, her face goes hard and I think she's going to shut it on me again. But then my best friend smiles at me, her whole face opening up with so much joy, it looks painful.

"Viv, old bean," she says, and takes my hand.

Chapter Eight

The story is horrible and Harp tells it quickly. She lies on the couch where I'd imagined a convalescent Raj, and closes her eyes. I sit on the coffee table and listen.

"After you left. I guess, a little over a month ago? We were going stir crazy. We went to your house to take a bunch of stuff from your cabinets—sorry—and bring it back to my parents'. We thought we'd stay there a while. We thought Molly would be better off in a house with a yard than cooped up in the apartment. Things were changing outside. I didn't understand as quickly as Raj and Dylan did. They wanted to go to Dylan's aunt's house in New Jersey. They said we would be okay there—safety in numbers. They said I could come. I said no."

Harp presses her trembling lips together. She opens her eyes, as if to see how I will react to this, but I don't. So she keeps going.

"What had happened was, people had started Believing. They found this passage in the Book of Frick—did you hear about this?"

"The Second Boat," I say, nodding.

"The Rapture, Part II. People went nuts. They found another quote, too. Verse 53, Line 6: '*The road to heaven is narrow, and overcrowded with the damned.'* You can guess how they interpreted that one. It means we're expendable. We're standing in the way. Like, if we're going to suffer the flames of eternal hellfire, why make us wait another four months? Especially if we're making it harder for *them* to get to heaven. Remember Melodie Hopkirk?"

"Oh God."

Harp closes her eyes tighter, shakes her head. "We started noticing these flyers around town, with her yearbook picture on it, and another Book of Frick passage: *'If she profane herself by playing the whore, she shall be burnt with fire.'* Then about three weeks ago, they burned her house down with her and her whole family inside."

"Oh *God*," I say.

Harp takes my hand again, squeezes it. "And then, Raj. After the Hopkirks died, I said, let's go to Jersey; let's leave now. We had a route planned and we emptied Mom and Dad's checking account and we were going to leave that weekend. The only reason we didn't leave earlier—" She takes a breath. "The only reason was it was Molly's birthday that Friday, and Raj said she shouldn't have to spend it on the road. So we were going to leave on Saturday. I mean, our bags were packed and everything. Then on Thursday night, the doorbell rings. We were always jumpy when we went out, to get food from your place, or that trip we made to the bank, but when we were inside our own home—I mean, even after the Hopkirks, we felt like we were safe. So when the doorbell rang, Raj just went to the door and opened it, like it was nothing. There was a whole group of dudes out there, Believers. I saw people I knew in the crowd, guys from school. B.J. Winters was near the front. He saw me sitting on the couch and said, 'What's up, Harp.' They asked Raj and Dylan to come outside with them. They said they had seen a bear." Harp begins to speak very quickly. "They said they'd seen a bear, and they were gathering up the neighborhood guys to try and contain it. And Raj and Dylan went with them. They took them to a soccer field over on Ellsworth and stopped and the Believers started praying. Saying that verse about the damned. Dylan got what was happening right away; he started to run, he yelled to Raj to run. But Raj must've been confused. He was so gullible, you know? If you told him you'd seen a bear, he would've believed you had.

"Dylan heard the shots as he ran away. They were shooting at him, too, but they missed. He got back and took me into a room where Molly wasn't, and told me. I thought maybe he had it wrong. I mean, B.J. Winters—he said hi to me, Viv." Harp opens her eyes now and looks at me. "He wouldn't say hi to me and then kill my brother. Would he?"

"I don't know," I whisper.

"They brought his body back to the house that night. That's when they spray-painted 'Sin' on the door. Dylan and I buried him in the backyard while Molly was sleeping. The next morning, we came to the apartment. Dylan still wanted to go to New Jersey; he wanted me to come, but I said no. I said, you're not my family now that he's gone. I said that to him." At this point, Harp finally begins to cry a little, and it's more frightening than anything I've seen so far, because Harp doesn't cry. Harp has never cried in my presence, not even the time when, a little high at a party, she leaned against a hot tray of chocolate chip cookies she'd just taken from the oven, and burned a deep purple scar into her midriff. "I told him if he was going to go to leave now, because I didn't want to look at him. The person Raj loved more than anyone. That's the kind of shit I said before he took Molly and went."

"Oh Harp." I sit beside her on the couch and pull her tiny body under my arm. "It's okay. He knows you were upset. You can apologize the next time you talk to him."

"See, that's the thing," Harp says. "I don't know that I ever will."

She picks up the remote and turns on the television. The channel is set to a twenty-four-hour news network, and I get the feeling Harp's been watching it for days. At the moment Harp turns it on, the screen flashes the headline HURRICANE RUTH DEVASTATION: THE EAST COAST'S RECKONING? in blood-red type. They show a terrible graphic—first, a map of the United States as we know it, and then the same map with portions of the East Coast faded away like ghosts. Maine, Florida, the slight curve that encompasses Massachusetts, New Jersey, Delaware. "The National Guard is flying in to assess the damage," says the newscaster solemnly, though she can't seem to hide the slight glow of excitement in her eyes, "but for now we can confirm: the death toll on the East Coast is at three hundred and eight people, and counting."

Maybe my grandparents changed their minds. Maybe they got on a train, or a bus, or a plane, and left. Maybe they're exploring the Grecian ruins or some old English castle right now—glamorous, rich, as far away from the Church of America as they can be.

Grandpa Grant told me to take the car and go. I try to remind myself of that. If I don't let myself believe he meant it, then I'm partially to blame. Maybe they climbed to the roof of their building and sailed away on a piece of driftwood. Maybe they slept through the whole thing.

For a week, we bide our time in Lawrenceville. Now that I'm here, Harp puts on clothes in the mornings—her own, not the stuff Raj left behind. She stops drinking her way through their makeshift liquor cabinet. She's got the $2,017.51 she withdrew from her mother's checking account, and a couple of conservative-looking scarves to tie around our heads should we need to go outside. But we go back and forth about what we ought to do now. We make a list on a piece of loose-leaf paper, which I add to the end of my makeshift diary:

REASONS TO LEAVE:
- We are in danger here.
- We hate it here.
- We've never gone anywhere else.

REASONS TO STAY:
- We are doomed no matter what.

Every day, there's something new. On Friday, the five o'clock Channel Eleven news begins to close each broadcast with a recital of Frick's Prayer. *"Frick, let me be patient. Frick, let me be saved."* On Saturday, Harp opens her e-mail to find a missive from the public school district, the last remaining secular stronghold, saying that the Board of Education has voted 8-1 to adopt the Church of America's Suggested Curriculum for the Promotion of Our Values. My heart sinks, thinking of Wambaugh. To distract us, I show Harp the pictures I've stowed away: my parents' baptisms, my mother the punk. At this one, Harp smiles wryly.

"Mrs. Apple," she says. "Secret teenage badass!"

"It was so weird to be in that apartment. Towards the end it started to feel a little . . ."

I trail off. I have a word in mind, but I think if I say it, Harp will laugh. But she just nods.

"Haunted," she supplies.

"Yes. The last night I was there the phone rang, super late, right as I was walking out the door. At first I thought it was going to be you, but the area code was wrong. Whoever it was didn't say anything, but I just had this *feeling* it was my mother. It's stupid," I say. "Isn't it? How could it be my mother?"

Harp shrugs. "It's not stupid. After Raj, I kept dreaming that my mom was standing in the doorway, screaming at me to get up and ready for school. I'd wake up angry at her and be half-dressed before—" She stops, shakes her head. "What was the area code?"

"415," I say.

"That's California. San Francisco." Harp smiles at my quizzical look. "I used to have an internet boyfriend there. It was a thing. Don't ask questions. Do you know anyone there?"

"Nope."

"Do you want to find out who it was?"

"I guess," I say, shrugging. "But it was probably nothing."

"Nothing is nothing anymore, Viv."

We stare at each other across the couch, and at the same time, it seems, we glance down at our measly What to Do Now list. Harp continues.

"Sometimes, I feel like if I could just be *doing* something, like if I could spend the next few months trying to get some particular thing done, it wouldn't be so bad. Like that would make it feel like I was actively trying to survive this thing."

"What is there to do, though?" I try to think back to Wambaugh's chalkboard full of ideas, but somehow I know Harp won't be satisfied by suggestions like 'Use energy-efficient lightbulbs' and 'Write letters to the editor.' "We have literally no plan."

"Viv," says Harp, a sly smile spreading across her face. "Don't you know me yet? I *always* have a plan."

At some point in the last month, after I left but before Raj was killed, Dylan stayed home and watched Molly while Harp and Raj went to pick up some essentials they couldn't find in my house—dishwashing soap, toilet paper, beer. It was a fraught trip. The Believer contingent had grown and Harp and Raj felt conspicuous wherever they went. Raj had put on a suit and made Harp wear a long skirt so they would blend in, but they kept getting suspicious side-glances. They paid for their items and walked out onto the sidewalk, relieved to be only a few blocks from home. And that's when they found themselves getting screamed at by a small group of protestors.

"My gut instinct," says Harp, as we put her new plan into action and drive into the suburbs the next evening, already feeling safer once we're on the highway and can't see how the people around us are dressed, "was obviously to scream back at them."

Which naturally she did. Harp shook her fist at the group—about twenty people in all, she estimates—and called them motherfuckers, and it took a couple moments of Raj tugging on her sleeve and the group falling slowly silent in confusion for Harp to realize they weren't Believers at all. The group that faced her was comprised entirely of young people, who held signs that said things like: NOT MY GOD, NOT MY PROBLEM and a number of ironic plays on one of the Believers' most popular signs: GOD HATES FIGS; GOD HATES BAGS; GOD HATES FLAGS. The New Orphans. They quickly determined through her proficient cursing that Harp was not, in fact, a Believer, and they invited her and Raj to come with them to their meeting in the echoing front hall of Cathedral of Learning, the ornate and now-abandoned central building of the University of Pittsburgh.

"I saw them, in New York!" I tell Harp excitedly. "They're part of the reason I even considered running away! I felt like they were actually doing something, you know? Like they weren't just sitting around waiting for the apocalypse to come."

"I felt like that, too, at first," says Harp. She's examining some handwritten directions in the dashboard light. "Take this next exit, then turn left. We thought they seemed serious. That they had plans that were already being put into motion. At the very least, we figured they'd be a good support system. We thought if we knew they were out there and on our side, we wouldn't be so afraid of the city itself."

The second meeting was two days later. Harp and Raj attended again, and this time they brought Dylan and Molly. It was nearly a two-mile walk, Harp reminds me, through hostile territory, and this time they had a seven-year-old with them, slowing them down. But Harp and Raj assured Dylan that it would be worth it: that the New Orphans would restore his faith in humanity, his hopes for Molly's future and his own.

They were wrong.

"There was a fucking drum circle, Viv," Harp explains. "They drummed for like twenty minutes, and then everybody had to stand up and say one thing they liked about the United States, and one thing they didn't like."

"What did you say?"

"That I didn't like drum circles and I liked being in a place where there weren't any."

But the problem wasn't that the Pittsburgh New Orphans were, in Harp's words, "dirty hippies"—just that that was all they were. They had no plans, Harp says, no definitive course of action. They were like us, in other words, only they had given themselves a name, and the appearance of organization. The group's camaraderie had a certain level of appeal in a city where a sexually active girl could find herself waking up in a house on fire, but camaraderie was about as far as they had gotten in their attempt at political action. Harp says that when any individual in the group wanted to speak, they had to first be handed the "Stick of Peace"—a small branch someone had picked up off the Cathedral lawn. There was no tension, no disagreement, no sense of the clock slowly winding down. No ideas.

"Everyone just sat around agreeing with everyone else," Harp remembers. "Everyone 'had a point.' 'You have a point.' 'I think you make a good point.' The girl who brought an electric keyboard with her and played us 'Imagine' in the middle of the meeting 'had a good point.' But nobody had anything to say."

"They were just unorganized, Harp," I say. "They were new."

"They were *meek*." Harp nearly spits the word. "They were meek, and they thought that's what made them strong, that's what made them good, that's what made them better. But you know what the thing is about the Believers? For all their talk about submitting and obeying, they're never anything but unstoppable."

The only useful thing about the New Orphans, explains Harp as we pull into the parking lot of a boxy brick apartment building in South Park, is that it put her in touch with the person we've come here to see. She met him at her first New Orphans meeting; he was introduced as the group's "information guy" and he gave Raj his home address, in case they ever needed a hand. This had meant a lot to Raj, and it meant even more now to Harp. Also, she adds, this guy wasn't in the drum circle. "I feel like he has his finger on the pulse," she murmurs as we walk up to the front door, keeping our eyes open for movements in the shadows. "I think he can tell us what to do next, where we're needed. I don't feel like he's trying to recreate the Summer of Love."

I'm skeptical. Harp has spent the last half hour describing the epic ineptness of the Pittsburgh New Orphans, so the claim that their "information guy" would be something other than incompetent seems dubious. More likely, I think, he's cute, or into Harp. I know Raj only died two weeks ago, and that the Harp before me is more hollow-eyed and tired, less rapid-fire than she once was. But still I don't believe she'd skip an opportunity to flirt.

Harp rings the buzzer next to the name "P. Ivey" and the second she hears the crackle of the intercom she starts to speak. "Hey," she says. "I'm Raj Janda's sister. You met him at a New Orphans meeting last month. He's dead and I need to talk to you."

"Jesus, Harp," I mutter.

After a second, the door buzzes and unlocks—maybe P. Ivey is used to this sort of greeting—and Harp barrels in with me at her heels. His apartment is on the first floor, at the end of a dank little hallway that smells vaguely of cat, cigarettes, sad people. Harp bangs on the door.

"Harp," I whisper, as we hear the lock turn, "relax."

The door opens. P. Ivey stands before us. It turns out that he *is* cute—he's very cute. He has soft, messy brown hair and long fingers. P. Ivey has blue eyes. Very blue. Bluer than blue. The bluest eyes I've ever seen.

I would have had no way of knowing that Harp's information guy would be Peter from the Rapture's Eve party,

97

but still I wish I'd had some suspicion—I would have stayed in the car, or better yet, dug myself a small hole to hide in. I'm still mortified at the memory of my vapid conversation that night, and standing here in the cramped living room of his apartment, so close to all his clothes and books and guitars and things, I feel huge and obvious and awkward. Like I have a sign hanging over me, reading "Remember This Moron?" in blinking neon lights. Peter has no couch—there isn't enough room for one—so the three of us stand around his desk chair, staring at each other. I don't know what to do with my arms. My arms have suddenly become two useless flopping appendages.

"Um," says Peter. "Do you guys want anything to drink?"

"Do you have beer?" Harp sits in the computer chair and I inch closer to her. The closer I get to Harp, the more invisible I'll be. Perhaps she can send me some sort of secret signal as to how a regular person holds her arms.

Peter frowns. "Water?" he offers.

Harp sighs. "Fine."

When he's left the room for the next one, an equally small kitchen whose every surface seems covered in dishes, I lean down and hiss in Harp's ear, hoping the running water will drown me out. "What are you doing? Why didn't you tell me it was him?"

"You know him?" Harp whispers back, startled.

"He was at the party. The Rapture's Eve party. I thought he was cute. You told him we should have babies together. Harp! This isn't funny!"

"Viv!" Harp's eyes are wide and she covers her mouth to hide her laughter. "I swear I didn't remember. Really,

I didn't. If I remembered, I would have told you. I promise!"

Peter comes back into the room carrying two glasses of water and I stand straight again.

"It's Harp, right?" says Peter, handing the first glass of water to her. Harp nods. He turns to me now, a smile on his face, and hands me the other glass. I brace myself for some awkward allusion to Rapture's Eve. But he says, "I'm Peter."

I stare at him for a moment—is it a joke? But his smile is blank and welcoming, and there's no reason for him to lie. Besides, even I know I wasn't very memorable that night. "Vivian," I manage to squeak.

Peter turns his attention back to Harp. He sits down on the floor at her feet. "Your brother was Raj?" She nods. "What happened to him?"

Harp tells an abbreviated version of the story. Her voice doesn't break once, though she does take a moment, right after she mentions Raj's body on the stoop, to take a long drink from her glass of water. I move my hand from the back of the chair to her shoulder. Peter watches her face the whole time she speaks. He looks disturbed but unsurprised. When she's finished, he doesn't speak for a while. He picks thoughtfully at the carpet.

"You probably already know that certain groups have been targeted over the last month," Peter says. "Basically anyone who's mentioned in the Book of Frick as being unsaveable. There've been a lot of attacks on other religious groups, gays and lesbians, any girls or women who are seen as or can be proven to be 'promiscuous.'" He makes air quotes around the word "promiscuous." "I've heard some awful stuff." He looks up at Harp, right into her eyes with those blue ones, and the sadness on his face is so genuine. "I'm sorry about your brother. I only met him that once, but I thought he seemed like a really good guy. He didn't deserve to die like that; nobody does. I know how hard it is to lose somebody close to you. I'm just really sorry."

I can tell she's trying to stay cool, in control, but despite herself Harp raises a hand to her face to wipe her tears away. "Thanks," she says. Her voice is a little hoarse.

A few moments go by where we all stay very still, saying nothing. I can hear the drip of the kitchen faucet, the tinny noise of a television in what must be Peter's bedroom. I feel my face flush. There's so much pain in this room; I can feel it—I can feel Harp trying to contain all of hers and I can feel Peter's, too, just below the surface. And there's mine as well, hardening into a fist somewhere in the center of me. It's been six weeks of loss upon loss, and what I should be thinking of is the magnitude of all our pain combined. But what I'm thinking is: this boy has a sweet face and blue eyes. He is speaking softly and kindly to my best friend. He made air quotes around "promiscuous." For the first time in I don't know how long, I feel the knot of stress in the center of my spine begin to loosen. I feel a little bit safe.

Peter clears his throat. "The thing is," he says hesitantly, "I'm not totally sure what you came here for. I want to help you; don't get me wrong. If I can help you, I will. But I'm not really into the vengeance thing." He shrugs a bit, apologetically. "So if you're asking to me to spearhead a manhunt or something . . ."

"No," Harp says. "Nothing like that. It's just that Viv and I feel useless. We want to do something. At the New Orphans meeting, they said you had connections to the Church."

He grimaces. "I wish they hadn't said that."

"You mean you don't?"

"No," says Peter slowly. "I do, technically. But nothing solid. Nothing that will help you take them down, if that's what you're looking for."

I had a feeling this was the sort of mission Harp was after, and she looks disappointed. She glances up at me with a resigned expression, and I can tell she's about to suggest we leave—she's frustrated by this meeting, embarrassed at having cried in front of an almost total stranger, scared about returning to Pittsburgh too late at night. But I speak before she's able to.

"What sort of connections?" I ask.

"What?" Peter seems startled, like he's forgotten I'm standing there.

"What are your connections to the Church?"

"Oh." He shrugs casually, but I see a little twitch in his face before he answers. "My father was a Believer. From way, way back. So I've seen more of the Church than most."

It's clear Peter doesn't want to talk about it, so I don't try to make him. But his nerves make me nervous, and I try to remember we can't blindly trust anyone anymore, no matter how badly we want to put our lips on their lips.

"Do you have anything else? Anything about the New Orphans? Are they less useless in other cities?"

Peter smiles at this. "In some they are. In some they're worse. The ones here are pretty bad, though. I'm assuming that's why you came to me and not them?"

We nod. Peter stands, and pushes past me to open a desk drawer. I take a step backwards, stumbling a little, hoping that Peter hasn't noticed.

"From what I gather, the New Orphans movement got rolling a few months ago," he explains, rifling through some papers in the drawer. "A high school kid in South Dakota—his parents went Believer and he started the group for people who'd gone through the same. It didn't take off until the Rapture itself, though." He produces a small slip of paper from a manila folder and hands it to me. I'm surprised by this; it should seem obvious to anyone that Harp is in charge of our team of two, but then I remember that I'm the one who asked the question.

"Spencer G. @thenewestorphan. Keystone, South Dakota," I read out loud.

"That's right by Mount Rushmore. He's the one you'd want to talk to," says Peter. "He's got a bunch of converted Non-Believers working for him—Believers who converted back. He probably knows more about the inner workings of the Church of America than anyone who hasn't recently been sucked up into the atmosphere."

"Mount Rushmore?" I say. "Isn't that on Frick's list of Sacred Sites?"

In the Book of Frick, Frick claims that in the late 1970s, Jesus personally appeared to Frick in a powder-blue

102

Chrysler convertible, which had the power to travel instantly through space and time. Jesus used the vehicle to usher Frick to seven different spots in the United States that were personally blessed by God for one reason or another, at which Believers and Non-Believers alike could expect to find redemption. The list includes everything you'd think it would: the Grand Canyon, the Pentagon, Wall Street (*"For God saw that Americans were industrious, and made money in His name, and he saw that it was good"*). It's one of the many parts of the Book of Frick that make you wonder whether or not Frick was just straight-up on shrooms when he was writing it; make that accusation to a Believer, however, as I did to my parents in their mission to convert me, and they will whine that "it's only a metaphor!" and imply that your inability to grasp nuance is a large part of what ensures your eternal damnation.

Peter nods. "I don't get how he does it, but it makes me inclined to trust him. Anyone who can build a Non-Believer community in the center of a Church stronghold has to be some kind of force of nature, right?"

Harp takes the slip of paper from my hand and stares at it for a moment, saying nothing. Peter gingerly steps around me again, and takes my and Harp's empty glasses. He holds them for a moment, watching us courteously—waiting, I realize, for us to leave.

"Great," says Harp finally. She stands up. "And just real quick, before we go—is there anything we should know about that's going on in California?"

Very abruptly, Peter tries to cross his arms, but he's still

103

holding the two water glasses and they clink loudly in mid-air. He looks at Harp suspiciously.

"What do you mean?"

"I mean," she says, "does the Church have any particular history of being in California?"

Peter chews for a moment on the inside of his mouth, frowning. Then he says, "How do you know about this?"

I say "Know about what?" at the same time Harp says "How do *you*?" Immediately she looks at me and groans. I realize a second too late what Harp was trying to do. Peter smiles wryly at us.

"Why don't you tell me why you asked about California?" he suggests. "And then I'll tell you what I know, or what I think I know."

I'm expecting some wild improvisation on Harp's part, so I'm surprised when she tells him the absolute truth. "Viv got a phone call at her grandparents' house in New York. Late at night. About a week ago now, the night before Hurricane Ruth. It was a San Francisco area code. They didn't say anything, but she thought it was her mom."

"I mean," I interject, realizing how crazy this must make me sound, "I didn't *think* it was. I just had this weird feeling, that's all. Intuition, whatever you want to call it. It doesn't mean anything." I say this part specifically to Peter, as an apology for stumbling onto whatever it is that he knows. "I didn't come here thinking it meant anything."

"I know you didn't," Peter says. "But it kind of might." Without warning he turns and walks the few feet into his bedroom. I look at Harp to gauge her level of confusion, and Harp instantly, as if she's been waiting this whole time

104

for me to look at her outside of Peter's line of sight, takes an invisible head into her hands and mimes making out with it. I punch her shoulder, hard, and she stifles her giggles as Peter re-enters, carrying with him a stack of mail that he drops on the seat of the office chair. I pick up one envelope, already torn clean open, and Harp does the same. We read the printed flyers that make up the contents, then switch.

The one I picked up says: "*If you lovest them, make them listen; for otherwise you shall spend an eternity apart—with you in the golden light of heavenly splendor, and they in the shadows of torment and calamity* (The Book of Frick: Verse 18, Line 2)."

Harp's says: "*I see thee and know thee to be my child; dost thou recognize me as thy own Father?* (The Book of Frick Verse 58: Line 3)."

Peter turns over the envelope in my hand, and points to the postmark. Olema, California.

"I've been getting these for about three weeks now," he says. "Every day a new one. Never handwritten, always a verse from the Book. Usually it's something about redemption, about Believing before it's too late. But this one," he touches the envelope I'm holding again, "this is the one that came today. '*Dost thou recognize me as thy own Father?*' It's a line from the story of Frick's first vision—the one he had in a dream, where he and God chat over frappucinos at Starbucks for a few minutes before God condemns secular morals and burns all the baristas' eyeballs out. It's what God says to Frick while everyone else is rolling around on the floor, screaming for mercy. '*You are my child, I am your Father.*'"

I nod. Of course I know the Parable of the Starbucks; everybody does—it was probably Frick's most marketable vision.

"This mail could be from any Believer," Peter says. "I realize that. Some old lady in California could have gotten my address off the internet and thinks that converting me is her best shot at the Second Boat. I'm totally aware of the probability that it's this scenario and not any other one. But. Like I said. My father was a Believer before Frick even predicted the Rapture." Peter trains his blue eyes on me as he speaks and doesn't look away. "I was ten years old when he joined the Church—that was eight years ago. The people who followed Frick after the Rapture prediction; they were scared about the weather, the economy, all those weird incurable viruses that started going around a few years ago. They at least had a little reason to think that this guy had the answers. The people like my father, who joined up way before that—they're not well. That's the best way I can describe him. The way his mind works, his ideas about things. He's not well. My mother left and took me with her. He would call periodically and say a lot of things that didn't make sense. He worried about the state of my soul. He described, in detail, the specific sort of hell I would endure, all the ways I had let God and Frick down. But he didn't know me at all. He didn't—" Peter stops and takes a breath. "My mom died, last year. Ovarian cancer. He didn't call. The next time I spoke to him, and the last time, was Rapture's Eve, and to say that he was incoherent would be a major understatement."

"You think it's your dad sending you this mail," I say.

"I feel like it is," Peter says. "It's just a feeling; I don't know. It might mean nothing."

"But it might mean our parents didn't get Raptured."

"Why are the letters postmarked California, though?" asks Harp. "Wasn't the Church of America headquarters in Florida? Wouldn't it be washed to sea by now?"

"Florida wasn't the only place where Frick owned property," Peter says. "He had a personal compound in northern California, not far from San Francisco, right in the middle of some state parks." He shrugs a little sheepishly at the looks we give him. "My dad was in pretty deep. I *know* stuff."

I feel it throbbing in me suddenly, barely palpable and yet somehow so intense I have to clear the one chair in the room of the mail that rests on top of it, and sit down. Harp is pacing Peter's small apartment. She has that manic glint in her eye, the kind that means she's coming up with a plan. "Have you told anyone else?" she asks Peter.

"I've spent the last three weeks trying to convince myself that I'm crazy," he says. "I only told you because—I don't know why I told you! Because you want to do something, and so I'm offering you the only thing I have. The only thing I have is the tiniest sliver of a suspicion that my Believer father is alive in Northern California. That's nothing."

"It's not," I say.

"It really is."

"It isn't." I look up at him. "An hour ago, our parents were gone, and we had no idea where they'd gone or how they got there. Now we have the tiniest sliver of a suspicion.

107

And if they're not in California, maybe someone else is, someone who could explain."

"We could get in touch with the guy in South Dakota?" Harp suggests. "And then he can connect us to some San Francisco New Orphans? I guess we're risking major incompetence there. We would need to scope out the San Francisco chapter first, stalk their Facebook pages a little, see how Drum Circle-y they are on a scale of 1 to 10."

"No," I say. My heart is beating fast.

Harp looks at me. "No?"

"No," I say. "We go."

"We do?"

"There's no reason for us to stay here," I tell her. "If there's a person on this planet who can give me some idea of where my parents are, I want to be the one who talks to them. Let's go. We'll drive there. We have a car. You have some money. We'll do it ourselves."

"Viv." Harp kneels down in front of me and looks at me with concern. "This could be a total dead end. We could uproot our lives and drive all the way across the country just to find your call was a wrong number and the mail is just a weird coincidence. Then we wouldn't get any answers and we'd be stuck in the middle of nowhere for the end of the world. Alone."

"We wouldn't be alone. We'd have each other. And if things really get dire, I have an aunt in Salt Lake City we can stay with." *An aunt I've never met before who may not know I exist*, I think but don't say. "And anyway, I feel like if we don't go—Harp, if we stay here, we're meek. Aren't

108

we? And I don't want to be meek anymore. I want to be unstoppable."

For the second time in an hour, Harp's eyes well up. But she's smiling, too. "Vivian Apple, you emotionally manipulative bitch," she says. She takes my hands into hers and squeezes. "Of course I'll go with you on this completely futile suicide mission. Of course. I would be honored."

I grin at her, in part because I'm happy, and in part because she has absolutely no idea what I'm about to do next. I look up at Peter, who is watching us with a strange mix of emotions in his expression—bewilderment, yes, and a slight undercurrent of what is possibly concern for our mental health. But there's yearning there, too. I had a feeling I'd see it.

So I say to him, "Are you coming?"

And after a moment he says, with a face so bemused it's like he doesn't even mean to say it, "If you'll have me."

Chapter Nine

"Very smooth, Apple," Harp drawls a few minutes later. We're standing outside of Peter's apartment building, waiting for him to get his stuff together. "The old Invite the Cute Boy on a Cross Country Road Trip Even Though For All Intents and Purposes You've Only Just Met move. I should have seen it coming."

"Harp—"

"The classic Don't Give Your Best Friend a Head's Up Even Though She Too Will Be on Said Trip and Is Not Really Looking Forward to Constantly Cockblocking You strategy," she interrupts. "Expertly done. Grade A, top of the line scheming."

"Harp," I say. "It might be his dad. You know?"

"Old Slick Maneuver Apple over here, with her It Might Be His Dad excuses and her Are You Coming come-ons."

"Harp, seriously." I know she's sincerely annoyed with me under her sarcasm, and I don't blame her—I have broken the code, put bros before hos, and now she's unwittingly signed herself up for who knows how many days of my nervous bumbling around Peter. But in the last year, the two of us have attended countless parties where Harp wandered off to the back bedrooms with some boy, while

I sat awkwardly with my beer in the kitchens, panicking that she'd be hurt or Magdalened. So I don't plan to beat myself up over inviting Peter to come with us. And anyway, I'm jumpy. "I get it, but for now can you just keep an eye out?"

I'd like to point out to her that I don't have a chance. It's not like I'm not heartbroken over it. I've always been invisible to the boys I like; it's the superpower I never wanted but must somehow learn to cope with. Before the Rapture, it bothered me more, especially every time I looked at my happy parents, so dependent on each other, so in love after well over twenty years. They were barely older than me when they met, which means both must have had the ability to make themselves seen. I used to wonder how they'd done it, why they wouldn't teach me. But things are different now. I don't know how much time I have left. And while that's made me, in many ways, less meek than I was before, in this particular area it just makes me tired. I'm not going to spend the next four months moaning over the fact that Peter didn't remember me, didn't even remember not liking me. I'm not going to think about how much more of an adult he is than me: a literal adult, at eighteen, one who's been an orphan for so much longer, and so much less suddenly. In what world would such a boy look across a distance of a year, at a girl whose life has been marked by indecision and inaction, and want her?

The front door opens behind us and Peter stands in the doorway. He's wearing black-framed glasses, a soft gray T-shirt. He's got a backpack slung over his shoulders, a guitar case in one hand, and a grocery bag filled with the contents of his kitchen cabinets in the other. We've decided to leave right now, while the adrenaline is still pumping wildly through our veins, but I'm starting to realize all the holes in our plan, all the things I haven't thought through yet. For instance, food. For instance, gas. For instance, the fact that we don't know this person.

"Hey," Peter says, stepping out from the light above the door and towards us in the shadows. "I'm glad you guys are still here. I'm glad I didn't just hallucinate that whole thing."

I laugh. I want the witty rejoinder to just fall off my tongue, but all I can come up with is, "Yeah. Right?"

Harp stares at the guitar case in his hand, and I can practically hear her thoughts: *drum circle drum circle drum circle*. The three of us move quietly to the car. Peter told us his neighbors are mostly young Non-Believers who keep to themselves, but I'm still jumpy. The fates of Raj and Melodie Hopkirk still reverberate in my mind like bad dreams. We drive back to Pittsburgh in the unnerving dark, and Peter stays with the car while Harp and I run to her apartment to grab our stuff. There's a loud, small, drunk-seeming group of men at the end of the block; we can make out their formal Church attire from Harp's front door. They're moving away from us but still Harp whispers, "Fuck, fuck, *fuck*," under her breath, and I don't exhale until we're inside, the door shut firmly behind us.

"Peter's nice, right?" I say as we head upstairs. "I mean you can't pretend he's not nice."

"Very nice," Harp agrees. "I'm sure a lot of serial killers are nice, too."

"Is that really something you're worried about?"

She shrugs. "He's not being one hundred percent honest. I know you noticed it, too. He got jumpy when you asked him about the Church, about how he knows so much."

"It's a sore subject for everybody," I point out.

"Maybe. Or maybe he's deliberately hiding something from us."

I understand Harp's concerns in theory, but it seems impossible to me that Peter could be anything but good, that his apparent interest in helping us is anything but forthright. And also I'm annoyed—I've just done what Harp has for months been trying to get me to do: something wild. I would've expected a parade, not a lecture. "You're the one who wanted to go to him in the first place," I say. "You're the one who wanted to *use* his Church connections."

"That's before I knew we'd be hanging out in a car with him for who knows how long!" Harp exclaims. "If I'd known we were going to take a road trip and bring strange dudes along, I might have made a few calls."

"So make a few calls, then, if that's what's really bothering you."

We've reached Harp's apartment door. "Obviously that's not what's bothering me, Viv," she sighs, taking out her keys. "This night is just not what I expected. And I'm sorry, but I guess I'm wondering if this trip is such a good idea."

"Listen," I say, as she unlocks her door. "If you don't want to come, you don't have to. But I'm going, and I think Peter should, too. It's his father, after all. And anyway, we might . . ."

I trail off. Harp has turned on the light and we see that the floor of the living room is showered in broken glass. The large window facing the street is shattered. Harp stands still with her hand on the knob, looking around wildly for a person, but there's nobody there. I point at the center of the carpet. There's a large portion of red brick sitting there, with a white piece of paper tied around it with twine. I unwrap the note. DYKES, it says in hand-written scrawl, and just below it, in someone else's writing, SLUTS. Like the Believers who threw it couldn't come to a consensus. I hand the note to Harp and she reads it, then sinks to the ground. Her face has gone gray. She's thinking of Raj, I know. I'm thinking of him, too.

"California?" I say.

She looks up at me. "California," she whispers.

Harp packs a suitcase full of sequined blazers, vintage dresses, boots, hoodies, fascinators, and then sits on top of it, chugging from a large plastic bottle of water she's procured from the kitchen. I throw everything I own—my six or seven remaining outfits, my mess of a diary, my dead useless phone—into my own bag. When I drag it into the living room, I notice my parents' sledgehammer propped up in the corner—Harp and Dylan must have brought it here when they escaped Shadyside. I sling it over my shoulder.

"Are you sure you're going to need all that?" I ask Harp, nodding at her overstuffed bag.

"I've never been to California before," she says. "I don't know what they wear."

114

As we're leaving, I expect to her to pick up something of Raj's to bring with us. The apartment is filled with reminders that he left this place thinking he'd come back to it. A men's fashion magazine splayed over the arm of the sofa. A pair of his socks, curled up into a ball in the corner where he must have thrown them after he took them off, as I'd seen him do so many times before. There's a note on the refrigerator door from him: HARP. BUY. MILK. FORFUCKSSAKE. If Harp sees these things, she doesn't say anything. She lugs her suitcase and her water bottle to the front door, and stands there waiting until I follow. On the landing, she takes out her keys and fumbles ineffectually with the lock for a couple of seconds.

"Hey," I say, "breathe."

But she just laughs and tosses the keys down the stairwell. "I mean," she says, "it's not like we're coming back here."

Out on the street, Peter leans against the car with his arms folded, his expression as nervous as Harp's and mine must be. His eyes widen when he sees us approach.

"Wow," he says. "That's a good look for you."

I glance at Harp, whom I assume he must be talking to, then back at him. But he's staring right at me. His eyes move to my shoulder, and I remember the sledgehammer I'm carrying.

"Oh," I say, flustered. "It's just . . . in case. You know?"

"I know." Peter smiles as he opens the door to the backseat. "It just suits you. You should carry one around all the time."

I feel a buzz of excitement at the top of my spine as I heave Harp's and my suitcases into the trunk. Is he flirting with me? Harp takes the passenger seat, slipping a pair of sunglasses over her eyes despite the late hour, and I get behind the wheel. I lay the sledgehammer across the center console. I take the photographs of my parents out of my coat pocket and place them on the dashboard. I want to be able to glance down at them while I'm driving into the great unknown, and remember why I'm doing it.

I put the key in the ignition and hold it there. I realize I'm waiting for someone to say something, to commemorate our leaving. But it doesn't happen. We just sit in the car in silence for a second too long, and then I've turned the key and I'm driving away. One minute we're here and the next minute we're leaving. It's that simple.

By the time the sun rises on the trees lining the highway, we've crossed the border into Ohio. It's a beautiful May day, and I'm exhausted. I'd expected Harp to stew over her reservations in silence, but the minute we left Pennsylvania she began chattering mindlessly about nothing in particular, about what she wants for lunch and whether or not our route will take us past the Grand Canyon and where is the Grand Canyon, anyway. I'd expected her to be rude to Peter, but of course she starts to flirt with him. "Play us a song, Peter!" she coos, swatting his arm playfully. I drum my fingers on the steering wheel and try not to feel hurt. Harp likes boys and boys like Harp—this has been a fundamental truth about my world for nearly a year now.

Abruptly, several exits from Cleveland, Harp asks me to pull over.

"I'm tired," she whines. "I can't nap up here. I want to switch with Peter."

"I thought you were going to take the second shift," I say.

"I'm too tired. Do you want me to fall asleep at the wheel?"

I pull onto the shoulder and Harp flings the door open. She walks to a point several yards from the car and hunches over with her hands on her knees. Peter gets out and stares at her a moment, then leans down to talk to me.

"I can take over, if you want to get out and take care of her."

I shake my head. "I've got another hour in me. And anyway, she's fine."

Peter shrugs and gets in the passenger seat. Immediately I smell that clean boy smell of him, campfires and soap and cinnamon. After a moment, Harp gets back in the car, lying flat across the backseat and throwing an arm dramatically over her eyes. We've barely hit the speed limit again when we hear her gentle snores drifting up from the backseat.

"She's had a rough couple of weeks," I say apologetically.

"We all have. It's no big. She's funny."

"Well," I say. "She's also kind of a brat."

Peter laughs. "Kind of," he agrees. "But I can see why you're friends with her."

There's a beat of silence, and then before I can stop myself, I say, "You don't remember the first time we met, do you?" Inwardly, I groan. Peter brings out the girl in me who says out loud every thought that pops into her dumb

117

brain. I glance sideways and see he's staring at me, a confused half-smile on his face. I can tell that he's racking his mind to place me, and failing.

"It's okay," I say. "It was only for a minute, at the Rapture's Eve party. Harp threw that, and I helped a little, I guess. Did you not realize that?"

"No . . ." says Peter slowly. "I honestly didn't."

"We only talked for a minute. You asked what I believed in and I couldn't tell you. I said that thinking about the apocalypse was a downer. I was going for 'delightful ray of sunshine' more than 'cool, disinterested chick,' but either way, I'm pretty sure you thought I was an idiot."

Peter grimaces. "It kind of sounds like I was a dick to you."

"No," I assure him. "You just moved away pretty quickly. I would have done the same."

"I was having a bad night." He picks up Harp's water bottle from the cup holder and starts fiddling with the ripped wrapper. He takes a sip from it, pauses. "Before I got to that party my dad called me for the last time. He was . . . barely lucid. So I was a little jumpy. Plus, I'm not good at talking to new people. I've gotten a bit better at it in the last month, but only out of necessity—now everyone's new people. I'm sorry."

"Don't worry about it!" I say brightly. I feel bad for having taken us into this awkward territory, and like magic my gut instinct is to revert back to the cheery voice the Church of America magazines have implanted in me. "I'd completely forgotten about it until yesterday!"

"Are you sure? It kind of sounds like it's stuck with you."

"No! Of course not!" The magazine voice is a couple octaves higher than my own—more of a coo. The magazine voice speaks in exclamation points. "Don't be silly!"

"Well," says Peter, "I'm still sorry. Do you want to meet for the first time again?"

I'm so thrown by this that I'm snapped out of my false cheer. "What?"

"Like this. Ready?" He holds the water bottle like it's a plastic cup and gazes around the windshield, nodding his head a little to a beat I can't hear. He turns and looks at me, gives me a welcoming nod. "What's up," he says. "I'm Peter Ivey. I just got off the phone with my dad, who—in addition to being a total deadbeat—is psychotically focused on my impending eternal damnation. Cool party, though, right?"

I laugh. "Oh, hey," I say. "I'm Viv. I think this Rapture business is a complex and nuanced phenomenon, but probably this isn't the best environment for me to explain my many intelligent thoughts about it. If I had to sum it up flippantly, though, I'd say it's a downer."

"Reasonable," Peter allows. "Let's take a road trip together!"

He laughs then, a nervous happy laugh, and I laugh, too. I'm glad Harp's asleep. It's like being alone with him, like having another shot to show him the real me. After a moment, Peter picks up the photographs from the dashboard.

"Now that we're finally acquainted," he says, "can I know who these people are?"

"Oh! Those two on top, getting baptized, those are my parents."

I expect him to flip quickly to the next picture, but he stares hard at my father's face, and then my mother's, as if trying to memorize them. "And what's going on here?"

"I found that one at my grandparents' apartment. See that girl with the blue hair in the second row? That's my mother at, like, seventeen."

Peter laughs in appreciation. "Ah," he says. "So badassery runs in the family?"

I don't understand what he means at first. I'm shaking my head to correct him—no, I want to say, that's *my* mother—but then I realize that he knows what he's saying. The thought of it makes me blush a little, and it also makes me sad, because he doesn't know me yet. In the last few hours, he's gotten an impression of me that makes me seem much cooler than I actually am.

"Not really," I explain. "I guess it maybe seems that way since I spearheaded this crazy thing? But usually I'm the exact opposite of how I am right now."

"I find that hard to believe," Peter says.

"Trust me. The badass in this car is asleep in the backseat."

"Hey, man," says Peter after a moment. "I know I'm just going by what I'm seeing here, but what you're describing is a Viv I don't know yet. The Viv *I* know—and again, not an expert, because I only just officially met her within the last five minutes—is a sledgehammer-wielding badass. She's the only person I've met in the last two months who's said, 'I don't know what's going on here; let's find out.' You know it's a lot easier not to try, right? It's a lot easier to just curl up in a ball and let the world end."

"I know that," I say. "I have to fight the urge not to every minute."

Peter shrugs. "Well, it's pretty brave to fight it." We sit in silence a moment, and again I have to silence the magazine voice in my head (*"Examine his compliments for hidden meaning. Is he admiring your face, your body, the more unsavory parts of your person? Then he's a heathen who's trying to destroy your virtue! Is he complimenting your godliness and obedience? HUSBAND MATERIAL!"*). I try to believe what Peter's telling me. He clears his throat.

"Also," he continues, "maybe this is none of my business, but you should probably know that your badass friend back there? Is pretty much wasted right now." He holds up her water bottle. "This is full of vodka. Did you know?"

Chapter Ten

After another hour, we pull over and switch, and Peter drives us across the Indiana border. It's half past eight, and Harp's still asleep in the backseat. I haven't noticed her so much as stir since she lay down there, so now I am constantly turning in the passenger seat to put my index finger under her nose to make sure that she's breathing. What do I do with the revelation that my best friend has gotten drunk on the sly today? Part of me says it's just Harp being Harp, and another part of me is weirded out—as much as I realize that she and I are different people, it's strange sometimes to recognize the things Harp does that I never would. *She's having a hard time right now*, I think, the sixth or seventh time I turn with a vision in my head of her choking on her own vomit. But then I think, like Peter said—*we all are*.

Meanwhile, in the front seats, for those fifteen-minute periods when I can successfully shake all my anxiety about Harp away, Peter and I talk. We talk about books and movies and bands and his mom; we talk about what we'd be doing right now, if there'd never been any Pastor Beaton Frick. Peter can see himself at college in New York City, walking down a street of a million people, reading on the subway, lying in the grass in Central Park on a sunny day. I'd be getting ready for my junior prom right about now. I'd have gone dress-shopping with my mother, and split the cost of a limo with Lara and the others, and when Harp walked in, stumbling a little in high, high heels, wearing something slinky and slutty and sparkly, I'd have judged her. As penance for this alternate reality, I check Harp's breathing, brush her hair back from her face.

She wakes when we park at a rest stop near South Bend; she sits up in the back and wipes the drool from her cheek. "Fuck," she says, sounding dazed. "I need to pee."

Before I can say anything, she's out the door and on her way inside. While she was sleeping, Peter and I agreed we'd have to tread carefully from here to California. Believer culture seems to shift so quickly, from benign to terrifying and back again. We were planning, when Harp woke, to collaborate on personas to adopt in our interactions with strangers, characters that would lend us some level of protection—i.e., a Believer older brother shepherding his sinful sister and friend back into the fold. "It will be like a game," Peter had said cheerfully, and he almost made me believe it. But now here's Harp, running for the entrance without devoting even a shred of energy to wondering how much danger she faces.

Peter and I follow. "All these cars," he says, and I notice for the first time that the parking lot is full. "What is everyone doing here on a Monday morning?"

"I don't know," I say. "I can't tell if it makes me less nervous, or more."

Inside, there are lots of people milling about: standing in line for fast food and coffee, or sitting with their families around tiny Formica tables, sharing little bottles of energy drinks. They're dressed like normal people. They're talking and laughing and their children are chasing each other in circles. The women don't seem subservient to the men, and there might even be a gay couple here, happily sharing a soda—there are too many people to tell. Beside me, Peter exhales in relief, and we smile at each other, and I feel that rush of giddy energy I'm beginning to associate with proximity to him.

"You wanna grab some food and I'll get some water?" he suggests. Then he clarifies, "Some actual water."

We split up. Last night before we left her apartment, Harp and I divided all the cash she'd drained from her parents' checking account into different purses and pockets and rolled-up pairs of socks. We don't want to carry too much of it on ourselves at any given time, in case the worst-case scenario happens, and we're separated. Even so, right now I have $338 on my person, stuffed into different pockets of my jeans and my coat and in the lining of my bag. It feels like a lot, until I think about how long this money has to last us. The sign outside says the gas at this stop is $9.82 per gallon—I have to believe this is an error in order to not start crying in front of a rest stop burger joint. And even if we scrimp and save for the next few days as we make our way across the country, we will still need money to live on when we end up wherever we end up.

I'm standing in front of the BurgerTime register, examining the menu options for which items will cost the least money and/or provide maximum nourishment over the highest amount of hours—fried grilled chicken? Cheesy

124

cheeseburger salad?—when I hear a voice suddenly chirp, "Vivian? Vivian Apple?" I drop my eyes to the cashier. She's my age, lit up under the fluorescents, wearing a red-striped visor and a white polo shirt to match the BurgerTime logo. Her black curls are twisted into a tight bun at the top of her head. I open my mouth to tell her, sorry, she has the wrong person—but she can't have the wrong person, she's said my name. And even though I can't place her in my immediate memory, there's something familiar about her sad eyes, her pleasant smile. I smile back at her, a little quizzically.

"Jesus." I haven't heard Harp sidle up beside me, but she's there now, smelling vaguely of stale vodka and hand sanitizer. "Where the fuck are we? Why is Edie Trammell here?"

Of course it's Edie Trammell. Why wouldn't it be Edie Trammell?

Edie was in our class for years, a cheery presence on the yearbook staff, a decent softball player. But we haven't seen her since her parents pulled her and her younger brother out of public school when we were in the sixth or seventh grade. A rumor went around that they'd done it for religious reasons—they objected to the books we were reading in English and the evolution we were starting to learn in science. This was just before Frick's Rapture prediction, but as far as I know the Trammells weren't early Believers—they belonged to some other church, but believed what they believed with a fury. At least, that's the story that got spread around. It's funny now to think that we were ever confused by extreme action taken in the name of God. Now Edie's parents seem just like everyone else's. This is the first I've seen of her since she left school. The last I remember hearing about her was from Lara Cochran, right before she converted—she'd been working afternoons in a gelato place in our neighborhood, and she told me Edie had come in with a much older man whom she claimed was her fiancé. Lara had been scandalized at the time, had wondered aloud in her prudish way whether this meant that Edie Trammell was Not a Virgin. But to my mind, none of this explains what Edie is doing here, by the side of a highway in Indiana, flipping burgers.

"I knew it was you!" Edie sings. "Vivian Apple! And Harp Janda—I'd know you anywhere! I can't believe it!" She steps back from the cash register and comes around the counter to hug us, and that's when I notice that she's hugely pregnant. She leans across her swollen belly to hug me around my neck, and when she does the same to Harp, Harp looks at me over her shoulder with wide eyes.

"Edie," I say. I'm still not sure what the right way to acknowledge a woman's pregnancy is, even though I've watched a few girls my age go through it at this point. "It's so . . . weird to see you. How did you end up here?"

But she doesn't get a chance to answer, because a man with a walrus-y blonde moustache has stepped up to her place behind the counter. His hands are on his hips. "Edie? I'm sorry, am I interrupting your social hour?"

"Oh, gosh! Sorry, Mr. Knackstedt!" says Edie. "These are just some old friends of mine from home!"

"You know they don't get free ValuMeals just for knowing you, right?" Mr. Knackstedt eyes Harp and me—and then

Peter, who has wandered up behind us with a plastic bag full of water bottles—with total contempt.

Edie nods. "Of course, Mr. Knackstedt!" She turns to us, still smiling in genuine delight. "Okay, gals, I gotta get back. But I have a break in twenty minutes, so stick around, will you? And then we can catch up properly!" She plants a kiss on Harp's cheek and then on mine, and flits as daintily as a very pregnant girl can back to the register.

We can't handle the awkwardness of buying lunch from Edie, and we don't want her to get in trouble from her manager. We buy three slices of greasy pizza (I picture in my head our total sum of money trickling down, down, down), and I watch Harp wolf down hers while I eat mine in slow, deliberate bites, thinking if I get full enough now, I might not have to buy dinner later. After a while, Edie comes shuffling up to us, tossing her visor down on the table.

"Hoo boy," she says, dropping into the chair next to Peter. "What a day! I've been up since dawn, with no end in sight."

"Edie," I say, because I have dozens of questions to ask her and this one seems the most innocuous. "Is this place always so busy?"

"It has been, the last two weeks," she explains, "but that's only because most of these people come from a small town not too far off I-80. I guess the Church of America folks were making things a little unfriendly for all the Non-Believers—not saying that they meant to, of course— and so they're living out of their cars right now, and spending most of the day here."

"How'd you get knocked up?" Harp asks abruptly, through a mouthful of crust.

Edie blushes. I want to give Harp a warning look, but I resist my instinct to mother her, which I'm positive she hates. "You don't have to tell us anything you don't want to, Edie."

"No, that's alright! I don't mind telling the story to old friends—or even new ones!" Edie smiles at Peter and it doesn't seem worth reminding her that neither Harp nor I were ever really friends with her—she was just a girl we knew from school who was gone one day, who we never tried to find. "You might remember I started getting home-schooled towards the end of junior high? We belonged to a Baptist church at the time. Well, my parents still might—I don't know!" She smiles as she speaks, but her left knee bounces wildly with nerves. "What happened was that—gosh, over a year ago now—one of the youth pastors in our church converted to the Church of America. We stayed in touch after he left and he kept trying to convert me, too—he gave me a nice copy of the Book of Frick, and he had me read a chapter every night. And then we'd discuss the things we found. You know," she says, beginning to sound a little defensive, "I know how a lot of it must sound, to Non-Believers, but there's a lot of good in there, too. The Church is very big on fostering community, supporting one another, protecting one another. I don't think I'd have converted if it hadn't been for all that. But," Edie says, looking bashful, "it's true that I wouldn't have even considered it if I hadn't liked Christopher so much.

"He was older than me; he would've been twenty-three

just last week. He told me I had to be baptized secretly, so my parents wouldn't try to stand in the way of my being saved, and so I told them I was going to Jubilee. That's the big annual Christian Youth Festival over in Akron?" She looks at Harp and me like we'll know it, but we both just shake our heads. "I had to beg their permission to go, but finally they said okay. They put me on the bus to Akron," Edie's voice wavers, "and that was the last time I saw them."

"Did Christopher get Raptured?" Harp asks. Her voice is softer now, more sympathetic. It's hard not to feel bad for Edie when she's sitting in front of you, pregnant and on the verge of tears, wearing a BurgerTime nametag that says, in small print, *Ask me about our hot dog fries!*

"I'd imagine," Edie says. "But I haven't seen him in about six months."

Peter inhales a sharp, angry breath, just as I say, "Oh, Edie!"

Edie laughs a little nervously. "I'm making it sound so much worse than it was. He did marry me, after all! The Church pastor who baptized me performed the marriage ceremony right afterwards, so that we could—"

Harp raises an eyebrow.

"So that we could be together as God intended," Edie says. "Christopher said that being married would make my transgression against my parents moral in the eyes of the Church, which was important to me—I felt so bad about it. Well, anyway, then I was blessed with this pregnancy, and only two months after that was when he got transferred to a Church in St. Paul. I didn't mind leaving Pittsburgh. The only thing I minded was we didn't get a chance to say goodbye to my parents. I thought we'd be able to, but Christopher said there wasn't enough time. We were driving to St. Paul, see. Christopher wanted me to see the country; he wanted to visit other parishes as the Rapture approached. He was so excited. I was—" Edie stops a moment and swallows. She smiles apologetically at us. "I was not so excited. I was scared about what would happen to us, and to my parents, and all my Non-Believer friends. Christopher tried to be patient with me, but I think my doubts were too much for him. They might have been testing his own faith. I don't know. Anyway, one morning six months ago I woke up in a motel room just off the highway here, alone. He'd left me a note saying he'd had a vision that he was meant to continue on to St. Paul alone, but that it would be okay, because we'd see each other in heaven."

"Did he leave you any money?" asks Harp.

Edie shakes her head. "He paid for the motel room, though, so that was good. And anyway, I didn't think I'd need money—it was only four months until the Rapture. It never occurred to me that I wouldn't be saved, especially since I was carrying an extra soul." She rubs her pregnant belly mournfully. "So I walked back to this rest stop, and asked for a job, and waited. And the Rapture came and went and I'm still waiting."

"Where are you living?" I ask, afraid of the answer.

Sure enough, Edie waves a hand around, to indicate here. "There's a break room upstairs with a couch they let me use. I keep it real nice," she says to me, "so don't look at me like that. And I can eat at BurgerTime for free, any time I want. There are a lot of people out there who have

130

it worse than me, and I know it. Soon I'll have a little guy to keep me company, and hopefully we'll get swept up in that second Rapture they're talking about."

Suddenly Edie starts, and stands. She looks over at the BurgerTime station and gives a cheerful thumbs-up to Mr. Knackstedt, who pantomimes looking furiously at a watch.

"My break's over," she says. "Harp, Viv—it was so nice to see you. I'm sorry I've been chattering away this whole time and haven't heard a word about what you're up to. And—I never caught your name."

"Peter."

"Peter," Edie says, sighing. "Now that's a beautiful name. Peter, it was a pleasure to meet you. I hope I didn't bore you too much. God bless you three."

She picks up her visor from the table and waddles back to her register. Harp takes the pizza I've abandoned from my plate and bites into the rubbery cheese, stretching it into string.

"Well, *that* was depressing. Poor Edie. Fucking *dudes*, man. No offense," Harp says to Peter. "But fucking *dudes*."

I don't say anything. I feel sick to my stomach. It's hard to describe how I feel. I'm depressed by Edie's story, by this big rest stop filled with displaced people. But I'm angry, too. I'm suddenly so angry that I feel like I need to stand up, kick, punch, run for hours and hours. I am full of energy right now. I want to destroy the Church of America. I look at Peter and find he's looking back at me. He has no expression on his face but somehow I know exactly what he's thinking, and I know he's thinking what I'm thinking, even though I haven't even articulated it yet to myself. Edie needs our help.

"It's fine with me," he says quietly.

I look at Harp.

"What's fine with him?" she says, confused. And then it begins to dawn on her. "Wait. No. Please tell me no. Viv. That's not our job. It's not our responsibility. She's fine. Viv!" she calls out to me, as I stride across the rest stop towards the register behind which Edie stands, glowing, waiting. "The car's not that big!"

At first, Edie doesn't understand. "You want me to come with you to Mount Rushmore?" she echoes. "For fun? Are you visiting the Sacred Sites?"

"Not exactly," says Peter. He and I stand to the side of the register, trying to persuade her to join us in the gaps between customers. Harp is behind us, silent. Edie's exuberant friendliness has worn off just slightly, and she glances around nervously for her manager as we speak. "We're going to visit some friends of mine in the town there. Friends from . . . the internet."

Peter shrugs at me, clearly realizing how weird this sounds. But I have the same instinct to keep our true mission hidden from Edie. She's probably the most genuinely kind person in the entire ending world, but a Believer is a Believer.

"That sounds fun!" Edie says, after punching in an order from an elderly couple for two ValuMeals. "I think I'll stay here, though. I appreciate the offer, but I can't leave my job, not in my condition. Take a lot of pictures, though, and if you ever swing back this way . . ."

Mr. Knackstedt, standing at the stove in the back, puts a tray on the order window and peers out at us. His brow furrows. "Edie!" he shouts. "Do you know how many hungry teenagers would sell their grandmothers for this job? Look alive out there!"

"I'm sorry!" Edie says, taking the tray and handing it to the waiting customer. "I'm sorry! My friends were just leaving!"

I take a step forward. "Edie, listen—"

"That's *enough*," Mr. Knackstedt barks.

"We'll be gone in a second, dude!" Harp yells at him, taking a step forward so that we're shoulder-to-shoulder. "Chill!"

"Edie," I say. "We're going to Keystone to talk to the New Orphans. Do you know who they are? They're an organization dedicated to bringing down the Church. We need information about where Beaton Frick's private compound is located in California, and then we're driving there to see if we can found out what exactly happened on Rapture Day."

Edie's eyes widen. "Oh."

"We don't know what we're going to find," I tell her. "And if you'd rather not be a part of it, that's okay. We'll take you somewhere else, anywhere you want to go, but—"

"Do you think there's anything in the compound that would tell me why I was Left Behind?" she interrupts. "Because that's the thing I just can't quite figure out. Why, when I did everything right, did I get Left Behind?"

"I don't know," I say.

Edie is very still for a moment, and then she pulls the

apron over her head and sets it down on the counter. "We will get a chance to visit Mount Rushmore, though, won't we?" she says. "That seems like it would be something to see."

We cover the whole of Illinois that evening. Somewhere along the way, we crossed whatever line we had to cross, and gained another hour. Harp insists on driving, because she's not interested in sharing the backseat with Edie, who since we yanked her and her one small backpack of possessions out of South Bend has been alternately crying loudly in gratitude, praising Jesus, and trying to get updates on our old grade school classmates. She sits in the middle of the backseat, wedged between Peter's guitar and me, and for the first hour I keep saying, "You're welcome! No problem! We're happy to have you!" but then I pretend to sleep so I don't have to say it anymore. I don't regret it, though— Edie's so happy—and I know Harp doesn't really regret it either, because it means she got to scream, "FUCK YOU, OLD MAN," at Mr. Knackstedt as we walked out the door. I can see Peter's face in the rearview mirror through my partially closed eyes; he's got a smile on his face.

Peter and I had a moment in the rest stop where we read each other's minds—it felt so nice. I can't remember having that before. Part of the joy of being friends with Harp is that I never know what she's thinking. There must have been a time with my parents, before the conversion, before we set ourselves in constant opposition to each other, that they knew me well and I knew them, too. But if there was, it never felt as easy, as secret, as special as that.

134

We follow the signs for a cheap motel outside of Des Moines and decide to stay there for the night. Peter and Edie book the room, pretending to be a married couple—after they've gotten the keys, Edie whispers prayers under her breath asking forgiveness for the lie. Peter says he can't tell whether or not the proprietors are Believers. "There's a cross over the reception desk and the woman who checked us in had her shirt buttoned to the neck," he says, "but she also seemed as twitchy as we were." Either way, we won't risk letting them see Harp and me sneak in. If they're not Believers, they might charge us more; if they are, they might suspect an orgy.

There's only one bed in the room. We fight over who will take it—all of us suggest Edie, but Edie keeps claiming she's fine with the small couch in the corner. Peter insists that he take the couch, and Harp keeps saying he and I should take the bed, over and over, more sweetly innocent each time, until finally I have to pinch her. In the middle of the discussion, though, we all go quiet—I feel like something invisible has passed under my feet, trying to unbalance me. Am I about to pass out? The desk lamp edges forward on its own accord, and tips off the table with a crash.

"Um," says Harp, as Edie starts a solemn Hail Frick under her breath. "I don't want to sound like an idiot, but . . . was that a ghost?"

But Peter shakes his head, looking mystified. "That was an earthquake," he says.

Growing up in western Pennsylvania, I've never experienced an earthquake before. Mild as it was, it's an awful feeling—like the ground itself is turning against us. Now nobody wants to sleep alone; we turn off the lights and the four of us lie horizontally across the bed, over the covers. We have to maneuver so that Edie's not next to Peter—she is, as she reminds us, a married woman—or poised on the edge, where she might fall. I'm by the headboard and she's beside me; Harp's on the other side of Edie; Peter's at the foot of the bed. "This is snug, isn't it?" says Edie. I listen to her whispered prayers and then her steady breathing; I can hear Harp snoring as soon as her head hits the pillow. Peter, though—I can't tell if he's asleep or awake. I want to talk to him, to whisper jokes to him through the night. I want him to tell me stories about every single thing he's ever done or seen. But he's too far away. I take my right hand into my left and I squeeze it a couple times, pretending it's his. At the ceiling, I mouth, "Goodnight."

Chapter Eleven

When I wake the next morning, Edie is snuggled next to me, slumbering, angelic. Peter and Harp are gone. I sit up, and notice Harp standing at the window, biting her finger-nails and peering through the curtain. She waves for me to come over. I have to step over Peter, who at some point during the night must have rolled onto the floor and either not woken up or decided to stay there. I fight the instinct to sit on the edge of the bed to watch his sleeping face—the dark outline of his long eyelashes forming little half-moons, his lips parted, the dark scruff of an incoming beard. I walk to the window, and Harp pulls the curtain open further so I can see.

"It's a Christmas miracle," she whispers.

Outside, snow falls lightly onto the parking lot. I can see my grandparents' sedan where we left it, covered in a dusty layer of white. It's the middle of May. I don't know much about the weather patterns in Des Moines, but I have a feeling this isn't normal.

"I had to get up. She prays in her sleep." Harp jerks her head towards the bed to indicate Edie. "A girl can only take so many Our Fathers mumbled into her ear."

"Harp," I say, "do you want to talk about yesterday?"

She shrugs, watching the snow fall. "Not really. I know I'm being whiny, but Edie's harmless. And I am seriously glad she's not living in a BurgerTime supply closet anymore."

"Not that." I can't help getting a weird nervous smile on my face, because I'm trying to make this not sound like an intervention. "I meant your water bottle full of vodka."

Harp doesn't answer for a minute. She picks thoughtfully at her fingernail. "I was freaked out. Okay? The brick freaked me out. Going on this trip freaks me out."

"You could have said something. You could have drank all the vodka you wanted, but you could have given me a heads-up."

"I don't know, Viv," she sighs. "Historically, you're the one who curls up in the fetal position, while I charge ahead, getting shit done. I'm not saying it's not nice to let you take the reins, but it's embarrassing, too. It's embarrassing to feel scared and small and helpless."

"I know it is."

"I know you do. And don't get me wrong: I'm into Vivian 2.0. She's headstrong and willful. She's a delight. But I'm starting to wonder if it's going to be easier on our friendship if at least one of us is always coming apart at the seams."

I want to tell her that I don't believe this—I believe we both can and should be as strong as we can at any given moment. We'll get more done that way. But behind us, Peter and Edie have started stirring, and Harp looks about ready to pull down the jokey, deflective mask of insincerity once again. I take her hand.

"If you feel yourself coming apart at the seams, tell me, okay?"

"Don't worry, Viv," she says. "Next time I'll share the vodka."

When we've stuffed our clothes back in our suitcases and wiped the windshield clean of snow, we sit in the car with the heater on and examine our road map. The distance to Keystone doesn't seem that great—on the map I can pinch the drive between my thumb and forefinger. But Peter says it will take something like ten hours, and then who knows how much longer to actually find the New Orphans. He's the only one who has a phone that's still in service, so we use it to tweet Spencer G. "Where is the compound located?" Peter writes. "Heading to Keystone, need help." I hold the phone in my lap while Peter takes the first shift driving, but a response from the Orphans never comes.

We try to break the driving as equally as possible between Peter, Harp, and myself; Edie offers to take a shift, but also admits that she doesn't technically have a permit. It seems like an unnecessary risk to take, so as a result Edie gets extremely bored, and drives Harp crazy with her attempts to initiate sing-alongs. All the songs Edie knows are obscure Baptist hymns, so the rest of us can only sit and listen politely. For Harp, this involves a lot of sarcastic comments every time Edie launches into a new one—"Oh, gosh, you literally know a million of them! How neat!" and "Wow, this sure has a whole lot of verses, doesn't it?" When Edie runs out of songs, she asks us each to recount our particular Rapture stories, and the results are four dismal tales about waking up to find the world completely different, each of us to some degree abandoned. Harp tells Edie a succinct version of the story of Raj's death. She tells it in a bored, drawling voice, like she has no interest in Edie's sympathy, but she leaves out the fact that Raj was gay, which makes me think that she at least wants to avoid Edie's disdain. But as a result, Edie is confused.

"Did they kill him because he wasn't white?" she asks Harp.

"No," Harp says. Then she pauses. "I don't think so . . ."

"The Church is very white," says Edie. "I know I said it's a community, and they all care for and protect one another, but I have to say that didn't always feel true. I think some of the Church Elders might have given Christopher a hard time about marrying me. I can't prove that, but it was always just something I felt."

There's a long silence, and then Harp says gently, "They killed Raj because he was gay, Edie. Not because he wasn't white. I'm sure your family is safe."

"Oh!" Edie's clearly flustered, but relieved. I glance in the rearview mirror and watch her compose herself. After another long moment, she says, "That's a tragedy, what happened to your brother. It makes me sick that that could happen in the name of my God."

Harp smiles weakly at her. "Thanks, Edie."

After that, both Harp and Edie seem a little less manic. They pass out granola bars and grapes from Peter's bag of food, and in the late afternoon start up a new sing-along, focusing now on Christmas songs, as a nod to the snow

140

still making the roads slick outside the cozy car. All of us know Edie's religious carols, despite our varying levels of secularism, and Edie is game to learn the ones Harp teaches her—"Winter Wonderland," and "Grandma Got Run Over By a Reindeer," and "Baby, It's Cold Outside," which Edie is scandalized by. In the early evening, after Harp has driven her three hours and is dozing peacefully against Edie's shoulder, I take over. We've left the snow behind: now the landscape is huge and empty, just parched-looking grass on all sides, and above us the huge unending sky. The sun has just set and the clouds are a deep, aching blue. It looks like what I used to imagine heaven looked like, when I was a child and had been explained the concept by my parents. Even then, they subscribed to the idea of heaven, but from their description it seemed to me to be nothing more than a peaceful cloud palace populated by all my dead fish.

"What are you thinking about, Vivian Apple?" Peter asks. He's been sleeping behind his sunglasses in the passenger seat, his feet up on the dashboard, but now he sits up straight.

"Nothing." I say it automatically, then change my mind. "Actually, I was thinking that I feel very small, out here. Like I'm just a speck on this highway on this planet in this universe. It's really, weirdly comforting. Like, that must be how Believers feel all the time. That there's just so much more going on in the world than whatever's going on with me."

Peter says nothing. I glance away from the road and see that he's smiling. "What?"

"It's just, that came dangerously close to a statement of belief. Which, if I recall your claim correctly, I've been apparently trying to get out of you for two months."

"Peter," I say, very seriously. "I finally trust you enough to tell you: I believe in the sky."

As it gets darker, the wind picks up, until literal tumble-weeds blow across the road and we can feel the car shuddering slightly against the force of it. Peter asks me if I want him to take over, but I'm too afraid to slow the car down, to stop it. I imagine myself stepping out and getting blown away. Soon we can see nothing but what's directly lit by our headlights: a few feet of highway, and the red dust swirling above it. Suddenly an owl appears in the glow, struggling to flap its wings against the wind, and before I can react, we hear the thud of having killed it.

"What was that?" Harp yelps, waking up.

"A bird." Peter puts his hand on my arm.

"Yiiiiiiiiikes," she says. I hear her turning in her seat, like she's trying to see the owl's body on the road behind us, but we're already well past it, and anyway, it's too dark. "Cold-blooded, Viv. This really is a whole new you."

"Are you okay?" Peter asks me.

I nod, but my vision starts to blur with tears.

"Pull over," he says firmly. "We'll be okay, I promise. Pull over and let me drive."

The wind whips at my face as I step out of the car, but I can still walk solidly in front of the parked car. He meets me there halfway, and again, he puts his hand on my forearm. His skin is warm to the touch. He is looking down at me in the dark.

"Are you okay?" he asks again.

I shake my head. "I killed it."

"It happened too fast. It was an accident."

"I know. It just makes me sick that I killed it."

"Hey," says Peter, and he pulls me into a hug. I'm predisposed to be wowed by the warmth of his hug, seeing as I already consider his eyes the bluest, his face the kindest—but he holds onto me so tightly, for just the right amount of time, that I am immediately comforted, deep in my bones. When he pulls away, he tips his head backward and indicates for me to do the same. The sky is black and enormous and freckled all over with stars. "Look at how small we are, Viv. Look at how little of the universe we occupy."

I say nothing. I think, *I could love this boy. Someday soon, I could find myself loving him.*

When we get back in the car, Harp is snoring again and the wind has died down. Peter gets back on the highway, and I close my eyes, too. Then Edie leans forward, sticking her head between the front seats.

"I hope this doesn't embarrass you," she says, and I don't know at first which one of us she's talking to, "but you two seem to have a very beautiful, godly relationship. I'm so happy you've found each other."

I start to giggle nervously, and then even more so when I notice Peter isn't laughing at all. "We're not together, Edie," he says, and it sounds pleasant enough, and Edie makes some flustered apologies, but then none of us say anything for a long time. We just drive along silently, not together, in the dark.

We stop at a cheap motel in Keystone, and Peter books the room by himself, borrowing from Harp a handful of twenty-dollar bills. When he comes back to the car with the keys, his face is tense and nervous. He has us huddle behind the car as he carries the bags into the room by himself, and then one by one, with him keeping lookout, he sends us into the room.

"Maybe this wasn't such a good idea," he whispers, sliding the deadbolt behind him. He's turned on the desk lamp, and in its dim glow, we can see how grim the room is—dead flies swatted flat against the white walls, the sink in the bathroom dripping noisily, the huge and grue-some crucifix hanging over the bed. "The owners are not faking it. After I paid, I turned around and there was a line of obvious, real Believers behind me. They're all here for Mount Rushmore, obviously. And they seem a little testy."

"How is this possibly New Orphans headquarters?" Harp hisses. "How do they manage it, if it's crawling with Believers?"

"I don't know," says Peter. "I didn't realize how bad it was. Either my information was wrong when I got it, or it's wrong now."

I feel a tension headache crawl up between my eyes. Edie sits on the edge of the damp-smelling bed and hugs her huge stomach; she begins to cry as silently as she can.

"I'm sorry," she whimpers. "It's probably the hormones, but I'm just so *hungry*."

"It's okay, Edie," says Peter. "I'll go out and bring us back some food."

"I'll go with you," I volunteer.

"That's okay, Viv. You've had a rough night. Harp, do you want to?"

But Harp sinks down next to Edie on the bed. I notice she's brought her slowly depleting supply of vodka in with her. Her eyes are wide as she shakes her head. "I can't," she whispers.

Peter and I dress in the most conservative outfits we can put together out of our four suitcases. I have a shirt I can button to the collar, and Edie gives me a long black skirt to wear. Peter puts on a tie, and shaves. Just before we leave, Edie clears her throat and then hands me a small gold band.

"Oh, Edie," I say. "That's alright. We'll pretend to be brother and sister."

"You'll be safer if you don't go out there as a single woman." She puts the ring in my hand and folds my fingers over it. "Just bring it back to me, okay?"

We turn off the light before we leave so that nobody appears to be in the room. Harp and Edie are happier to wait for us in the dark than attempt to see what it's like out here. When we reach the street, Peter points to a restaurant in the distance—La Casa de Millard Fillmore: Mexican Done American Style—and we head there. Peter walks in short, staccato steps, and keeps turning to look at me.

"What do we do?" he says. "What do you think I should do? Should I hold your hand?"

"No. They never hold hands. You just walk and I stay a step or two behind you."

"Right." Peter continues to walk, turning his head every few feet to assure himself that I'm still in his peripheral vision.

It would be one thing if we were in Keystone pre-Rapture, when I thought Believers to be maybe a little unhinged, but fundamentally not too unlike my own parents—capable, I would have thought then, of changing their minds. But the Believers swarming around us now, eyeing one another suspiciously and muttering tersely and practically inaudibly to their wives and companions—these people have a dangerous sort of glint in their eye. The Believers before had a smugness about them, a sureness that they'd go to heaven and the rest of us wouldn't; these Believers aren't quite so sure, and that makes them angry and violent and desperate. I do my best to keep my eyes on the ground, off their faces, because I am supposed to be playing the part of subservient female, and because to look at them scares me. Because I can feel them leering at me—just subtly enough to not subvert the Book of Frick's teachings (*"Let not your attention be swayed by your neighbor's wife, though she be a temptress and the devil himself"*), but a second too long for me not to notice. It's amazing to see up close the difference between how they treat Peter and how they treat me—for him it's a sober nod, a muttered greeting of "Brother"; for me it's a scrutinizing gaze that makes me feel exposed and dirtied and ashamed.

Peter orders quickly at La Casa de Millard, and not much: the prices are way high, in that this is a tourist trap, and it costs us $50 to get two chicken burritos and a small plastic box of nachos to share. But I can tell what he's thinking—if we order more food than two people can eat, will they wonder about us? Will they follow us back to the room? How well can we play the role of young married Believers?

I carry the bag of food as we walk back down the street to the motel. Peter won't let me stay too far behind; he keeps slowing his step so that we're practically in sync.

"You're being too courteous," I murmur to him. "You have to walk more like you don't give a damn about me."

"Well, that makes me sick," Peter mutters back. "I can't do that."

"You have to," I say. "It's what's keeping us safe."

This convinces him, and he bolts ahead a bit, as I scurry to stay within my rightful place. It would feel like a flirtatious game, if there weren't couples all around us doing the same thing, worried to slip out of their roles lest they be judged by other Believers or God. When we turn down the side street, within sight of the motel, Peter slows down again. He looks around to make sure no one's watching, then grabs and squeezes my hand.

"Vivian Apple," he says with satisfaction. "And she claims she's not badass."

I keep my head down, because I'm blushing, thinking, *You bring it out in me. You make me brave.* And then suddenly my heart thumps in my chest, and I know I'm about to do something even braver, something the old Vivian would have never dared. I want to tell Peter how much I like him, that I've liked him from the moment I saw him at the Rapture's Eve party. I can hear my own voice in my head, telling him: I know I'm seventeen, and my bangs are too long, and I don't yet know how to carry my own arms; I know it's the end of the world. But I would be his if he wanted me; I would be so happy to be his. We're nearing the motel, and I'm running out of time to say it. But I only have to be brave. I take a breath, and—

"Viv," Peter says, almost breathlessly, again somehow reading my mind. "I have to say something I don't want to say, but it would be unfair not to say it: I can't really imagine . . . *being* with anyone right now. I think there's just too much going on, in our lives, in the world, and I think that if . . . any two people, per se, thought it would be a good time to be with each other, they'd be wrong. I think they'd be doing each other a disservice. Does that make sense?"

"Yes," I say. *No.*

"It's all happening so quickly," he says. "Too quickly. And there's just not enough guaranteed time left to . . . We could all be dead in September. It would be bad enough to be dead in September, but to have to watch someone I . . . That's why I don't think it's fair."

"Of course it isn't," I say. "I agree."

"You do?"

"Absolutely."

"Okay." We're standing at the door of our motel room, and all I want to do is get inside. I want to sit and share a burrito with Harp, and get out from under the buzzing white bulb hanging in the motel corridor, which must be lighting up my face in all its mortification. I wish more than anything at this moment that a trap door would open in the concrete and the earth would swallow me whole. Peter has a worried look on his face as he gazes down at me. I need to get inside before I start crying at it. "It doesn't make me happy," he says softly, "to have to say that."

I use Harp's trick, and summon the stone mask of complete indifference. I shrug. "It doesn't make me feel anything. Can we go inside now?"

Chapter Twelve

In the morning, Peter returns our keys in the motel lobby and grabs a map of Keystone for the four of us to study. It's a small town with only three main streets. Peter's plan is that we'll dress in our Believer garb and circle Keystone for a half hour at most, looking for any sign that could suggest a nearby New Orphans compound. At the end of that time, if we've found nothing, we leave. Harp has been using Peter's phone all night to tweet at Spencer G. with increasing desperation—"WE'RE IN KEYSTONE WHERE U AT, SPENCER"—but has gotten nothing in reply, although his account is active and retweeting posts by New Orphans in other cities. I don't say it out loud to anyone, but I no longer expect to find them here, in the middle of what's basically Believer City. Maybe they were here once, but they're gone now. Which means we'll be running blind once we hit California. The insanity of our plan is beginning to sink in, and it's taking all the strength I have not to lock myself in the bathroom with Harp's vodka.

"The main thing is getting out of here safely," Peter says, looking right at me like he can hear my thoughts. "As long as we can get out of here safely, we can make our way to California and figure it out from there."

Harp and Edie murmur their agreement while I stare out the motel window, like a brat, pretending Peter doesn't exist. This morning when he was in the shower, I hurriedly whispered to Harp what he said to me last night, and she rolled her eyes at my despair.

"Girl, please. Don't you realize what that means? You're already in. You just have to make him want it."

She suggested further indifference, aloofness, as much distance I can manage in a small four-door sedan. And at the moment, I'm just embarrassed enough to try it. If I pretend to be less than interested, I can avoid the looks I keep noticing Peter give me, which read to me to be full of humiliating sympathy and guilt.

Outside, South Dakota is hot and dry, as far from yesterday's snow as I could possibly imagine. We leave the motel parking lot and get onto the main road, and when I see Casa de Millard in the distance I feel a little twinge of pain at the sight of it, at the thought that I'd just been about to declare how I felt when Peter declared his necessary non-interest. The rational part of me tells me to relax: not to work myself up into a state over a boy I've really only known for a couple of days now. But I can't help it—the looming apocalypse heightens every emotion, makes attraction more powerful and rejection more dire. Peter might've been my first shot at a boy who really saw me, and liked what he saw—and now it feels like he might be my last shot, as well.

In the last three years Keystone has been majorly revamped. Where once it must have been a Mount Rushmore tourist trap, it is now essentially a Church of

America playground. The buildings along Route 16-A are polished red wood, meant to resemble the Old West of cartoons and Disneyland. But every sign features some nonsensical marriage between patriotism and Belief: The All-American Christian Family Restaurant, Fine Holy Leather Goods (WE SELL AMERICAN FLAG COWBOY BOOTS AND ALSO WWJD BRACELETS), Li'l Ronnie Reagan's Heavenly Jelly Beans. We creep down the increasingly Believer-friendly main road, and I feel tears like pinpricks gathering at the back of my throat. I don't know why I'm so disappointed—it was always a long shot—but it would have been nice to see some sign of the New Orphans out here. It would have meant we aren't alone.

Suddenly Peter, in the front seat, points and says, "There!"

At the corner of the intersection is a tan brick building with a sloping red roof and no visible crosses or flags. It's surrounded by a tall, menacing barbed-wire fence, with two armed guards in full riot gear standing in a small opening. There's a large makeshift white wood sign on the grass on the front lawn, and on it someone has spray-painted WE ARE THE NEW ORPHANS in red. Harp sighs.

"I swear to you," she says, "that if I hear so much as one *beat* of a drum, I am going to crack some skulls. I mean that literally," she clarifies, turning to Edie. "Not figuratively. I'm going to straight-up murder some hippies."

To say this was not what we were expecting would be an understatement. I'd imagined the New Orphans headquarters to be a large green farm out in the country, populated with long-haired women kneading dough in the kitchens.

Failing that, I thought we'd find just some powerless kid like us, in a basement. The reality is so much more impressive than either of those possibilities. It's hard to tell what the building used to be, but Spencer G. and his cohort have taken absolute possession of it, and it sticks out in Keystone boldly and unapologetically, a direct challenge. At the sight of it, I feel this soaring sensation in my chest, a feeling I haven't felt in days, weeks, months. It's hope. For this place to exist in the midst of a Church of America stronghold means that Spencer G. must be more powerful than any of us would have imagined.

We park around the corner and try to de-Believer our outfits as best as we possibly can—we imagine the guards wouldn't take kindly to being approached by four apparent Church-goers. Only Edie stays in what she's wearing, proclaiming to be comfortable. We walk up to the guards with our hands in the air, and they just watch us from behind their reflective sunglasses with expressions we can't read.

"Hey," says Peter, doing what seems to me to be not a particularly good job of acting casual in the face of a huge automatic weapon. "Is there any chance of us getting in there? We're not dues-paying members, or anything, but we don't mean any harm. We're not like a secret cell of Church terrorists or anything, ha ha ha."

Harp groans softly behind me. I know I'm supposed to be acting indifferent to him, and that even if I wasn't, I should be slightly concerned about the terrible job he's doing of ensuring our safety right now, but I can't help it: I find his nerves adorable. One of the guards sighs. The other, his face dry and cracked with sunburn, seems crankier. He doesn't speak, but his upper lip curls up into a sneer, and he shifts his gun from one hip to another, causing us all to flinch.

"We have money?" Harp says. I glance back at her and she shrugs at me, her hands still lifted in the air. "I mean, we have some money, if that what it takes to get in."

I think about what I have in my pockets—a little over $150, and Harp probably doesn't have much more than that. I don't know if this will be enough to bribe the guards. If it's not enough, what do we do? How much of our money can we afford to give them?

"Vince?" says a voice behind the guard, and he shifts to reveal two people—a boy and a girl of indeterminate age who are standing behind the fence, peering out at us with interest. "We wondered who you were talking to."

"They say they're *not* terrorists," Vince replies, and he and the other guard laugh then, like they've been waiting to laugh the whole time. Peter makes a face.

The girl steps between the two guards. She's in her late teens and has a sun-bleached, beach-y look—long, honey-colored hair that hangs down her back, freckled shoulders, flip-flops. She holds an armful of fresh-picked flowers. The boy is a little younger; his sleek black hair is shaggy over his ears, and he wears a green hoodie and no shoes. He carries a basket of skimpy-looking radishes, still speckled with soil. He indicates for us to lower our arms and move closer. When we do, an unmistakable scent of weed hits our noses.

"Welcome," he says. "Are you Orphans?"

Harp, Peter, and I nod uncertainly, not sure whether he means orphans with an upper- or a lower-case "o". "Are you Spencer G.?" Peter asks.

The boy looks back at the girl and both of them laugh at this. Peter gives me a puzzled look, and I quickly turn away.

"Sorry, friend," the boy says. "My name is actually Gallifrey. Around here, it's a great honor to be mistaken for Spencer G. But also, he's not known as Spencer G. anymore. Please, come in; let us show you around."

The four of us move past the guards, who immediately lose interest in us and stare again into the heart of Keystone. It's clear that these men are neither Believers nor Orphans—they must be free agents who take their guns to wherever they receive a steady paycheck. We follow Gallifrey and the girl across the dusty front lawn, towards the building's entrance.

"Sorry," says Harp. "Did you say your name is Gallifrey?"

"It's not my given name," Gallifrey explains. "It's a recent New Orphans initiative. Lacking parents, we must rebuild ourselves as new and complete individuals, rather than part of a family unit. So we've all disposed with the names we were given, and chosen words that better describe the people we've raised ourselves to be. I chose 'Gallifrey,' which to me represents exploration. Have you ever seen *Doctor Who*?"

Harp shakes her head. Gallifrey looks disappointed.

"Well," he says. "It's a reference to that."

We step inside. The building is cool with air-conditioning, and dark—the windows of the front room have been boarded up. Gallifrey and the girl, whose chosen name turns out to be Daisy, explain that we're in what was once a presidential wax museum, a popular tourist spot for families who'd come all the way to Mount Rushmore only to find that after twenty minutes of staring at those four stone faces, you'd run out of things to do. As the town turned Believer, the owners abandoned the building, and Spencer G., a local who was growing more and more disturbed by his parents' behavior, took it over as a hideaway and head-quarters. This room we're standing in was once the gift shop, but is now a communal meal room, with a small kitchen to one side, and a long table where three New Orphans now sit, waving at us, eating cereal. Gallifrey and Daisy take us on a tour of the building—the old diorama-like exhibits have been renovated into bedrooms, but their painted presidential backgrounds remain, so that we see various replicas of the Oval Office, but with beds where the desks should be, and New Orphans lounging around in them. Some are asleep; some are reading books or knitting; some are curled up with members of the opposite or same sex, in various states of undress. We see maybe thirty Orphans in all, and they all look alarmingly happy.

"Will you be staying long?" Daisy asks.

"We just came to talk to Spencer," I say. "I mean, the guy that used to be Spencer."

Gallifrey points to an empty exhibit just down the hall from us—two big empty unmade beds lit up under the museum lighting. "This used to be the Reagan-meets-Gorbachev room," he explains, "but it's yours now, if you want it."

I shake my head, glance at my friends for backup. "No, that's okay, thank you. We'd really just like to talk to him and move on."

"You have to stay for dinner," Daisy insists. "Goliath will want you to stay for dinner."

I stare at Daisy a moment, at her pretty, imploring face. I wonder if I've heard her wrong.

"Goliath?" Peter echoes.

Gallifrey beams. "That's the name of our leader. The man you knew as Spencer G. We'll take you to him now, but Daisy's right—he's going to want you to stay for dinner."

They lead us further down the hallway, which takes a sudden horseshoe curve and leads back, I see, into the communal room from which we just came. On the way, Edie takes my hand and squeezes. When I look back at her, I see everything I'm feeling expressed on her face. She looks terrified, hopeful, dazzled. At the end of this hallway is a boy so powerful, so fearless, that he's set up shop in the middle of a Sacred Site and renamed himself Goliath. At the end of this hallway lie answers, a path to California. My mother and my father. It doesn't seem so impossible now. I feel as I did when I first stumbled upon the New Orphans in New York, before Harp and Peter recounted their disappointments. I feel, for the first time, like this trip has not been the most needless and foolish and dangerous enterprise four teenagers have ever undertaken. When Gallifrey and Daisy reach the end of the hallway, they turn to us, smiling.

"Goliath," Daisy says to whomever is sitting inside the last exhibit, who we can't see yet. "We'd like to present to you some new New Orphans."

The four of us catch up. Unlike the rest of the Oval Offices we've passed in the museum, this last has not been renovated into the bedroom. Its centerpiece is still a huge, cherry-wood desk, bearing the presidential seal. The boy they call Goliath sits behind it, typing furiously at a laptop, but he stands when we're assembled before him. Goliath is tall—taller than Gallifrey and Peter both—and broad-shouldered, with high cheekbones and golden-blonde curls that fall just past his ears. He looks like the star of a movie about a really handsome surfer.

"Brothers," he says. "Sisters. Orphans. Welcome."

Chapter Thirteen

Goliath grins around at us with his perfectly straight teeth. He reaches out and takes my right hand, clasps it between his two thick ones. He is at most eighteen, yet he handles this interaction with the confidence and geniality of a middle-aged CEO. He's dressed as though he's about to attend a board meeting, in pinstripe suit pants and a red tie, his white sleeves rolled up. None of us know what to say to him. He is ridiculously good-looking.

"I'm Vivian," I begin. "This is Harp, and Peter, and Edie. We—"

"Vivian," says Goliath, looking into my eyes. Then he takes a step to Harp, and grasps her hand as he has just done mine. "Harp."

Harp giggles, bats her dark eyelashes at him. He's Harp's type exactly—she always goes for all-American boys with confidence to spare; it's what had me so worried for months that she'd be Magdalened. Goliath must note her interest, because he gazes in her eyes an extra second before moving on to greet Peter and Edie. When he finishes, he sits behind his desk, and leans back in his chair with his feet propped up.

"Please," he says, waving his hand in our general direction. "Take a seat."

There are no chairs in the immediate vicinity. Gallifrey

and Daisy scramble into the common room to get us some. We edge slightly closer to Goliath's desk.

"We came here to see if you could give us some information," Peter says.

"I can try!" Goliath says pleasantly.

"We were—we're heading to California," continues Peter. "We'd heard . . . well, we know for a fact that at one point, Frick had a personal compound there, north of San Francisco." He waits a moment, but Goliath just watches him. "We want to go there and see what we can find. Maybe see if anyone there was Left Behind. Anyone important."

The head of the New Orphans makes a steeple of his fingers and peers at us from behind it. Meanwhile, Gallifrey and Daisy have set up a half-moon of folding chairs. Goliath waits until we've sat, and then he waves his hand, dismissing Gallifrey and Daisy from the three-walled room. He stands and walks over to a small cart, on which sit a few half-empty bottles of alcohol that I can only assume he procured from his parents' liquor cabinet after they were Raptured—Scotch, amaretto, Bristol Cream. Goliath pours some amaretto into a glass, and then mixes it with some orange Gatorade. Peter catches my eye and makes a face.

"I'm sorry, gang," says Goliath, turning to us, "does anyone want anything to drink?"

We all decline except for Harp, who takes an amaretto-and-Gatorade and drinks it down like water. Goliath leans against his desk and regards us again. I have an urgent, anticipatory feeling, like he's about to tell us something big, something we'll really be able to use.

"Peter, I'd be interested to hear who confirmed the California compound to you," he says finally. "Only if you're willing to reveal your sources, obviously."

We look to Peter. "My father was Believer for many, many years," is all he says.

"A lot of people's parents were Believers," Goliath replies. "But I've never heard any of them state with confidence that Frick had any connection to California."

Peter stares ahead and doesn't elaborate. Goliath raises an eyebrow, but doesn't push any further. "Well, to tell you the truth, I've heard whispers. A few tweets coming out of the San Jose airport claiming the simultaneous arrivals of small groups of Believers over the last year. One flight attendant told me he had at least a dozen of them on Rapture's Eve, but when we tried to get more information out of him, he played dumb—a Second Boater. Then I had a barber over in Point Reyes Station DM me to say he cut Frick's hair every month and a half for the last twenty years, so he doesn't understand why Frick says he lives in Florida."

Peter takes out a small notebook. "Point Reyes Station, you said?"

"Yeah," Goliath says, frowning at the sight of Peter jotting this down. "But again, Peter—nothing confirmed there. For months, the rumors were he was living in some mansion in a forest in California. Someone gave me the name of a road once . . . I can't remember it. King Arthur Lane? But anyway, it's all myth and legend. Right before Rapture Day, the live feed from the Church of America website showed Frick praying, constantly, at his home in Florida."

"I mean," I say as he pauses to let this sink in, "is it

possible the feed was, you know, lying? That they were trying to bait and switch us? If we think Frick's in Florida before the Rapture, and then after the Rapture he isn't . . ."

"Then surely he must have been Raptured," Peter finishes for me.

"I guess it's *possible*, Vivian," Goliath allows, sounding dubious. "But like I said—they were always just whispers. No one ever came forward with any proof that Frick spent any significant time there. The truth is, you get all kinds of nutty theories thrown at you when you run a network as extensive as this one." He winks at Harp. "Once I got a really long, involved e-mail claiming that Frick was actually the Pope, and the whole thing was a scheme to bring more people into the Catholic church. To me, that claim and the one you're making about California hold the same amount of water. The only proof I've got is that someone's saying it."

"Have you ever considered sending people out there?" Peter asks. "Recruiting your San Francisco chapter to try to track Frick down?"

Goliath shakes his head, smiles at Peter a little sadly. "Peter, I'll be honest with you, I haven't. And I'll tell you why. Maybe at first, the New Orphans were about trying to take down the Church. I had a lot of former Believers giving me all the dirt they could give on their local pastors. Lots of weird sex shit going down. I mean, I was the one who started the hashtag #beatonfrickisadipshit, which was trending worldwide for a week back in February, so trust me when I tell you that I feel you on that nihilistic impulse. Back then, I was mad. But the more people who contacted me, kids our age, whose parents were about to trade them in for eternal splendor, I began to realize we were dealing with something different than just an Us vs. Them scenario. We're trying to rebuild here, guys. The Church of America is in the past. We're the future. Do you hear what I'm saying?"

"But they *aren't* in the past," says Peter. "They're still active. It feels like there are more people in the Church now than there ever were."

"It does feel that way out there, Pete," Goliath nods. "I definitely agree. But I think if you spend a little time with us, you'll begin to find that the Church no longer feels like a concern. We have a great community here. We feed each other, nurse each other. We provide emotional, spiritual, and—sometimes, if necessary—financial support. I know some other chapters of the New Orphans have destructive goals in mind—the New York one was planning a violent takeover of the NASDAQ building before the hurricane, and earlier this week, the Chicago New Orphans took the mayor's family hostage in an effort to get the Church of America megastores in the area permanently shut down. It didn't work out; the mayor's wife and three New Orphans were killed in the process—" Goliath stops, bows his head briefly as if in prayer. "I have never been a violence guy. I have never called for that. I've said from the beginning, we can change this thing peacefully. We're young; we're smart— we can figure out a way. Here in Keystone, we're content to move on. Put the Church behind us. Love one another. See, this community I've created? It would've never been possible without the Church. You know? I'm saying that in its own way, the Church created *me*. And I know a lot of people around these parts who are grateful for that. So let's not focus on destroying. Let's focus on building something, together."

What he's describing sounds impossible. You'd only have to take a few steps beyond the fence and into the Believer mecca outside to know that it is. But Goliath's confidence is weirdly magnetic. His focus on us now is so razor-sharp, so friendly and warm, that I feel like he may be on to something—like all it would take to change the world is a bunch of young, smart people who care about it. Goliath stands then, and claps his hands together

"Did Gallifrey and Daisy give you the full tour? Why don't we take a walk around?"

Goliath takes us on another loop around the building, this time introducing us to each individual New Orphan, all of whom scramble out of bed, put down the dishes they're washing, their laptops, their video games, to talk to us. They tell us stories, not unlike our own, of mothers and fathers and friends disappearing into the ether, of having nowhere to go. They love it here. They love Goliath. Always their stories end with declarations of where they would be without him and the New Orphans—lost, they proclaim. Dead. There are young children, who hug Goliath around the knees as he approaches like he's a favorite uncle. Goliath takes us out back, where once there was a mini-golf course but now there is a reasonably functioning greenhouse and a small, struggling garden. "Any green thumbs among you guys?" he asks us, and when Edie tentatively raises her hand, he pounces excitedly, pointing out the various crops they're trying to harvest in the dry Dakotan soil, asking her advice. She seems flustered, but pleased.

Everyone here is happy, and—they all assure us—safe. The fence and the guards are nothing but a precaution. The Believers who swarm to Keystone with increasing frequency are not interested in sacrificing rebellious teenagers to get to heaven; they're on expensive vacations with their families, trying to get the Sacred Sites checked off before the next Rapture comes. Once, Goliath remembers, a few Believer dudes got wasted at the All-American Christian Family Restaurant, and came over to the commune looking for a fight, but almost immediately they got sick at the feet of the guards, and crawled back shamefaced to their hotels. Otherwise, the Believers barely acknowledge that the New Orphans are here.

By the end of the tour, I can feel it all around me—the New Orphans have managed to turn an abandoned presidential wax museum into a real, vibrant home. I'm suddenly achy with a longing I've been burying for months. All I want is to stay still in a single place for a while, and feel like I belong.

When Goliath says, "Will you stay with us tonight?" and Harp looks at me with pleading, mischievous eyes, I don't look to Peter for his assent. I tell him yes, and we do.

I think it will be a night, and then I think maybe it will be two. I think we'll stay just through the weekend, and then we've been in Keystone for three weeks, with no sign of leaving. It's easy to be there, to no longer feel like we're on the run, like we're racing against a clock. It feels like what I imagine a college dorm must feel like, when you first get there and are settling in. All of us are on our own but for each other. I can spend every second of the day surrounded, and not get tired of them. In the mornings, we eat breakfast together, then split up to perform various delegated chores. Afternoons, we're left to our own devices, until the evening, when we gather together in the community room to make dinner together. Goliath always makes a little speech before we eat—like grace, but more rehearsed. I'm grateful to him for this place, but sometimes it's a little hard to take him seriously. At a certain point he begins to seem like one of those ambitious kids I went to high school with, back when ambitions were something worth having. I watch him gaze around, at the ecstatic nightly after-dinner parties that everyone but the very young kids and Edie attend, and imagine he's seeing this community he's built through the eyes of the admissions board at Yale.

But maybe I'm just jealous. On our first night, after a few shots each from somebody's Raptured dad's tequila, he and Harp began to make out sloppily against a wall in what used to be the Unelected Presidents exhibit. They went at it so hard that Harp didn't even notice or care when the drum circle started up shortly thereafter. It feels like they've been attached at the mouth ever since. Every night, after she thinks I'm already asleep, Harp slips out of the bed we share in the Gorbachev exhibit, and wanders off to wherever Goliath's bedroom is.

"Do you call him Goliath when you guys are having sex?" I ask her one morning while we're brushing our teeth.

"I don't know what you're talking about," Harp sniffs. I suspect she's trying to keep their hook-ups as private as she can, that she likes the shroud of mystery about him. The Orphans don't know where he sleeps, have never seen him wear anything but a suit, know little about who he was before he was Goliath. I get the sense she likes having a secret to keep, that she still feels the need to play the rebellious child around me.

Edie, meanwhile, is having a much better time than I would have expected. Despite the constant partying and everyone's giddy adoption of Woodstock-level free love principles, she seems to get happier by the day. She watches after the younger New Orphans, makes sure they're eating vegetables, reads them the few storybooks they've packed, and when they run out of those, she writes new ones. Every night, she'll come out into the community room, sleepy-eyed and huge in her striped pajamas, and sweetly ask us to turn the music down. The first time she did, I worried about the New Orphans turning on her, resenting her for the maternal pall she casts, but they all did as they were asked, anxious to please her. One of the guys here, Estefan, turns out to be a registered nurse from Wyoming, and he's at Edie's side day in and day out. He's assured her when it comes time for her to give birth, he'll be there to take care of her. Edie glows here, happy and useful and beloved by all.

And if Peter is anxious to get back on the road, he doesn't show it. He proves himself to be an excellent cook, contributing to every meal—he makes sweet potato chili, pumpkin bread, pizza dough, tacos; one night he makes a blueberry pie from scratch. In the late afternoons, he sits out back with Gallifrey and the others, who are trying to teach themselves basic carpentry from YouTube videos, but usually just end up whittling small animals out of firewood. Goliath is the New Orphans heartthrob, but there's a small group of girls, not unlike me in their shy, desperate awkwardness, who flock to Peter when he's strumming his guitar in the Andrew Jackson exhibit down the hall, who sit around and worry each time he volunteers to leave the compound for supplies. Our first night, as Harp made out with Goliath at the party, Peter slipped in beside me at the table where I sat with Gallifrey and the others, and handed me a beer.

"You know," he said into my ear, "I really think at some point someone should tell him that Goliath *dies* at the end."

I said nothing. The warmth of his breath on my ear made my whole body seize up with desire, but I was taking Harp's advice and saying nothing. I smiled weakly and sipped.

"Viv," Peter said then. "Are you upset with me?"

I looked at him. He looked like he was genuinely hurt, like I had hurt him.

"Of course not." I should have apologized; I could have just explained: it's hard to be close to someone I like, who I know likes me, and not be able to have him, for reasons dramatically noble. But it was, easier, of course, to say nothing. The nearby Orphans got louder then—they'd been having a conversation about science-fiction television shows, but now they were discussing what they would do if they could travel through time.

"You can't just go back in time and kill Beaton Frick as a baby," Gallifrey scoffed at a pixie-haired New Orphan named Eleanor who smoked a clove cigarette.

"Why not?" she asked. "Since when are there rules about time travel?"

"Since always!" Gallifrey replied. "You can't interfere with the past in any way—you have no way of knowing the impact. It's called the butterfly effect."

"I'll tell you what," an Orphan named Kanye interrupted. "I wouldn't go after Frick. If I could kill any of them, I'd kill Adam Taggart."

"Is no one listening to me?" said Gallifrey incredulously. "You're all going to theoretically rip a hole in the fabric of the space-time continuum!"

Peter cleared his throat. "Why Taggart?"

There was a challenge in his voice. He sounded a little like he did during our conversation on Rapture's Eve— thoughtful and curious and controlled.

"Because Adam Taggart was the fucking worst, man," Kanye said. "Frick was all myth and bluster and crazy-ass stories. Taggart was the dangerous one."

I'd never thought of it that way, but I nodded when I heard Kanye say it. Adam Taggart was always more visible than Frick; the Church website sold T-shirts imprinted with his image, and the words "The Enforcer" printed beneath. My mind flooded then with some of the disturbing asser- tions Adam Taggart made in the three years preceding the Rapture. "The cup of God's wrath has been poured out on a nation whose women demand abortions and applaud infanticide," was his statement on behalf of the Church on the most recent anniversary of 9/11. Harp and I read the quote online repeatedly to memorize it, and then we'd say it out loud at random moments to make each other laugh.

Sometimes all I had to do was pick up an empty cup and pretend to pour to send Harp into a spiral of Adam Taggart hysterics.

"Who would you kill, Peter?" asked Eleanor, exhaling a plume of sweet-smelling smoke.

Peter shrugged, took a long sip of beer. "Nobody." He glanced at me quickly and then stood up. "I don't want to be the one to fuck up the space-time continuum."

Since then, he's avoided me as much as one can in a small renovated wax museum filled with approximately thirty-five other people. Sometimes I can feel him just on my periphery, hesitating as if to speak to me, but I can never bring myself to turn my head and smile. At this point, it feels as though the hole I've dug myself into is just too deep. It would be too embarrassing to approach him now, to act as though nothing has happened. And anyway, in the last few nights, I've noticed Daisy edging ever closer to him at the dinner table, on the couch where he usually sits during the parties. I've seen them sitting together, their heads bent in conversation, and last night, I saw Peter throw his head back and laugh.

I start to get lonely. After the newness of the New Orphans has worn off, once I've become acquainted with each of them and their individual dramas and tragedies, I begin to feel restless. One day I borrow Gallifrey's laptop, and spend a few long hours searching for information on all the people I've lost. My parents. My grandparents. Dylan and Molly. Nothing. Too many people are missing now; I find long lists of their names on blogs and in newspapers. Nobody is looking for anyone's family but their own. Wambaugh's name and e-mail is still listed on our high school's website, but that might mean nothing. All I know is that I'm back to waiting. I'm sitting here in South Dakota with the New Orphans, waiting for the world to end or not end. I send Wambaugh an e-mail:

> *Wambaugh,*
> *I hope you're safe. I don't know if you're in Pittsburgh or someplace else. I'm with Harp Janda at a New Orphans commune in South Dakota. Do you know about the New Orphans? I think you'd be into them. I know you made it seem like the world isn't actually going to end in September, but be straight with me here: do you think it is? If it is, is there anything we can do to stop it? Or should I just stay here? It's nice here; there's food; we're safe.*
> *I'm sorry to bother you but you're the only adult I know anymore.*
> *Viv*

After I send it, though, I remember it isn't true. There's still my father's sister in Salt Lake City, my Aunt Leah. I've never met her or Uncle Toby, but whatever kind of people they are, they're further west than here. Closer to California. I search what I believe to be their names—Leah and Toby Meltzer—and I find a Salt Lake City address that can only be theirs. I write it down, and stick it in the pages of my diary so I won't lose it.

One day after the two-week anniversary of our arrival in Keystone, I decide I want to see Mount Rushmore. I put on my Believer clothes and ask Edie to come with me, because I can't find Harp anywhere and I don't have the guts to ask Peter. Edie's delighted to come, of course; there is still, after everything that's happened, a little Believer in her, and she's breathless on the drive over. When she catches sight of the faces on the way up the mountain, she actually gasps.

We pay the entrance fee, and follow the crowd as they shuffle through the stone entrance and closer to the Holy Terrace. When they find themselves as close as they're going to get to the rock itself, they drop to their knees, start swaying and praying. I see one woman tear off a bonnet and start gesticulating wildly, screaming gibberish—the people around her don't shrink away, but instead flock to her like she's imparting wisdom. We kneel with the crowd on the granite terrace. Everyone around me is weeping, holding their hands to their chests and gazing up at the mountain with wide, shining eyes. Beside me, Edie murmurs under her breath, trying not to let me hear her praying. I look up at those faces. Excepting those late-adopting Believers, those who are play-acting at being born again so as to not miss the next trip to heaven, everyone around me can stand in this place and feel something good. They feel love. They feel awe. They feel like they are not alone in the universe. There's nothing I can think of that makes me feel as at peace at this. The best I can hope for is the occasional moment of loose happy freedom—found usually with Harp but once or twice on this trip with Peter—that tells me it's okay. That if I was put on this Earth for any particular reason, it was to experience love and joy, just like anybody else. That nobody gave me life only to destroy me.

We walk the trail that brings us to the foot of the rock. At the bottom of the trail Edie stands with her head lolled back on her neck, staring up, mouthing wordlessly, and I stay to the side, trying to look demure. Without meaning to, I catch the thread of a conversation two Believer dads are having nearby, while their wives try to wrangle the kids together for pictures.

". . . bold as brass! Sitting out there right off the highway."

"I've seen it."

"But they're killers! You only have to check the Church's feed to know that. They'd sooner kill you than look at you. Lots of Believers have died at the hands of the Orphans—martyrs gone to their reward, yes, but—"

"That's in other cities, brother. You've just come to Keystone. My family and I, we've been here for a month now. Waiting for the Second Boat. And I can tell you, those Orphans, they aren't a threat to anybody."

"No?"

The second man laughs. "You think we'd let them stay if they weren't? A bunch of dumb kids, that's all. Scared of their own shadows. Don't trouble yourself, friend. The New Orphans aren't a threat to us."

Chapter Fourteen

Back at the compound, I find Peter at the kitchen table, whittling something unidentifiable out of a small block of wood. Daisy dances around him, twirling a hula-hoop around her hips, cooing, "You'll never catch me! You'll never catch me!"

"Peter?" I say, straining to make myself heard over her. "Can I talk to you a second?"

He looks at me, then puts down his knife. "Can you give us a second, Daisy?"

She stomps out of the room with an exaggerated pout. When she's gone, Peter gazes at me, his expression neutral. If he's mad at me, he has every right to be. I don't know how to apologize for the way I've behaved these last weeks.

"I can't stay here anymore," I say. "I'm getting too comfortable. I want to get on the road tomorrow. I found an address for my aunt in Salt Lake City—I want to stop there next. She might have nothing at all to tell me about my parents, but I feel like I want to see family right now. Obviously you're welcome to come, but I totally understand if—"

"Say no more," Peter smiles and picks up his knife again. "I'm already packed. Tomorrow, you said? Morning?"

"That's what I was thinking."

He nods in satisfaction and turns back to his project. I take a step towards the museum hallway, to search for Harp among the exhibits, with my heart beating a little faster than before.

Harp is less visibly enthused by my plan when I corner her after dinner, before she's able to sneak away to Goliath's room. "Tomorrow?" she balks. "What's the rush? Is the world going to end slower the faster we get to California?"

"We're not getting anything done here, Harp. Remember when we were going to be unstoppable? We've literally just stopped."

"Are you having a bad time? Is that what this is about?"

"I'm having a fine time, Harp," I sigh. "Really. I'm having too good of a time. I just don't want to spend the end of the world here."

She sizes me up through narrowed eyes. There are plenty of things I want to say to her. Mostly I want to ask her why she's pulling away. What good is it doing her to pull away? But I just stare back, waiting for her answer. Harp sighs.

"Fine," she says. "But tomorrow's too soon. Let's just wait until the end of the week and see how we feel then."

Harp's already looking past me, trying to signal to Goliath with her eyes, but I don't let her slip away. "I'm leaving tomorrow, Harp. I really want you to come, but if you want to stay here, I can't blame you. We're leaving at nine a.m., so you have time to make up your mind."

"Vivian Apple," Harp says in mock astonishment. "Are you giving me an ultimatum?"

"I love you, Harp," I say quietly. "I want you to go wher-ever you want to go, or stay wherever you need to stay. But I can't let you make this decision for me. This one decision, I have to make for myself."

The Orphans have turned on the music and set the bottles of alcohol out on the community room table. It's a goodbye party, for me and Peter and whoever else decides to come with us. But I don't have the energy for them tonight. I saw the look in their eyes when I told them I was leaving; they think I'm crazy. Crazy to leave, crazy to believe there's anything else to do out there but hide and wait and die. They may be right. I leave Harp in the doorway, the party spinning away from me, louder with every step I take, and I climb into bed for what might be my last night of security, my last safe sleep, between now and whenever the world finally does decide to stop turning.

Early the next morning, not long after sunrise, Peter and I stand in the yard halfway between the front door and the entrance to the compound, and the New Orphans file past and say goodbye. I didn't see Harp when I woke up, and I haven't seen her in the hour between then and now. The Orphans kiss my cheeks and tell me we'll meet in another life. I don't know what that means to them, but it sounds very hopeful. Docile, too. I want to tell them there's no guarantee of that, but I think it would make me sound ungrateful, which they must already believe me to be.

Edie is staying behind, as I suspected she would. I told her yesterday afternoon that I was leaving, and she instantly told me she wouldn't be joining us. I can't blame her. I think this is the right place for her, the place where she and her baby will be safest. She has a kind of power over the New Orphans—she exudes a serene authority that makes everyone turn to her for comfort and guidance. They'd be devastated if she left, and they'll protect her. Now she stands before me, smiling and crying, and hugs me tightly.

"Thank you for getting me to this place, Viv," she says into my ear. "I think I might have died if I hadn't gotten to this place."

"You're welcome, Edie."

When she pulls back, she beams at Peter and me. "Actually," she says, "it's not Edie anymore. Or it won't be, after my official renaming ceremony tomorrow."

"What name did you pick?" Peter asks.

Edie gets shy and ducks her head. "Estefan helped me look up names online last night. I'm going to call myself Umaymah. It means 'young mother.' Do you think that sounds okay?"

"It's perfect," I say. "It suits you."

She hugs Peter, looking pleased with herself, and moves down the line. Harp is still nowhere in sight. The fact that she's not even going to say goodbye to me before I go has worked its way up to my throat and stuck there, and I'm finding it increasingly hard to breathe. I might be wheezing a little.

"She's not coming," I say to Peter, and he takes my hand.

Daisy and Gallifrey come up to us next. Daisy seems entirely unaffected by the sight of Peter holding my hand;

she hugs me as tightly as anybody else did, and when she pulls back, she says, "Gallifrey and I want to give you something to remember us by."

Smiling at us, Gallifrey reaches into the satchel bag on his hip and takes out a handgun.

"Holy shit," Peter exclaims. His instinct, like mine, is to instantly put his hands in the air in supplication. But Gallifrey, laughing, shakes his head, and hands the gun to Peter. To me he hands a small box of bullets.

"It's dangerous out there," he explains. "Believe me, I wish all our problems could be solved with nothing but intellect and a recognition of our common humanity, but they make it impossible. It's not smart to go out there without protection. To be honest, when you first got here, and we heard how far you'd come, we were surprised you made it at all."

Peter and I look at each other. "Well, thanks," Peter says.

Gallifrey nods. "No problem, my brother. Go in peace."

During this transaction, I've noticed Goliath has stepped onto the front stoop in his shirtsleeves, and is glaring at us from across the lawn. At first I think he's just mad at us for leaving—last night, when I announced our plan at dinner, he remarked with unpleasant surprise that this was the first time anyone had come to the New Orphans compound and not wanted to stay forever. We must be throwing a hitch into his social experiment, lessening it by not loving it. I imagine his interviewer at Harvard asking, "What would you say is your greatest failure?" and Goliath crossing his legs, looking wistfully into the distance. "There were these two people, at my commune . . ." he'll say. But then I realize that's not what Goliath is angry about. Harp has finally appeared beside him, wearing a shimmering black dress, a blazer, some huge black sunglasses. It is a completely inappropriate look for anywhere in the post-Rapture United States, but I'm thrilled to see her in it. Because behind her she drags her packed suitcase. She says no goodbye to Goliath, ignores the line of New Orphans who reach out to her; she just strides to where Peter and I are standing, and when she gets there, she shakes out her messy black hair.

"Ready when you are, chief," she says.

It's a ten-and-a-half hour drive across Wyoming, a state that from the road looks nothing like any place I've ever been before. It's hard to believe people actually live here—all that surrounds us is dirt and rock and sky. Harp is beside herself. "We spent seventeen years in Pittsburgh living practically on top of each other, when all the time there's just this empty state out here in the middle of nowhere?" she cries. We're alone on the road for miles and miles. Towards the end of the drive, when the sun starts setting in front of us and we haven't seen a sign of life in hours, I have a weird, half-dreamed moment where I think the apocalypse has already happened. The world has already emptied itself of people, but somehow it forgot about us, and now we are eternally stuck here, in this car, in the dust.

Because she's here, I guess I thought the distance between Harp and I, which I've felt gaping wider and wider since the trip began, had closed. But I'm wrong. She never offers to drive. Shortly after we get on the road, I hear a rattling noise, and glance in the rearview mirror to see her shaking a couple of pills out of a small orange container.

"What is that?" My voice sounds sharper than I'd intended. "Harp, what are you taking?"

She pushes up her sunglasses so I can see her roll her eyes. "Relax, Viv. It's just Xanax. Goliath gave me some to deal with my anxiety."

"Anxiety?" I echo, confused.

"Yeah," Harp drawls. "I know it's, like, totally no big deal or anything? But I'm going to die in a couple of months. We all are, actually. The whole world is going to die. And I guess I'm just feeling a *little* stressed out about that fact."

I don't have anything to say to this. I can't really blame Harp, although I wish she'd gotten the pills from an actual doctor. I find myself missing Edie's calming presence, that genuine goodness in her that had cowed Harp, for just a little while. I know Harp is grieving, and I know she's afraid, but it isn't fair. Because I hold grief and fear inside me, too. So does Peter, so does Edie, so does everyone. And we still manage to stand up straight.

It's dusk when we enter Salt Lake City. Peter starts pointing out signs for motels.

"I don't want to wait for the morning," I say. "I want to go there now."

"Viv, she doesn't know you're coming," he points out. "She doesn't even know whether you're alive. Why don't you call her tonight, and we'll head there in the morning?"

But I shake my head. I need to get this over with. Since

180

I found the address online and made the decision to visit, visions of all the hypothetical outcomes have started to fill my brain. I imagine Aunt Leah's a die-hard Believer now, that she'll drag me into the house by my ear and torture me into contrition. I imagine her dead, missing, in hiding. I imagine a woman with my father's kind face, sitting me down on her living-room couch and telling me exactly how to live my life from this point forward. "Listen, kid," she'll say. "Rome wasn't built in a day." And she'll serve me a home-cooked dinner and give me a bed to sleep in, and it will be different than if I'd stayed in Keystone, because she'll be an adult, a member of my family, and she'll know what's good for me in a way the New Orphans never could. I don't know which of these possibilities is the correct one, and the not knowing makes me sick. So I shake my head at Peter. "I want to go there now," I say again.

"You heard the boss," says Harp from the back in her careless way.

The Meltzers live on a leafy street in a western neighborhood of the city. I'm driving, so Peter reads out loud the numbers—"562, 564, 568, 570." It's a one-storey house with an American flag in the window, an old satellite dish on the roof. The lawn is green but for one big dead patch. There's a busted-up station wagon in the driveway. I park out front, and the three of us stare out the window, searching for a sign. Do we stay or do we go? It seems impossible to me that inside that house lives a woman who knew my father when he was young, before he Believed in anything at all. I turn to Harp and Peter.

"I don't know what's going to happen now. I don't know how long this will take. If you want to stay out here, that's fine."

"And miss the extremely urgent family reunion?" Harp balks. "I don't think so."

So together we cross the dying lawn. I stand on the top step and ring the bell. Peter stands one step below me. Harp stays a yard behind us, her black shades slipped again over her eyes, her arms folded. I imagine how we must look to the neighbors peering out their curtains. I wonder if they're Believers or New Orphans or nothing at all. I wonder what they think we are.

The door opens enough for part of a woman's face to be visible in the crack. Her eyes narrow when she sees me standing there. "What?"

"Leah? Are you Leah Meltzer?"

"Why?" asks the woman, opening the door slightly wider. She is in her mid-fifties, a few years older than my father would be, with a head of hair too coppery-red to be natural. I only have to gaze at her another moment to know that she must be my aunt, because it's like looking an artist's rendering of me in the future. Aunt Leah has my strong brows, my dark eyes, the slight gap between my two front teeth. Her body is what my father called the Apple body: she's small-breasted, wide-hipped, skinny-armed. I could cry just looking at her. She's family.

"I'm Vivian. Vivian Apple. I'm your niece," I explain.

This was the part in my imagination where she'd pull me in from the unknown and embrace me. Where she'd make me a cup of hot cocoa and talk to me about boys.

But Aunt Leah's face stays wary. She glances over my shoulder at Peter and Harp, and then back at me.

"What are you doing here?"

"We—" What *are* we doing here? The two weeks in Keystone have made our objective seem sillier, less attainable. I don't know where to begin. "My friends and I, we're driving to California," I begin, "and I remembered you lived in Utah . . ."

"Do your parents know you're here?" Leah interrupts.

I shake my head. "They were Raptured."

Leah inhales through her nose. She's still eyeing me with vague distrust. Maybe she thinks I've come for money. I don't know how to explain it: I don't want your money, Aunt Leah. I just want to sit for a while with someone who knew them. Finally, she pulls the door all the way back, and pushes the screen door open. She doesn't invite us in. She just waits until my hand is on the door, holding it open, and then retreats into the belly of the house.

I follow her, and Peter and Harp trail behind. We cut across the living room and into a den, where the television's blasting, playing a repeat of an old sitcom. There's a man in a recliner there, eating a meal off a plate he balances on his own wide stomach. He mutes the sitcom and watches us curiously. Leah sits on the couch. Her brow is still furrowed and she stares at me like she's never seen my species before.

"Lee?" the man says. "Who are they?"

Aunt Leah purses her lips. "*Ned's* daughter."

"Goddamn," says the man. He puts his plate on the table and stands. He's a huge man with a big black beard and

183

no hair on his head. He has nice eyes that skip over our faces curiously. Eventually he must decide I'm the most likely candidate, because he comes over and pulls me into a hug, his beard scratching pleasantly at my face. "Look at you. You're the spitting image of your father. Leah, doesn't she look just like Ned?"

Leah stares, and doesn't answer.

"I'm your uncle Toby," the man continues. "We've never met. Can you believe that? You must be—what—fifteen? And we've never met? Vicky, right?"

"Vivian," I say, blushing, feeling bad to correct him since he's being so nice. "Actually, I'm seventeen."

Uncle Toby slaps a hand against his forehead. "Vivian!" he says. "Of course. Goddamn! Are your folks outside? We haven't seen them in—"

"They're gone, Toby," Leah interrupts him. "Raptured."

It sinks in slowly. I watch the emotions move across his face—blank surprise, followed quickly by sorrow. Uncle Toby turns the full force of his gaze on me. He looks at me like he sees through whatever front I've haphazardly dashed together in the last year, right to the core of me, where all the pain is. He claps a heavy hand down on my shoulder.

"Oh, Vivian," says Uncle Toby. "You poor kid. I am so, so sorry to hear that."

At first I don't feel it coming, and then I can and I'm begging myself to stop, because the last thing I want to do is start crying in the den of some strangers, even if they are my aunt and uncle; they're just trying to eat their dinner and here I am, on a Wednesday night, a true orphan, huge and sore and messy with grief. Uncle Toby goes blurry and I make a tiny, pathetic whimpering noise, before he helps me over to the couch and sits me beside his wife. Aunt Leah looks uncomfortable, watching me wiping my eyes with my sleeve, but she doesn't reach out.

"At any age, that's a loss." Uncle Toby is babbling now, sitting precariously on the edge of the coffee table. "But at your age. That's just hard. Going it alone at your age. It's not an easy age to be alone."

I nod. I'm embarrassed now, to have cried in front of them, and I feel bad for Harp and Peter, hovering nervously behind us, and for Uncle Toby, clearly racking his brains to give me advice. He keeps shooting imploring glances at Aunt Leah beside me, but she just leans back into the couch now, folding her arms across her chest.

"Of course," she says after a moment, and her voice sounds different. Colder. "It was hardly a new experience for your mother, was it? Abandoning a kid."

"Leah," Toby says once, like a warning.

I think they must be talking about something private between them, something that has nothing to do with me. But then I get a sick sort of feeling in me, a cold panic sliding up my lungs. "What?" I say.

"All I mean is, it couldn't have been too hard," Leah continues. "Probably it's like riding a bike. You think you've forgotten but then it turns out to be easy."

"What are you saying?" I ask her. Uncle Toby stands abruptly. He picks his plate off the table and takes it to another room. I have a ringing in my ears. "Aunt Leah." I grab her left arm so she looks at me. "What are you talking about?"

She yanks her arm back, and gives me a wounded, annoyed look. "Are you making fun of me? I'm talking about the baby, of course."

"What baby?"

"What baby?" Aunt Leah seems so angry, and so confused. "You know perfectly well what baby. Your mother's first baby. Your sister."

Part Three

Chapter Fifteen

What remains is a world-falling-away feeling. An unrealness in everything. Like if I were to look down at my own fingertips, I'd find them fading.

"I don't know anything about this," I tell Aunt Leah.

She turns to me, raising an eyebrow, but as soon as she sees my face in the flickering blue light of the television screen, her expression softens. "You really don't?" she says.

I shake my head. I feel both Harp and Peter move forward, flanking me on either side, to protect me. Harp puts her hand hard and reassuring on my shoulder.

"What is your fucking *problem*, lady?" she snaps at my aunt. "*That's* how you deliver earth-shattering news to people?"

"I didn't realize," Aunt Leah says, a little desperately. "I really didn't. There was a time when Mara wouldn't shut up about that baby. I haven't seen her in twenty years; how was I supposed to know she'd stopped?"

"I don't know about this," I say again. My mind is racing through a million different memories of my mother, of my mother mothering me, flicking through the scenes like a flipbook to find any clue that I was anything but the first. But there's nothing. There's my mother brushing my hair after a bath when I was little; there's my mother taking my picture on the first day of kindergarten; there's my mother teaching me how to scramble an egg; there's my mother. The only thing that makes me believe my aunt is telling me the truth is the memory of a photo, hidden in a drawer in my grandparents' apartment. An anonymous baby in 1986. The shiver that went up my spine at the sight of it. My sister.

Aunt Leah sighs. "What do you know about how your parents met?"

"They met at college," I reply promptly, because their love story has been drilled into me like a fairy tale. Set up on a blind date by pushy roommates. Went to a movie off-campus, shared Sno-Caps and Coke. Dad nervous; Mom sweetly thinking, *This is the man I'll marry*.

But Leah shakes her head. "No," she says. "They met in New York when they were both just at the end of high school. You really don't know this?"

"She doesn't *know*," Harp says through gritted teeth.

"Listen," Aunt Leah says. She picks up the remote and turns off the TV. "Here's what happened. At the end of his senior year, Ned went on a trip to New York City with his Model UN club. He had to beg our parents to let him, only because he'd never been outside of Pittsburgh without them before. Till he went, he hadn't given them any reason not to trust him. I was out of college by that time, working downtown; Toby and me were two years married. I was home for Sunday dinner when Ned comes back. And we've

190

barely asked him how was his trip when he tells us he's met a girl.

"Okay, so he's met a girl. So what, right? He says they met in the park; her name is Mara; she lives in New York. That's it. That's all he tells us, so that's all we know. But suddenly he's on the phone with her four, five hours a night. He's taking eight-hour bus rides back and forth to New York on weekends. Meanwhile, she never comes to *our* house. I don't know what my parents thought, but I figured Ned was ashamed of us. I thought he'd convinced his fancy New York girlfriend that he came from a family of hicks or something.

"But that wasn't it. The truth was, your mom was pregnant. She'd been pregnant when they met, about five months along. I don't think she knew who the father was. Later Ned explained to us she'd gotten in with a bad crowd, was seeing older guys, guys who pushed her around. She was maybe on drugs, I don't know. Her parents kicked her out and she'd been staying with friends, and Ned didn't approve. All those weekends he went up there, he was trying to find her an apartment, paying for it with the money he made working at the pharmacy. And then she turned eighteen, and then he turned eighteen, and they got married. Before we'd even laid eyes on her.

"Finally, he brought her out here. She was probably eight months along, getting real big. She looked terrible— her skin was all waxy, her hair dyed blue at the ends. She had a big safety pin through her nose. I thought my mother was going to have a heart attack, I really did. And

191

we're asking them, why did you do this, why didn't you tell us? And Mara's just sitting there, biting her nails, not saying a word. Ned says they got married because *they're in love*. They didn't tell us 'cause *we wouldn't understand*. My dad asks him, does he realize how much work a baby is? Does he really think he's capable of raising another man's child?

"And then Mara finally talks. She says she's giving it up; she wants a clean slate. And I can tell by Ned's face he isn't happy. Probably he had some fantasy about them playing house. I knew him his whole life; I know how he thinks. The man can fall in love with a pregnant teenage punk, but all the time he's harboring these *Brady Bunch* delusions. You can't convince me it was your mom pushing to get married at eighteen. She had plenty of wild years left in her. But he must've made it sound pretty appealing to give it up and be good, because that's what she did.

"And the other thing that happened, if you want to know the truth," Leah says, and her voice takes on a fresh wave of coldness, taps into some ancient store of anger and recrimination, "is that we told her we would take it. Toby and me. We had no children, not by choice, and we told her we'd raise it and love it like our own. And she told us no. She said it would be too painful to have it close, to know too much about it. So she had it, and she gave it to strangers. And it doesn't make any sense, either, because she stayed in touch with the adoptive parents for years and years after that. Up to the point where we stopped talking, because it hurt too

192

much to hear about. 'The Conroys sent us a picture of Winnie!' she'd say. 'Winnie's learning how to ride a tricycle!' Like it was just some friend's kid, instead of her own flesh and blood. One day, I finally said, 'Mara, I don't want to hear about Winnie. Every time you talk about her I think about how you wouldn't let her be mine.' That shut her up. Ned calls me later, yelling, telling me I should be ashamed of myself, but I wasn't then, and I'm not now. Then about ten years after that, you were born. My parents told me, because Ned and Mara weren't speaking to me anymore. They'd been married ten years when you were born. If you ask me, that's too much. You settle into routines in ten years. How do you make room for a baby? How do you know for sure, if you're her, that you even want one?

"So, yeah," she says, and she folds her arms. "You've got a sister, and no cousins. And I don't think it's surprising that Mara let herself get caught up in the Rapture and taken away by it. Because she hasn't had any trouble leaving her kids behind before."

When Aunt Leah's done I ask her where the bathroom is. She points me down an adjacent hallway, with a wary expression, like she'd expected more questions or more yelling. But I don't want to speak to her anymore. I don't want to have to listen to her speak, ever again. Harp makes a motion like she's about to follow me, but I wave her away.

In the bathroom I just stand under the fluorescent light and examine my face in the mirror. I have my mom's freckles and my dad's dark hair. I am the person they chose to create together. I am their blank slate. A child born out of the choice to be good. I'm angry. I've never been so angry. It isn't the fact of my sister; it isn't my wild pierced mother's unprotected sex, or my brave dumb father's stepping in to play the hero. I'm angry because I didn't know. Because I had to sit on Aunt Leah's couch while she told me. Because they left. They told me they were going and they went, and they made it seem like it was an absence in me that was worth leaving. Now I know: it was only ever their story. If I was part of it at all, I was just a footnote.

When I leave the bathroom, Uncle Toby stands outside, waiting. He hands me something, an old photograph. It's a picture of my parents at their college graduation. They're in navy-blue caps and gowns, their arms wrapped around each other. They look so happy. According to my aunt's timeline, they'd been married at this point for four years. Winnie was long gone, and soon Leah and Toby would be as well. After that, my mother's parents. After that, me.

"Leah loved your dad," Toby says softly. "She really did. He was her baby brother. I remember how she used to talk about him when we first started going out. She made him sound like this genius, this movie star. When he was just this dorky kid. It hurt her that your parents didn't want us to raise Winnie, but that was nothing compared to how she felt when they stopped talking to her. For weeks, she called them every day, three times a day, begging forgiveness. But they were done with her." He snaps, to show how quickly and easily it was done. "I can't imagine them as Believers. I can't think of what your last few years have been like. But they were really fun once. And I never saw two people so in love. I thought you should be able to remember them like that."

In the picture, my mother's hair is no longer blue. It's her usual strawberry blonde. You wouldn't know by looking at her that she'd ever been pregnant, that any man had ever pushed her around. She looks like a normal young woman on her graduation day, excited and loved.

"Can I use your internet?" I ask Uncle Toby.

First I search her name. "Winnie Conroy." There are pages that lead to nothing: historical records about floods, fires; an obituary notice for a Dallas woman born in 1943. Then I find what I hoped I might. A social networking page with nearly all its information hidden, but a profile picture that shows a woman in her mid-twenties, grinning in the sun, her face practically obscured by large sunglasses. Winnie Conroy. A Masters student at UC Berkeley. Who one night, last month, must have tracked down her biological grandparents' phone number, and called it. Just to see what happened. Just to hear what they sounded like. It wasn't my mother's silence that I heard. It was my sister's.

I check my e-mail and find a reply from Wambaugh. She's happy I'm safe; she's happy I'm with Harp. Wambaugh gave her notice when the high school went Believer; she moved to Sacramento, where her parents live. She gives me her number and tells me to call it if ever I need her, but she also says:

Viv, you're going to live a full and happy life. I still believe this, despite everything that's happened in this country in the last two months. But I would be remiss in my duties as a Responsible Adult if I didn't encourage you to stay where you are in South Dakota. It sounds like it's a safe place, and there aren't many safe places left at this point. Just keep your head low until it all blows over.

Whoops. I write her phone number on a piece of paper, and slip it into my pocket. I hide the picture Uncle Toby gave me in the middle of a pile of bills next to the keyboard. I don't want it. I don't know those people; I never have. It doesn't matter to me whether it's Leah or Toby who finds it, or when, or what they'll think when they do. By then I'll be long gone, a girl who came and interrupted their dinner one Wednesday night in June.

In the living room, Harp is pacing, tugging nervously at her skirt, while Peter leans against the wall with his hands in his pockets. When I walk in, he stands upright and Harp stops moving. They look at me with wary eyes. I can hear someone bustling around in the kitchen, the clatter of silverware and plates.

"She wants us to spend the night," Peter murmurs. "She feels bad. She ordered a pizza for the three of us to split."

I shake my head. "I want to get out of here," I whisper.

Peter opens his mouth, like he's going to question me,

and he's probably right to do it—I shouldn't blame my aunt for things my parents never told me. But before he's able to, Harp steps up to my side and links her arm through mine.

"Let's not bother with goodbyes, okay?" Harp says. "At this point, I'm worried she'll pull a literal skeleton from the closet."

Chapter Sixteen

It's night when we leave Salt Lake City. I offer to drive, as I'm the one depriving my friends of beds and pizza, but Harp won't hear it; she opens the door to the back-seat to let me in and moves her bottle of vodka to a spot where I can easily reach it, then gets behind the wheel. We can't see much outside our windows, but after a while Peter, who's been studying the map, says we're in the salt flats—that all the land surrounding us is covered in salt, and if the sun were out, it would shine silver and white. It makes me want to come back here someday, if the world is still turning. I wish I could see these things, these things I've never seen before, without this mess of anger and anxiety clanging in the back of my head like a gong. Neither Harp nor Peter say anything to me, and I'm relieved about that. I wouldn't know what to say back. I can't even bring myself to tell them that it must have been Winnie, my half-sister, whose call I answered in New York City. That there's probably some logical explanation for Peter's mail, too. The trip can only end in ways that will hurt us. I know this now. But still I don't tell them.

The one thing I do mention is Wambaugh. I explain to

Harp the e-mail I sent her and her reply, and Harp is nice enough not to scoff when I tell her that Wambaugh recommended staying in South Dakota. "We can stop in Sacramento on the way," Harp suggests brightly, and I know she's just trying to make up for her attitude and my aunt's bombshell, but I appreciate it anyway.

I drift in and out, aware of the increasingly rickety sound the engine makes now that we've pushed it so hard across the country. At points I hear Harp and Peter talking to each other in worried voices. "But what do we do when we get there?" I hear Harp say. Somewhere between awake and asleep, I mistake them for my parents—they are driving me home from a trip to the county fair, a movie that went on later than expected, and when we get there they will tuck me in to my bed, and I will hear their voices recede as they walk down the hallway to their bedroom. I will be so sleepy and safe then that I'll forgive them. This betrayal will just melt away. It is an unbearable sadness, a kind of suffocation, to wake up and realize my mistake.

I've woken because the car has stopped and the passenger door has slammed. Outside the window I see a sign for a motel, and Peter walking towards the office. Behind him shines the blinking neon of a casino. *Sinners—If You're Going to Hell, Don't Go Broke.* Harp turns around in her seat, yawning. The radio clock reads 2:30 a.m.

"Sorry, dude," she says. "I couldn't drive anymore."

"Where are we?"

"Winnemucca, Nevada." Harp shrugs. "It seems decent. I mean, if Sinners Casino is still unscathed, we'll probably be able to spend one safe night."

I hate that I've led us all the way out here, to the middle of nowhere, based on the most dubious of hunches. I hate that my hunch has turned out to be wrong. I can't let Harp go on thinking I believe it. "Listen—"

But she holds up her hand. "We should have a serious talk sometime soon, I agree. But for now let's just acknowledge that we're best friends forever, and I'm not just saying that because there's a possibility forever's only gonna get us to September. Okay?"

I nod at her. She grins and steps out of the car. Peter's already back with the key, which he hands to Harp. He gets into the backseat beside me. Harp takes her suitcase from the trunk and walks backwards to the stairs, wagging her eyebrows suggestively at me. I look at Peter.

"Sorry," he says. "I just wanted a chance to talk with you, alone."

"Okay?" I don't mean for the word to end in a question mark, but I'm instantly made nervous by his proximity, by the fact of being alone with him.

Peter looks cautious, concerned. "Are you alright?"

"I don't know," I say.

"That was really messed up tonight," Peter says. "And it's fine if you don't want to talk about it now, or ever. I just wanted to ask when Harp wasn't around to make pithy comments. I just wanted to say, you know, that whatever you're feeling is totally normal."

"Yeah?" I'm immediately angry, not at him, just at everything. It's so easy to slip into anger; it fits so much more comfortably than any of the other emotions I'm feeling. "That's a relief. You know, I meant to Google 'normal reactions to have at the discovery that your life has been a lie' when I had the chance, but it totally slipped my mind."

"Your life hasn't been a lie," he says softly.

"Yes, it has, Peter!" I cry. "It absolutely has! Since I was a kid, all they did was tell stories about how they met and where they had their first kiss and how easy it's always been. It was always them, this invincible duo, and for a long time I felt like if I was good enough—like if I was really, really good enough—they'd let me into their club. But they never did, Peter. And now I know that they never even considered it. Because all I was to them was proof— proof that my mother had been reformed, that my father was the one who reformed her."

I'm crying now, but Peter only gets closer. He holds my hand. "You were more than that to them, Viv. They loved you."

"You don't know that. You have literally no way of knowing that."

"They had to have loved you," he says firmly. "You're Vivian fucking Apple."

The car is silent then, except for my sniffling. Peter holds out his arm and I look at him quizzically; he uses his sleeve to wipe my face. "Look," he says. "You're angry at them, and you should be. They lied. They told you about a made-up version of themselves, who did made-up things. They shouldn't have done that. But Viv, if I've learned anything at all in the last eight years of my life? It's that people just like to tell themselves stories about where they came from. They can't help themselves. They don't trust

201

the world around them—it's too good for them, or not good enough—so they tell themselves stories about it. They tell themselves an old magician who lives in the sky made them out of clay and put them here until whenever he makes up his mind to take them out again. Your parents didn't like their creation myth, that's all—it had pain in it, and chaos, and their own parents were ashamed. So they told themselves a story that was at least partially true: about two good people who deserved happy lives. And probably at some point they started to believe the story.

"But the thing is, really," Peter continues, "that it doesn't matter. For your parents or anyone else. It doesn't actually matter where we came from, or where we're going, or when. The only thing that matters is what we have to do while we're here and how well we do it."

The only light coming into the car is from Sinners Casino's blinking sign, so the outline of Peter's face appears and disappears, over and over again, as he speaks. I'm not crying anymore. I'm looking into his kind face as he gazes back at me.

"What do we have to do?" I ask.

He smiles a little. "Well, I don't know, Viv," he says. "Probably love each other."

I move the inch or two of distance that still remains between us, and find his lips in the blinking dark. He kisses me back so softly that I wonder if this is his kind way of rejecting me, of easing me out of the embarrassing moment where I'll have to pull away. But then he touches my hair, my neck. He runs his left hand up my bare right arm. Suddenly I am making out with Peter Ivey in the back of a stolen car in a motel parking lot in Winnemucca, Nevada, at nearly three o'clock in the morning, and the best part is that it's so easy. My brain has gone silent—all the question and worry and fear that had been swirling around up there not a minute before is now just white noise. I laugh into Peter's mouth.

"Cool!" he says, pulling back. "Laughter. Just what every guy wants to hear at this moment."

"It's just—this is fun." I kiss the side of his mouth, his chin, his jawline. He puts his warm hand against my cheek.

"I agree." He kisses me again. "But you know, just for the record? When I said we had to love each other, I didn't necessarily mean right this second, in the parking lot."

All we do is kiss. I have an urge to go further, to climb on top of him in this cramped backseat and see what happens, but I resist it. I don't know if the urge comes from actual desire, or some instinct to self-destruct. To null the pain of this day with as much mindless joy as possible. As it stands, I leave the car, thirty minutes later, feeling pretty happy. He carries our bags up the stairs to the room, and at the door puts them down so he can take my face into his hands and kiss me again quietly. Harp has left the door unlocked and a light on. She's lying in bed already. Peter motions for me to share it with her; there's a couch by the window where he'll sleep. I slip in beside her as he goes to brush his teeth.

Harp's eyes flick immediately open. She has a badly concealed smile on her face. "Oh hey, Viv," she whispers. "Your nose is a little red. How did that happen, I wonder?"

I touch it. It feels raw from rubbing against Peter's little bit of beard. I don't have to say anything to Harp; she's giggling silently beside me. I grin at her and close my eyes.

When I wake up, the lights are off and it's still dark outside. But there's a pounding on the door, a furious and terrifying banging. I sit up in bed, startled. I can see Harp's eyes wide open, shining in the bit of moonlight that peers in through the curtains. Peter is crouched by the door, listening. He holds a finger to the lips I've recently kissed.

"This is management," shouts the male voice at the door. "Open up, now."

The clock radio says it's five in the morning. I don't know what we're going to do. Peter checked into the room by himself; if the manager finds Harp and me here and has even the slightest Believer sympathies, I don't know how bad the outcome might be. We might be hurt. We might be killed. The man won't stop knocking. Peter frantically waves at us to move, to hide, but where is there to go? It's just a bedroom and a bathroom. Harp gets up silently and steps into the wardrobe; I rush to join her. Peter closes the door behind us, and then we hear the click of the bedside lamp and the opening of the door.

"Sorry," we hear him yawn. "I was totally out. Is there a problem?"

"Are you alone in this room?" says the man's voice.

"Of course," says Peter, and even from inside the closet I know that he's answered too quickly, too assuredly. I'm finding it hard to breathe. In the dark, Harp finds my hand with hers.

There's a silence then, a couple moments in which we're

just waiting, waiting. When we next hear the man's voice, it's too close to us. I realize he has pushed past Peter to check the room. I squeeze Harp's tiny hand so hard I worry her fingers will break.

"Sorry," the man says, his voice slightly more relaxed. "We got a phone call from another guest, who said somebody was fornicating in here. Now, that might fly at other motels in Winnemucca, but the Shady Pines does not hold to that kind of behavior. Not now, not ever."

"I understand," Peter replies solemnly.

"But now that I'm here," the man says, and his volume increases slightly; he's taken another step towards the wardrobe, "I see you're just a nice, normal, Christian young man. Aren't you?"

"Yes. Naturally."

"Yes," says the man. "Naturally. Only one weird thing about you—you sure did bring a lot of luggage. Didn't you?"

I can see them out there, in my head, at the foot of the bed. My suitcase, and Harp's. Peter's duffel bag. All Peter needs to do is come up with a plausible explanation for them, and quickly. All we'd need to do after that is wait for the manager to leave, find a way for the three of us to sneak out of the room and back into the car. I am thinking *this is my fault, this is my fault, this is my fault*, and straining so hard to hear Peter's answer, that it takes me a second to register that the wardrobe door is being pulled open and the motel manager, a red-faced man with white-blonde hair, is yanking out a screaming Harp. I kick out at him when he reaches for me, but it's useless; he grabs me by my hair, and my scalp screams with pain. No one has ever deliberately hurt me like this before; I'm so surprised I can't even shout.

In an alternate universe, the scene is almost funny—the manager's in some blue pin-striped pajamas with a nametag pinned hastily onto the pocket; his name is Chip. He holds a writhing Harp by the arm, and he pulls my hair harder every time she tries to kick him in the balls, which is again and again and again. Chip mutters Book of Frick verses under his breath; they seem to be all the ones that justify hurt. *"Do not spare her the rod, lest she rise up to spite thee like the asp all thy life."* Peter runs at Chip, punching him the face, the neck, and Chip drops us. *"If she profane herself by playing the whore, she shall be burnt with fire,"* he says commandingly as he pushes Peter. Peter stumbles backwards over my suitcase handle and Chip advances. My skull is on fire. My eyes are filled with tears. *We're going to die here*, I realize. We are going to die here, and we are going to die like Raj died, like Melodie Hopkirk died—violently, and afraid. I think I'm in shock. I can hear some voice inside me saying, *Get up, Viv, get up*, but when I try to stand my knees buckle. Then I realize it isn't my brain speaking; it's Harp. Harp is trying to support my body with her own; she's half-dragging me to the door. Chip is distracted by Peter, who won't stay on the ground. I see him hit Peter, once, twice, hard in the face. Peter sees me hesitate. "Go!" he shouts.

We run.

We clatter down the stairs to the parking lot and race to my grandparents' car. Harp was the last to drive and she still has the keys; in the second it takes for her to fumble with them, I keep my eyes on the open door of our room. I can still hear Chip murmuring prayers, the sounds of a struggle; I can still see the shadow of movement on the doorframe. Harp has gotten into the car and turned on the ignition. She throws open the passenger door.

"Come on!" she shouts, but I can't move. Not until I see his face. Suddenly Peter bolts from the room and takes the steps down two at a time. Chip plods behind him with surprising speed. I get in the car and Harp peels backwards, then races to the bottom of the stairs to meet Peter there. I reach behind me to open the passenger door for him, but we're a second too late—Chip has caught up, and grabs Peter around the neck. He begins to drag him toward the office.

"Shit, shit, shit, shit," Harp whispers, but she doesn't slow down.

"Harp!"

"We can't *stay* here, Viv! The longer we stay here, the more likely a mob of Believers will come out and lend a hand. We'll get Peter back, I promise, but we need to figure out how first; we need to be careful!"

"I have a plan. Pull back around."

Harp's face stays pinched with worry; she acts as if she hasn't heard me.

"Do it!" I shout.

She leaves the parking lot and loops back around through the entrance. Chip has dragged Peter to just about the office door, and though Peter is trying to fight him off, he's losing. His right eye is pink and puffy; he has slick, red blood coursing out of his nose, all over Chip's beefy arms, which are clamped around his neck. Without really thinking about what I'm going to do next, I leap out of the still-moving car, causing Harp to yelp behind me.

"Hey!" I shout. Chip stops dragging and Peter stops struggling. It's hard to tell what sort of expression Peter's actually making, with his face as swollen and bruised as it is, but I think I can detect an undercurrent of concern that I have gone completely insane.

Maybe I have. For a brief moment, I think of my sledgehammer, waiting in the trunk. I think about the gun Gallifrey gave us when we left the New Orphans compound. Peter had stashed it in the glove compartment, seeming embarrassed even to touch it. I could reach into the car and use that, hold it with some confidence and buy Peter the distraction he needs to travel the ten or fifteen feet to the backseat. But I can't justify the act to myself, no matter how much I like making out with the boy I'd be trying to save. That would be playing by Believer rules: telling myself that violence and the threat of it is okay, if that's what it takes to get you what you want. "*For God so loved the world*," says the Book of Frick, "*that he sent us guns with which to protect our homes and women.*" The way Frick tells it, Eve—being weak—feared Adam's spear and destroyed it, when God had fashioned it especially for him. The serpent was just the straw that broke the Creator's back. No, I'm not going to pick up that gun. I'll figure something else out as I go along. I wonder if this is what bravery is: adrenaline plus love plus absolute stupidity.

"Are you serious, little girl?" Chip says, laughing. He's

beaten Peter bloody but he hasn't even broken a sweat. "You've got what we call a *reprieve*. Take it."

"The Book of Frick, Verse 78, Line 22," I call out to him. "'*And Thomas Jefferson laid his hands on Frick's brow. And he said: No man has a natural right to commit aggression on the equal rights on another. This is all from which the laws ought to restrain him.*'"

There's a sudden flicker in Chip's eyes—discomfort or disbelief, I can't tell. He says nothing. He doesn't let go. In the car, I hear Harp's breathless "Whoa."

"You've read the Book all the way through," I say, "haven't you?"

"Of course I've read the damn book!" Chip snaps, and then he quickly makes the sign of the cross in the air with his free hand. "You're taking that out of context!"

"Am I?" I ask him. Of course I am. It's been months since I skimmed the Book of Frick my parents gave me, and all I remember is the really absurd stuff and the one or two passages that actually made sense. But I have a feeling Chip doesn't know it. "Let's hope you're right, Chip, because what do you think the Prophet Jefferson would say, if he looked down here and saw you doing what you're doing? Right as the list for the Second Boat is being compiled?"

Chip loosens his grip just a fraction. Peter, no longer choking, gasps for breath, wipes the blood from his face with his sleeve. "What about, though," Chip asks, almost thoughtfully, "what about, '*The road to heaven is narrow, and overcrowded with the damned*'? That's in there, too."

Without thinking, I recite the next relevant quote that

comes to mind. "'*But I say to you, love your enemies, bless them that curse you, do good to them that hate you, and pray for them that persecute you.*'"

As soon as I've said it, I know it's wrong. Nothing in the Book of Frick is as reasonable as that. Chip's face clouds over. "That's not Frick," he says. "Frick didn't say that."

He pushes Peter out by his shoulders and brings one knee up, hard, into his spine. I hear Harp cry out behind me, and my own voice shouting, "No!" I turn to the car without thinking, the image of the gun in the glove compartment burning in my brain like a brand, but then I hear Peter's voice, barely audible.

"My wallet," he says.

Chip shakes his head, knees Peter in the back again. "I don't want your *money*," he spits.

"No." Peter shakes his head. "My dad. Give me my wallet. My back pocket. My dad."

I don't know what Peter's plan is. I want to take out the gun and point it at Chip until Peter is safely in the backseat. I want to protect him, this kind boy, this boy I could love someday; I want to hurt every single person who's ever hurt him. Chip, intrigued in spite of himself, pulls Peter's wallet out of his back pocket and opens it with one hand. He examines something in it, and then lets go of Peter abruptly, like Peter's skin has burned his own. Peter drops to his knees.

"That's not the name you signed in under," Chip says in a quavering voice.

Peter nods. He takes the wallet from Chip and pulls out a folded piece of paper, no bigger than a business card. He hands it over. Chip unfolds it and I watch his eyes widen. He holds whatever it is against his heart.

"Son," Chip says, his voice suddenly low and oily with respect, "can I just say how sorry I am for the baseless assumptions I made about you—"

"Forget it," Peter says, fighting to stand.

"You can understand my concern!" Chip moves forward to help him, but hesitates—he seems frightened of Peter now, of what Peter's going to do next. "These are dangerous times, as you well know. I hope that you'll keep me in your prayers."

Peter is on his feet now, wincing, holding his side. He starts to hobble to the car, but stops to look at me. He looks like he's going to be sick.

"I'm sorry," he says softly.

"Your father was a great man!" Chip calls after him, but Peter ignores him, opening the door to the backseat of the car and climbing gingerly in. "He was a patriot! Ma'am," he says more quietly after Peter's shut the door behind him, "do you think he'd mind if I kept this?"

He takes a step forward and shows me what Peter handed him. It's a small, wallet-sized photo, creased and uncreased many times, stuffed in wallets and pockets and in between the pages of books for who knows how many years. It's a close-up of a man holding a little boy. The boy is all big blue eyes and delight; the man is thick dark blonde hair and crinkled eyes, thin smiling lips. The picture is old, but still I feel my blood go cold when I recognize Peter's father. Adam Taggart. The Church of America spokesman. The Enforcer. There's no reconciling that man with the one I kissed in my grandparents' car tonight. There's no making sense of it. The sun is rising over Winnemucca and Harp honks the horn; I turn and find that Peter has slipped down, out of sight. Eight years he's been carrying this picture around with him. And this is the first time it's done him any good.

"It's all yours," I tell Chip.

Chapter Seventeen

"Your father is such a fucking *asshole*!" Harp shouts.

She's booking it out of Winnemucca, her hands clenched tight around the steering wheel. When I got in the car and we peeled out of the Shady Pines parking lot, Harp was terrified and confused. "What was it?" she shouted at us both. "Why did he let us go?" I was too stunned to answer, and finally Peter had to explain. That we're hurtling towards California because Peter thinks his father is there. That Peter's father is Beaton Frick's despicable psychopath of a right-hand man.

"I know he is," Peter croaks. "Of course he is."

"You don't think maybe you could have mentioned it a little sooner?" Harp continues. "Like, oh, I don't know, say, before you joined us on a cross-country road trip?"

"What was I supposed to say?" Peter asks. His voice is weak but there's some grit in it now. "'Thank you for the invitation, and by the way, my father is a hateful monster; hoping it's not genetic?'"

"Yes, actually! That would have summed it up nicely! But clearly that wasn't a priority for you, because you didn't even give us your *real fucking name*. What is 'Ivey,' anyway? Is that some kind of weird Church thing?"

Peter is silent a moment. "It was my mother's maiden name."

"What was *her* deal, anyway?" Harp snaps. "What made her think it was a good idea to get married to a woman-hating fundie lunatic?"

"Harp," I say sharply.

Harp exhales through her mouth. "Okay. I'm sorry. But Viv, seriously. You're going to tell me this doesn't bother you at all? That the dude you've been macking it to is the son of *maybe* the worst person ever? 'The cup of God's wrath'? That guy?"

"He's not his father," I say quietly. "He's clearly not his father."

"No, but—"

"We've been traveling with him for weeks," I continue, "and he hasn't hurt us. He's helped us. He didn't tell us who his father was, but if that was my dad, I wouldn't have told us either. And if it *was* Taggart sending Peter mail from California, that means we're working on more than a hunch. That means we're actually on to something real."

Harp is silent. I turn in my seat and look at Peter's face. He lies stiffly against the door with his left arm thrown across his ribcage. Even in the morning shadows, I can see the bruises forming on his face, the streaks of dried blood on his chin. He let himself get beaten so we could run. He watches me now with a look so scared and sad.

"Can we trust you?" I ask him.

"Yes," Peter says in a sigh. "Always."

We've reached California before we realize we've left our bags behind.

214

In addition to Harp's array of unusual outfits ("I had a poodle skirt in there!" she moans), this means we've lost a large portion of our cash. Each of us had about two hundred on us as we peeled our way out of the Shady Pines Motel parking lot, and there's an additional $660 stashed in various spots around the car, but the majority of Harp's parents' checking account was divided equally between Harp's and my suitcase. And gas is only getting more expensive. At the first station we pass once we've crossed the California border, it's $13.72 per gallon. We need food, a place to sleep tonight. I'm worried about Peter—he refuses a hospital, saying it will only slow us down and make us vulnerable. When he drifts into an uneasy-seeming sleep, I tell Harp about Winnie—that she lives in San Francisco, and is most likely the person who called that night. Harp tries to spin this as a good thing—a sign my sister knows about me, is trying to find me—but she knows, as I do, what it means. It means my hunch—the gut feeling that my parents are alive out there upon which this whole trip was initially based—is wrong. We're exhausted and broke; Peter's hurt and we could get hurt, too—anywhere, at any moment. If we're going to survive, we need to stop for a moment and catch our breath. We need an adult. And luckily, we know exactly one out here on this unfamiliar coast. We know the one I trust above all.

Harp gets off the highway in a resort town called Truckee, so we can get our bearings and something to eat. The weather is miserable as we pull in—a thick layer of cold, clammy fog obscures nearly everything. It's only eight a.m., and the only place that's open, for some reason, is a sad little BurgerTime, all rusted chrome and sickly pink. My eyes dart immediately to the register, as if I expect to find Edie standing there, but the girl managing it is a skinny blonde teenager chomping sleepily on a stick of gum. Harp takes Peter's phone and the slip of paper with Wambaugh's number outside, where she says she'll get better reception, while I get from the cashier a small order of hot dog fries, as well as a garbage bag filled with all the ice she can give me. Peter, propped up, purple-eyed in the closest booth, laughs when he sees me dragging it behind me, then winces. I sit beside him and he takes the bag from me, holds it against his torso.

"Hey," he says. "Remember when a Believer named Chip completely kicked my ass in a motel room in Winnemucca, Nevada?"

I pretend to think for a moment. "No. That doesn't ring a bell."

"Good. What remains of my dignity thanks you for that." There's a long pause in which it feels like neither of us knows what to say, and then Peter says, "I'm sorry. I should have told you earlier, but it's like you said—I don't like thinking about him."

"I get it," I tell him. "Really. I just wish I didn't know."

His face falls. "I don't blame you. And I understand if you want to pretend last night didn't happen—the nice parts of last night, I mean. If it's too weird now, I—"

"That's not what I mean." I touch his bruised cheek with the tips of my fingers. "I wish I didn't know because we have to be all serious and grim now, and have

216

Important Talks about it. When I'd rather just be, you know . . . making out with you."

It's so easy to believe in him then, as I watch his expression light up, all surprise and happy confusion. He begins to lean towards me, so slowly it's agonizing, but before he can kiss me Harp strides up to the booth, swinging the car keys on her index finger.

"Keep it clean, you two; this is a family establishment," she says, popping one of the greasy fries into her mouth. She scans the neon menu and calls to the cashier, "Hey, can you send a chocolate-banana milkshake over here? And a chicken-fried biscuit?"

"Money," I remind her as she slips into the booth across from us. "Try to remember that we're running out of money."

"Yes, Mother," she sighs, rolling her eyes at me. "Anyway, you'll be happy to know that Wambaugh was thrilled to hear from me and would be delighted to host us at her parents' home for however long we need. When I said we were having a rough time, she said she was literally turning our lemons into lemonade as we spoke. As in, she was making a pitcher of lemonade. She said that, Viv."

"I know, Harp." It's classic Wambaugh and goofy as hell, but I can't help but grin at the thought of it. "She says that kind of thing."

The drive to Wambaugh's parents' house takes less than two hours, on a foggy road through which I can just make out the ragged outlines of shaggy pines and snow-peaked mountains. Harp sits in the passenger seat, meticulously counting every last one of our bills, and Peter lies in the back, making very little noise except for the shift of the ice in the garbage bag we brought with us. I'm worried about the amount of pain he's in. I'm worried about fractured ribs, internal bleeding. But Wambaugh will know what to do. The prospect of seeing her has energized me all of a sudden, even though I'm exhausted and my stomach is empty except for one-third of a carton of hot dog fries, even though the weather hasn't improved since Truckee, and all we can see of California is a dense silvery fog. I think about Wambaugh the day after the Rapture: how she made me believe it was not over for us yet. I need that feeling from her again.

As we get closer, Harp reads out loud from the meticulous directions Wambaugh gave her over the phone. It's hard to determine where we are at any given time; the fog is so thick it obscures the road signs. But eventually we turn down the street Harp thinks is the right one. Behind all that fog I imagine there to be trees, big Victorian-looking houses, maybe. But we don't know for sure. The fog is so thick here, I half-wonder if it's smoke.

I park near where I imagine the curb to be, and we get out. Peter climbs out of the backseat, and I'm relieved to see he's standing a little straighter, grimacing a little less. From the sidewalk, we can see a little more clearly the dark outlines of homes. But there are no people visible, and no sound—we might be the only ones foolish enough to try to drive a car here.

"Wambaugh said they're halfway down the street," Harp says uncertainly. We look behind us, to gauge how far we've come, but there's no way of knowing. We move hesitantly forward, all my excitement and optimism suddenly draining away, because how can Wambaugh convince me that I'm doing the right thing if I can't even find her?

Suddenly Peter puts a hand out to stop us. I hear footsteps, the sound of shoes on pavement.

"Is that her?" whispers Harp. "What if that's not her?"

I'm not willing to stand here, to wait. "Wambaugh!" I shout. "Wambaugh!"

Harp tugs on my arm to get me to stop. We can hear the footsteps get heavier and louder. I shout her name again and Harp tries to pull me backwards to the car, but before she can get very far, a figure practically materializes in front of us, stepping out of the fog and into our vision like she's passed into this dimension from another. Harp drops my arm. That first burst of relief I feel upon seeing the person's face fades quickly.

Wambaugh looks like she's been through hell. Her eyes are ringed with dark circles; she has three inches of gray-brown at the roots of her dyed blonde hair. She's wearing jeans and a bathrobe and slippers, and she's probably lost ten pounds. But she still has her dimples, and that bright white grin that she grins now at us. She spreads her thin arms wide, as if gesturing to the wide world that surrounds us.

"Friends!" she cries. "Welcome to California!"

The fog, Wambaugh explains as she leads us carefully to her parents' house, started last week as a kind of misty haze, and it becomes more and more impenetrable with each passing day. Really, she tells us in her usual cheery way, it could be worse—it's practically impossible to drive, and it's a shame we won't be able to see the palm trees while we're here, but Believer activity has cut down by *a lot* since the fog rolled in. "A *lot*," Wambaugh says again to emphasize. She takes an abrupt left and leads us up what reveals itself to be a front path and onto the porch of a big old house with all its windows boarded up. As she's unlocking the front door, I glance at Harp and Peter. They both look a little nervous. Harp only ever had one class with Wambaugh, and knows her primarily from my descriptions. Peter doesn't know Wambaugh at all, and I can imagine what he sees—a middle-aged woman who seems hurt and scared and alone. This is the person I'm relying on to get us back on track.

"Mom! Dad!" Wambaugh calls out as we step into an ornate old-fashioned foyer with all its lights shut off. "My students are here!"

I don't know what I'm expecting from Wambaugh's parents. Seeing Wambaugh now, the tension between her eyes, the nervousness with which she closes the door behind her, I imagine her parents must be her total opposite. Cold and unforgiving. But we hear movement in the house, and then two elderly people shuffle into our line of view, wearing bright welcoming smiles on their faces.

"Well, isn't this just the surprise to end all surprises!" Wambaugh's mother says. She hugs me tightly and then does the same to Harp. Meanwhile, Wambaugh's father is shaking Peter's hand vigorously.

"Wish I could see the other guy!" he says, chuckling, and Peter chuckles too in his utter bemusement.

"We haven't met any of Matilda's students in *years,*" says Mrs. Wambaugh to me. "We used to meet them all the time when we were still in Pittsburgh, but then we retired out here and it's just been *years.* Of course, we didn't see much of Matilda herself during that time, either."

"Sorry, Mom," says Wambaugh. She instantly looks years younger, by virtue of having been reprimanded.

"I understand!" Mrs. Wambaugh says, putting her hands up in supplication. "Certainly I understand how busy a high school teacher's life can be! Not as busy as it might have been if you'd given us any grandchildren in that time, but—"

"Why don't we go into the living room?" Wambaugh interrupts brightly, gesturing to a room directly to our left. "We have lunch already set up for you guys there."

My stomach growls in response. Wambaugh and her mother lead Harp and me into the room, followed by Peter and Mr. Wambaugh, who's been talking to Peter the whole time about baseball. "Now, I *understand* it's been a trying couple of months," I can hear him saying, "but I'm sick to death of that dull as hell Church of America league. Do they have to follow up every home run with a stadium-wide Hail Frick? I want to watch real baseball!"

Peter murmurs in agreement. The living room is dark except for one desk lamp, and contains several cozy-looking couches on which I can already imagine myself falling asleep. There's a coffee table in the center of the room, on which a pitcher of lemonade and a platter of sandwiches already sit. There's a fire crackling in the fireplace, and above the mantle hangs a large crucifix. The sight of it makes my stomach drop. I stop walking, but Mr. Wambaugh just walks around me, ushering Peter to his seat while reminiscing about some classic World Series game from the 1970s, and Harp doesn't notice because she's made a beeline for the sandwiches.

"Viv," says Wambaugh, patting the spot beside her. "Come sit down."

When I do, Mrs. Wambaugh hands me a glass of lemonade and says, "Now, why don't you tell us about how you ended up coming all this way."

I start talking. I don't want Harp or Peter to tell the story, as neither one of them seems phased by the huge piece of Believer paraphernalia hanging not six feet from where we sit, and I don't trust them enough to leave out the dangerous parts—where we're going, and what we plan to do there. I tell them about my parents and Harp's, my grandparents, Melodie Hopkirk, Raj. I tell them a little about Edie and a little about how Peter got hurt. Wambaugh and her mother listen solemnly, their eyes bright with tears. The whole time my mind is racing. No wonder Wambaugh looks nervous and depressed, trapped here in this house with a couple of deceivingly pleasant Believers. Surely there has to be some way to get her out of here—we're four against two now, and Wambaugh's parents, though lively, seem a little frail. We'll get her out tonight, we'll make our way through the fog, and tomorrow, she'll come with us to San Francisco and help us find Frick's compound. In my story, I make it seem like we came to California because we had nothing else to do. Harp's on her third sandwich, not paying attention except to accept the Wambaughs' condolences when it comes time, but Peter is watching me carefully and curiously out of his swollen eye.

"Well," Mrs. Wambaugh says, when I've finished, blowing her nose into a napkin. "I don't know that I've ever *heard* of a braver group of kids than you three."

"Does your heart good," says Wambaugh's dad, "to see the youth of America flourishing like this. Makes the future seem a little brighter, doesn't it, Tillie?"

"Absolutely," says Wambaugh. She's beaming at me in pride, and I feel a little glow of pleasure when I think of how proud she'll be when she finds out our actual intentions. There's a little ding from another room, and Mrs. Wambaugh stands abruptly.

"That's my pie! I hope you kids like cherry. When Matilda told us you were coming, I thought you might need a little treat. Dear, will you help me clean up the kitchen? We should give Matilda some time alone with her kids."

Mr. Wambaugh elbows Peter in the side. "The old ball and chain," he says, not noticing Peter's flinch of pain. He follows Mrs. Wambaugh into the kitchen, and once I'm sure they are safely out of earshot, I turn to Wambaugh.

"You should have told us they were Believers!" I whisper to her. "We would have come sooner! We wouldn't have made you stay here on your own with them!"

"Believers?" Wambaugh echoes.

I nod at the crucifix behind her. When Wambaugh realizes that's what I'm talking about, she laughs. "Oh, Viv, I'm sorry; I see why you were confused. But my parents aren't Believers. They're super, super Catholic."

"That's a Catholic crucifix," Peter interjects. "You can tell because the eyes on the dead Jesus don't follow you as you move across the room, like they do on the Believer ones."

"Well," I say, unappeased, "Catholics are Believers, too, aren't they? I mean, technically anyone who Believes is a Believer. Why should I reject one and accept the other? They're all taking their cues from an invisible dude in the sky."

"Viv," Wambaugh begins, but I interrupt her.

"It's not like they're legitimate just because they've been around longer. In fact, that's just given them more time to do shitty things. What about the Crusades? What about all those bombed abortion clinics? What about *you*, Wambaugh? You look miserable. You don't look like yourself. What have they been doing to you?"

"*They* are my elderly parents," Wambaugh says, suddenly reviving the sharp snap of professional disciplinarian back into her voice, "and *you* need to back off, right now."

I set my jaw and stop talking. I've gotten carried away and I know it, but I'm still wary. Harp swallows a bite of sandwich.

"Wambaugh," she says, cautiously. "Are you Catholic, too?"

Wambaugh takes a breath. "Well, not that it's really

224

any of your business," she says. "But yeah, I am. I always have been—since I was a month old, in fact. And I've never bombed an abortion clinic or set someone's house on fire. So I'd very much appreciate it if you didn't conflate me with the people who do."

"How is that possible?" I ask. "How can you believe all that stuff?"

Wambaugh looks at me, her gaze softening. "We could sit here and have an in-depth discussion about why I believe the things I believe in, about the kind of comfort and guidance I've taken from my faith throughout my life, but it wouldn't matter to you one iota, Viv, because you don't believe. And that's okay! It's not up to me to tell you what you should believe in. That's the thing you've got to figure out for yourself. But let me tell you this: you can't go through life identifying the Believers from the Non-Believers and divvying up your love and trust accordingly. It's more complicated than that, Viv, and you know it. Don't be the kind of person who sees groups instead of people. That's the sort of thing Beaton Frick does."

It seems to me that Wambaugh has this slightly wrong—that Frick channels his hate into destruction and violence, while all I can do is hate, powerless and angry. But I've already upset Wambaugh and I regret it. So I say nothing.

"Now," she continues, "why don't you tell me what you're really doing all the way out here in California? Because something tells me that the Vivian Apple I once knew wouldn't embark on a cross-country road trip at the end of the world just for giggles."

I explain Peter's mysterious mail, what we heard from the Goliath about Frick's secret forest compound. I leave out the phone call; it embarrasses me now. Wambaugh listens with a worried look on her face. She never stops biting her lower lip. Towards the end of my explanation I realize that I'm starting to shrug a lot, to punctuate our rationale with "you knows" and "I don't knows," as if confirming with her face that this is a terrible idea.

"We had to do something," Harp explains. "We couldn't just sit around and wait."

Wambaugh smiles at us. "I think you're really brave. And I understand your frustration. It's just—I don't know, guys; everything is complicated, even the things that seem really simple. People disappear so you want to find out where they've gone. But what if you hate the answer? Or only find out some of it? You could spend years of your life trying to solve this mystery, and never be satisfied by it."

"But—"

"You have to try." Wambaugh completes my sentence for me, nodding. "I get it; I really do. That's why I'm proud of you. I just hope whatever you find out satisfies you. I hope you end up with more answers than you do questions."

"You could come with us," I say.

"I can't, Viv, but thanks. It's a nice idea, but I really need to be here."

"But you're clearly miserable here," I blurt out. "You seem really depressed!"

Wambaugh's eyes widen and then she bursts into a

226

familiar peal of her wild laughter. "Viv," she says. "I'm forty years old, unemployed, living with my parents. And the apocalypse is about to arrive! Of *course* I'm depressed."

The Wambaughs insist we spend the night, and Peter and Harp are relieved when I agree. We spend the day talking and laughing with Wambaugh, watching coverage of a tsunami aftermath in Japan. Mrs. Wambaugh is a registered nurse, and she patches Peter up as best she can. They serve us a huge dinner, roast chicken and stuffing and carrots and salad, with the cherry pie for dessert. Mr. Wambaugh pours us all big glasses of wine, and laughs at his daughter's disapproving face. "They've been through so much, Tillie!" Mrs. Wambaugh implores her. "Let them have a drink, for heaven's sake!" The wine makes us all sleepy, and the Wambaughs bid us goodnight, head upstairs to their respective bedrooms. Harp and Peter and I convene in the den, where the Wambaughs have made up a pull-out sofa bed. Peter picks a spiral-bound book off a side table—a road atlas of California.

"Mr. Wambaugh said we could take it with us," he explains, flipping open to a map of California. He points to Sacramento. "Here's us—" He traces his finger a short distance, to a point very close to Pacific. "And this is Point Reyes Station, where a barber apparently cut Frick's hair. And if you look more closely at this section . . ." He turns a couple pages and hands the atlas to Harp and me, his finger on a road marked Route 1—Sir Francis Drake Boulevard.

"King Arthur Lane," Harp repeats Goliath's faulty

information with a shake of her head. "God, he was a putz."

"So that's it then," I say. "Right? The compound must be somewhere in Point Reyes."

"That seems like our best bet," Peter agrees.

On the map, the area marked Point Reyes seems tiny, just a little sliver of green hugging the California coast. But I know it will be different once we're there—bigger and denser, yet another mystery to solve. I look up at Harp and Peter.

"The Wambaughs would let us stay, you know. They'll probably offer it in the morning. They'd keep us safe. There wouldn't be any shame in wanting that, in taking that."

Harp gives me a withering look, and stands. "Are *you* going to stay?"

"No," I say. "I'm going to see what's out there."

"Then of course there'd be shame in it," she replies, walking to the door. "You think I'm just going to chill here with my history teacher while my protégée is out there, fighting the good fight, having the adventure? Nice try, Viv." Harp yawns. "But you're stuck with me."

She slips out of the room, and in a moment I hear her footsteps on the stairs leading up to the guest bedroom we'll share. Peter is still bent over the map, tracing a road with his fingertip. He doesn't acknowledge me. I wonder if I've said something wrong. Or have I made the prospect of Sacramento sound too attractive to him? I know I could spend hours sitting here, willing him to speak to me, driving myself crazy wondering why he won't speak to me. But I won't let myself do it. I stand.

"Well," I say. "Goodnight."

I turn to leave but Peter reaches out and grabs my hand, pulls me down beside him. "Was that really your goodnight?" he asks. "That was pathetic." He takes my face into his hands and pulls me towards him. His lips are warm and soft; they make my whole body thrum with energy.

"I thought you were mad at me, or something," I say between kisses. "You were all mysterious and quiet!"

"That's not mystery; that's shyness." Peter tips his head to the side and kisses the hollow of my throat. "That's me not knowing how to say, 'Viv, you should stay here for a little while so I can kiss you.'"

"You should say it like that," I tell him. "That sounds really good."

When I'm kissing him, time seems to move in a new, dizzying way. Each second is sweeter, lazier, somehow shorter than the last. When we pull away, Peter stares at my face for a long moment and then grins, satisfied with whatever he sees there. It's one a.m.

"Get some rest, Vivian Apple," he says. "We have a big day tomorrow."

"I can't stay here?"

I only mean that I'm drowsy with wine and sleep and pleasure. But I realize once I've said it what it sounds like, and my face gets hot. Peter's eyes widen a fraction.

"I don't think so." He suppresses a little smile. "But only because I think the Wambaughs would disapprove."

I stand again and Peter stands with me. He wraps his arms around me and buries his face in my hair. "I have a little something for you, by the way. It's in the car. Remind me tomorrow to give it to you."

"What is it?" I ask.

But he shakes his head. "Tomorrow," he says.

Early the next morning, after we've slept enough and taken glorious showers, Wambaugh and her parents wait by the door with a big cooler, into which they've packed sandwiches, fruit, pretzels, water bottles. Mrs. Wambaugh has included a small first-aid kit, which she points out to Peter with a meaningful glance.

"I don't understand why you have to leave so *soon*," she says as she hugs us goodbye. "We'd be happy to have you just as long as you need."

"Thanks, Mrs. Wambaugh," I say. "But Peter has family further west."

"Well, you're welcome back any time," she says. "You really are."

"Just make sure you make it back here before the world goes kablooie!" says Mr. Wambaugh, laughing, and Wambaugh's mother elbows him, saying "Howard!"

Wambaugh walks us out to the car. The fog is still heavy around the house, and cold, but when we look up, we can see the faintest outline of a watery sun up in the sky. The car is safe where we left it; it's hard to imagine, as Wambaugh told us, that this neighborhood was ever a hotbed of Believer activity. Peter offers to drive—he's looking better today, and moving lighter on his feet. When she hugs me goodbye, Wambaugh says, "I hope you end up with more answers than questions."

"Are you sure you don't want to come with us?" I ask. Wambaugh nods. "This isn't my fight, Viv."

I watch her from the passenger seat window as we pull away. One second she's standing there on the curb in her bathrobe, with her arms folded. In the next she's been swallowed up by fog. A small voice inside me, one I don't want to listen to, tells me that I won't see her again. That person, a person who helped form me as much as anybody—I will never see her again.

Chapter Eighteen

The fog clears not long after we've left Sacramento, but the sky stays overcast. The road we're on is wide and winding, with acres of open space on either side. It's not long before we see signs pointing us in the direction of San Francisco and Point Reyes. Beside me, driving, Peter is fidgety and distracted. I know he still believes we'll find his father at the end of this road, and he has just as much a right as me to try. I reach over and take his hand into mine. Behind me, I hear the telltale rattle of Harp's bottle of Xanax. None of us quite know what to expect from this—I wonder if for Peter and Harp, as for me, the worst-case scenario would be nothing at all.

The road we take from Sacramento leads, after two hours, directly into Point Reyes Station, a town thoroughly abandoned. The buildings are short and squat and empty; some of them have charred-looking roofs and front porches, as though the people in them were burned out. We pass the barber shop Goliath told us about—the windows are all smashed in, and like Harp's old house in Pittsburgh, the word "SIN" has been spray-painted across the front door.

It's past noon by the time we finally find ourselves on Sir Francis Drake Boulevard. The road is long and winding and narrow, surrounded by dense trees on both sides. This is the point where our information just stops. We don't know how far onto the road we need to travel, or how deep into the forest we must venture once we do. I don't even know what we're looking for. I stare into the trees as we pass, thinking I'll see—what? I look for lights, for smoke, for signs of movement. Any sign or symbol that would indicate we aren't the only ones here. Eventually and accidentally, we get off the road, and onto one that brings us a bit south. This road is thin and seemingly untraveled, and the forest on either side is taller and more menacing. About half an hour into our drive we have to stop, because a fallen tree lies across the road, blocking us from driving further. The three of us leave the car to examine it.

"I didn't see any 'Welcome to the Church of America's Secret Headquarters billboards," Peter says. His voice is light, but he looks disappointed. "Did you?"

"Is this hopeless?" I ask. "This place is huge. How are we supposed to find a hidden compound in it?"

"It couldn't be that secluded," Harp says, "because Frick had to have been able to find it. And he was, like, really old, and possibly senile."

Peter nods and climbs over some branches and piles of leaves to the base of the fallen tree. "Also," he calls out, "this has been sawed down. It didn't fall naturally. I think this might be a good sign—a secret security fence. We should keep going on foot."

Harp fills a bag with water bottles and food from Wambaugh's cooler, and I grab the sledgehammer from the trunk—just in case. We climb over the tree and continue down the road beyond, which becomes even more over-grown and impenetrable; the grass is up to our knees. But it doesn't seem wild enough for an abandoned road—on the contrary, the grass is lush and green and level as far as we can see. There's an eerie calm all around us. I can't hear anything, not the chirping of birds or the distant highway, not even the wind rustling in the trees. Something weird is happening in this forest. Something artificial. Above all, I have this funny feeling that the three of us are being watched.

We walk slowly, for well over an hour, scouting everything in our immediate vicinity for signs of life. We stop by a creek to eat our sandwiches, but my stomach is in knots and Peter's hands are shaking. Harp takes a bite of hers and then wraps it back up in its plastic bag. While we're sitting there, the sun comes out, peeking down through the canopy of leaves, but that just reminds me that it won't be long until it sets. We continue forward, but I can't stop thinking about the approaching night. We don't have a tent; we don't have blankets; we don't have much food. We assume that at some point we'll have to leave the road and trek into the forest—but when will that be? What if we've already passed it? What if we never find it? I am more frightened now than I have ever been in the presence of Believers. Believers are just people—I know what they are and what kind of danger they pose. This forest is different, though, and unknown. I worry that it will swallow us whole.

"Maybe we should turn around?" says Peter after another hour. He's taken off his hoodie and slung it over his shoulder; the hair on the back of his neck is wet with sweat. Harp slaps bugs off her arms. I'm trying to catch my breath. "I feel like we should have passed it by now."

"Maybe we have," I say. My throat feels tight and the words come out in gasps. "Or maybe it's still ahead. We could keep going and have missed it, or turn around and never see it."

"Viv?"

I feel the dread rising in my lungs like smoke. I'm choking back tears. "We're never going to find it. It's hidden for a reason; it's hidden from people like us."

"We'll find it," says Peter. He reaches to pull me into a hug. "We're not in any rush."

"We *are* in a rush," I yell, pushing him away. "The world's going to end in three months, and we're going to still be in this forest, rationing bites of Wambaugh's sandwiches, looking for a secret place that might not even exist!"

"Uh . . . guys?" Harp says softly. She's wandered a few steps off the road and stands between two slim white trees. "I don't want to interrupt Viv's nervous breakdown or anything, but you don't think this could be a sign of anything, do you?"

We join her at the side of the road and look down. There, in the mat of dead leaves that makes up the forest floor, are six smooth white stones—four make a vertical line that ends at Harp's feet, and the other two lie on either side, turning the arrangement into a unmistakable cross. Harp points, several yards further into the forest, where another stone cross lies. When we look straight ahead into the trees, we can see another, and another, forming a path that leads to a point outside our line of sight.

"Holy shit," Peter whispers.

"I'm going to get credit for this, right?" Harp says giddily. "Like, when we all look back on this moment, you're going to say, 'And it was Harp who had the clear thinking to notice the path of crosses in the trees?'"

"You will get so much credit." Peter grabs her and hugs her with one arm. "I will personally ensure that those are the exact words engraved on your tombstone."

My best friends look at me. My face is still wet with tears. I take a step forward and put one arm around Harp and the other around Peter, turning us into a proper triangle.

"I'm sorry, guys," I say at the ground. "I got scared."

"It's okay, Viv," says Peter. "That's pretty understandable."

"Totes," says Harp brightly. "Now can we go find this motherfucking compound?"

We follow the crosses deeper and deeper into the forest. At first they're maybe three or four yards apart, but as we get further, more and more space lies between them, so that we'll pass one and have to keep walking uncertainly for a few minutes before another appears to assure us we're still on the right path. More than once we have to stop and recalibrate by moving back to the last cross and starting again. Once we're fairly deep into the forest, the crosses curve abruptly to the right, taking us several miles south and east, until I imagine we can't be too far from where we left the car. Nobody speaks. Each time we see a new cross, one of us points to acknowledge it, and we trudge on. All joking and talking has stopped; I don't hold Peter's hand or link arms with Harp. Dusk begins to fall, but I'm not scared of the dark anymore. I know we're being led to the end of our journey, and even though I don't know yet what that entails, there's a sense of relief in its drawing nearer.

It's becoming harder to see Peter and Harp in the dark, and the last cross we passed had to have been up to ten minutes ago, when all of the sudden the trees clear abruptly. In the dark, it's hard to make out just how big it is, but in front of us looms a large, beautiful wooden building, like a hunting lodge or a really wealthy person's version of a log cabin. We're still a front lawn's distance from it, and the forest floor in front of the lodge has been cleared of leaves and branches. There's a small garden of nearly life-size stone statues, guarding the lodge like sentinels. Without speaking, the three of us trudge across the fresh, new dirt, to examine them.

Peter takes a quick inhale of breath as we get closer to the first one. "Well," he says softly. "I guess we're in the right place?"

Even in the dark, it's impossible to mistake the statue for anyone but Frick. The sculptor has done a good job of capturing the businessman slick of his hair, each of his individual teeth. He stands with his hands clasped behind his back, staring up at the sky like an old friend. A small plaque at the bottom reads, *"Beaton Frick, Prophet and Messiah."*

"Ick," Harp says.

Even though there's no light emanating from the building in front of us, all three of us move carefully and quietly, and speak only in whispers. There are a number of additional

Frick statues, all portraying him reverently as an obviously holy man. "*Frick Receives Divine Inspiration*" reads the plaque on the one in which Frick scribbles furiously into a stone notebook, while three genderless winged angels stand behind him, looking down at him lovingly. "*Frick Is Shown the Holy Land*" depicts the chapter in the Book of Frick where Jesus takes Frick to the Lincoln Memorial, and Lincoln himself steps down to converse with them. Frick looks concerned and determined in this one, gesticulating his mouth open, while Jesus and Lincoln look interested and thoughtful, like they don't have better things to do. Then there are a number of statues of men in suits, none of whose names I recognize, and whose connection to the Church isn't explained. When we reach the last statue, Peter makes a quiet angry noise.

The man has thin, smiling lips and crinkled eyes. He stands with chest protruding and his hands on his hips, like a superhero. Behind him is a small group of women, all carved together out of one rock. "*Adam Taggart*," the plaque reads, "*Enforcer*."

"This is disgusting," Peter murmurs.

"I guess Frick really, really liked your dad," I whispered.

Peter shakes his head. "Not that. I mean the women."

I look again at the women gathered behind Taggart. They're the only women depicted in this garden of statues, and they are all cartoonishly buxom, wide-hipped. The artist has carved skimpy clothes onto them, so I guess they're meant to be the Church's interpretation of prostitutes, which is to say, most women. I take a closer look at their individual faces and am startled by the realistic

238

looks of pain and agony. It's only then that I realize that stone flames lick their bottom halves. In a circle around the unit of women, the artist has printed the words, "*She shall be burnt with fire . . .*" The statue depicts Peter's father burning a group of women alive.

"This fucking religion," Harp says.

I can feel my skin pucker with goosebumps, though I'm not at all cold. Now that we're here, I could not feel more sure we shouldn't be. I know we came all this way, through violence and hunger and hippies, but if one of my friends suggested that we turn back around at this moment, I would do it so happily. Peter and Harp bound up the steps to the cabin and up to the front door, and I follow. *Please let it be locked*, I ask the Universe, *let us not be able to get in.* It's locked, but Peter doesn't hesitate. He takes the sledge-hammer out of my hands, and uses it to smash in the nearest window. He leans the sledgehammer against the wall and climbs through, then helps Harps and me maneuver around the broken shards. Inside, we stand together in the dark, trying to let our eyes adjust, but the sun has fully set now.

"Is there a light switch?" asks Harp. She feels her way along the wall nearby. "Or do they just use fiery torches, Bible-style?"

"Harp," I say nervously, "I don't think it's a good idea—"

But she finds it, and flicks it, and everything in front of us is suddenly suffused with light.

I forget the sense of anxiety in my gut and gaze around in wonder. The inside of the compound looks like nothing I've ever seen before. We're standing in a huge open space, lit by an enormous chandelier that hangs from the high, sloping ceiling. The floors are made of sanded stone; the walls are red wood. It looks like the inside of a magnificent treehouse. Lining the walls are lofted walkways and staircases leading to several floors of doors shut on rooms whose insides I can't even imagine. Straight in front of us, there's a huge stone fireplace, and above that a giant, inexplicable movie screen.

"This is really nice," Harp says in naked admiration. Peter and I look at her. "Well, isn't it? It's like a fancy hotel in the woods."

"The Church of America is a multimillion-dollar corporation," Peter reminds her. "Frick was super-rich."

"I don't understand," I say. "Did he live here?"

"I thought so," Peter says, wandering off to examine what looks like a small office behind a panel of glass, "but this seems like more than that. What are all these rooms?"

Harp and I move in the opposite direction, studying the row of doors along the west wall of the building. As we get closer to the last one, we see that there's a handwritten sign suspended from a nail in the top center. "*Ulrich-Zaches*," the sign says. Harp looks at me and I shrug. She tries the door, and it opens.

I walk in first. The room is dark, but the light from the chandelier outside reveals three sets of stark-looking bunk beds lining the walls. The beds are tightly made, and there's nothing on them to indicate that anyone has slept in them recently. I turn and find a mirror hanging on the wall behind me, and a small writing desk. There's no paperwork on the desk, no pens or pencils. It's like the room is waiting for someone to come and inhabit it. But who? I run my finger across the surface of the desk, and it comes away dark with dust.

"This is creepy," Harp says. I look up and see that she hasn't moved from the doorway; her hand is still on the knob. Her face is tense, uneasy. "There's nothing in here. Let's move on."

We return to the main room just as Peter emerges from the office. He's got the same look on his face that Harp does, only he's directing it right at me. I feel my palms go clammy.

"There are some empty cubicles in there," he explains when he reaches us. "A couple of phones, disconnected. But there's also—Viv, I don't know that this even means anything."

"What?"

"There's a file cabinet. Locked. I tried to jimmy it open, but . . ." He shakes his head. His blue eyes are wide. "The labels on the drawers have last names on them. A to D, E to J, K to M. The first last name on the first drawer is Apple."

"Well, that could mean anything," I say. I can hear the panic in my voice but I don't feel it. I don't feel anything. I feel like my head has disconnected from my body and is floating several feet about us. "That could be just Church records, or—what do you think it means?"

"I don't know," Peter says.

"Let's get out of here now," Harp says again. "I mean it. I just—I have a bad feeling about this place. I think we need to go. I think we need to find the police."

"Oh, no point in that," says a voice behind us. "The sheriff is miles and miles away."

241

Harp cries out. We whirl around, and even though I know who and what I will see when I do, I still feel the floor beneath me lose some of its solidity.

He stands now in front of the stone fireplace with a pleasant smile on his lined face, radiating an otherworldliness, a ghostliness. He is tall and commanding and bigger than life.

"Frick," I whisper.

Chapter Nineteen

Frick takes a step forward, and the three of us step immediately back. I can see now that right behind him, stooping as though to hide, is Peter's father.

"You know me," Frick says kindly, in response to my whisper, continuing to approach. "But I don't think I know any of you. Do I? Have I ever had the pleasure?"

"Dad?" says Peter. When Taggart hears Peter's voice, he takes a small step out from Frick's shadow. He looks unkempt and unshaven, his expression vacant. He moans when he sees Peter; he sinks to the floor. Peter rushes forward to kneel beside him. "What's wrong with you?" Peter asks, but Taggart just stares into space. "It's Peter. Dad?"

Frick watches the interaction with a twinkle in his eyes that I recognize, when he looks up at Harp and me, to be tears. "Father–son reunions," he says softly. "They always get me. They remind me of a vision I had recently of my future reunion with my own heavenly Father. But—must be patient. Must be patient. You know me?"

Harp and I nod. I can't speak. I'm frightened, but the truth is I'm a little awed, too, to be in Frick's presence. It's not just proximity to celebrity; it's the fact that Frick gives off palpable vibes of power, of sureness. To stand here under his spell as he comes closer is to understand how he could convince so many that what he claimed to see was right and true.

"But I don't know you," he says. "What's your name?"

"Viv—Vivian Apple," I manage to squeak out. "My parents were Ned and Mara Apple, from Pittsburgh."

There's no flicker of recognition when I say their names. "And you?" he says to Harp.

"Harpreet Janda," she says.

Frick nods. "They seek me from all over," he explains, mostly to me. "Not just the States. Give me your tired, your hungry, huddled masses . . . that's in the Book of Frick, but it's also on the Statue of Liberty. Your friend here came all the way from the Middle East, all because she Believes. Have you read my book?"

"Um, parts," I say, while beside me Harp mutters indignantly, "I'm Indian-American." Now that Frick is only a few inches away from me, an alarm bell begins to ring. He is Beaton Frick—there's no doubt about that—but the smooth-talking, polished CEO I used to see in press conferences is gone. That blindingly white smile is gone—his teeth are yellow, coffee-stained. The Frick that stands in front of me now is grizzled and old; he's lost weight. He smells as if he hasn't bathed in weeks, and a muscle in his cheek twitches periodically. But it's his eyes that worry me most of all—those clear green eyes, piercing on TV or in magazine profiles, are wide, confused, manic. They're looking at me as hard as they can and not seeing anything at all. I've always believed Frick to be detached from reality, but I thought he was just a megalomaniac, a manipulator, a con artist. Now I begin to slowly understand. He's far more dangerous than any of those things. He's a true Believer.

"You have a question for me, Vivian Apple?" he says.

I shake my head.

"Yes, you do!" He wags a finger in my face. He turns abruptly on his heel and walks a few paces away. I realize for the first time that he is barefoot. "I can always tell when there's a question about to be asked. Ask it!"

I look at Peter, waving his hand slowly in front of his unresponsive father's face, and Harp, who stares back at me. I don't really want to ask it. I don't really want to know the answer. But Frick is here in front of me, alive. And this will be my only opportunity to achieve anything that even remotely resembles understanding.

"My parents were Ned and Mara Apple, from Pittsburgh, Pennsylvania," I say again. "They were members of the Church of America, and Believers. At some point on March 24th of this year, they disappeared. I'd like to know what happened to them."

"Certainly!" Frick grins as he turns back to me, like he's relieved I've asked him so easy a question. "Certainly I can tell you. What happened was that they were saved. While the rest of the world descended into hell, God blessed your parents and took them into his fold, in heaven."

I try to breathe calmly. "I don't believe you."

"No," says Frick, frowning. "I can see that. Tell me. Do you believe in heaven?"

I shake my head.

"Do you believe in God?"

I hesitate, then shake my head.

"What *do* you believe, Vivian?"

I've been asked this question so many times at this point—and asked it of myself even more—that I should have for him an articulate answer, one which encompasses everything I think is important about the world I inhabit, the world I think Frick has made significantly worse. I believe, like Peter said, that we should love each other. I believe, like Wambaugh said, that we are all people before we are groups. But what I'm feeling at this moment is something deeper than these platitudes. It's something huge and primordial and completely beyond my understanding. I believe in Peter. I believe in Harp. I believe in me.

"That you're lying," I say evenly.

Frick chuckles. He walks in a small tight circle, muttering things I can't hear. He does this for so long, I wonder if he's forgotten we're in the room. But then he begins to speak up.

". . . and when I first saw the angel, I didn't believe it *myself*, if you want to know the truth. Being at that time sinful, without God or vision. I stood up and I said, who are you? But the angel didn't have to tell me, for I was suddenly suffused with a holy light that clarified everything, made me see the truth in everything. I had been wrong. I had rejected God, and so had my country around me. And we were on a desperate path."

Frick looks at me again, and as soon as he does, his speech becomes oddly lucid. "See, the thing that I didn't understand about the God of the Bible was this—why would he go to the trouble of making us all, only to watch us fail, and eventually destroy us? If you were Him"—and Frick blesses himself and mumbles a quick prayer for forgiveness for even suggesting the notion—"and you decided to create a race of beings in your image, why wouldn't you build into them goodness, and wisdom, and strength? If you really loved us, wouldn't you make us unbreakable?" Frick approaches me suddenly then, and places his hands on either side of my head. I'm too shocked even to flinch. "That's the thing I didn't understand," he says, as begins to press down on my skull, "if he wanted us to live forever"—he presses harder and harder, his pinky digging into my lower eyesocket—"why did he make us so extremely fragile?"

I grab Frick's wrists, try to wrench them away, but he's surprisingly strong. I feel that he could squash my skull like a grape if he wanted to.

"Hey!" Harp shouts. She's at my side, suddenly, trying to push Frick back. He snaps awake, and steps lightly away, as though he'd just been standing in a door I wanted to pass.

"My apologies," he says. "But you understand me. The first angel I saw, so many years ago, he explained. We only appear breakable, he said, but God had given some of us a particular gift—or, if you like, a weapon. He had sent our souls to live in the United States. He had loved us so much He had given us that. That's why I don't feel so very bad for the damned, you know. They'll be tortured forever, but at least they'll be *here*.

"Anyway, that's when the wonderful thing began to happen. I had written my book, and spread it as far as I could, but the truth is, not many listened at first. They were happy; they were flourishing; they saw no reason to ascribe their success to God. A few sought me out, and followed me—blessed Adam over there, of course," and he gestures to Taggart, who still sits in an apparent fugue state next to a bewildered Peter, "and a handful of others, most of whom fell back into sin as years went by. But then, three years ago, I was standing outside a mall in Omaha, spreading the Word of the Church, and the people were passing me by, ignoring me as always, and then I just said it: 'The Rapture has been foretold for March 24th of three years hence,' I said. Now, at the time, I shocked even myself. I hadn't planned to say those words. I hadn't even thought them. And yet they came out at that moment, as if willed to. Of course, it was divine inspiration, I realize that now.

"And this was a message God wanted America to hear, so he began to show them the extent of his power. Earthquakes, floods, tornadoes, disease. Mass shootings, hurricanes, economic strife. And again and again, I told them. The Rapture has been foretold for March 24th of three years hence. And finally they began to listen."

He shoots me a quick, pleased grin. He looks like a child, showing his mother the plate off which he's eaten all his vegetables. Frick couldn't be more proud of himself.

"And, of course, that's when the Three Angels appeared."

He turns to look up at the blank gray movie screen.

"Three Angels?" Harp says. "Like the ones in the statue outside?"

"Yes, that's right!" Frick says, his volume ramping up a notch, as though Harp's first language is not English. She rolls her eyes at him. "The Three Angels contacted me and told me that I had done well, but not enough. For instance, I had not emphasized enough in the Book of Frick the reason *why* America was blessed above all other nations—capitalism!"

"Naturally," mutters Peter from the floor.

"They helped me to rewrite the Book," Frick explains, pacing again, this time with a little skip in every second step. "Then there was nothing to do but spread the Word as far and as best as I could, with the Three Angels to guide me. They spoke to me through the screen," he says, gesturing at it, "and they told me all I had to do was wait. Wait for the devastation to convince them. Wait for them to come to me."

Suddenly Frick stops and staggers, like he's gotten dizzy. He lowers himself to kneel on the floor, holding his hands behind his back. "They didn't feel like my other visions," he says quietly. "Not all the time. They didn't always have the light around them. They tested my faith. The angels asked me if I was sure it would happen, and when I said yes, they said, *how do you know*. And the truth was I did not know how I knew, but the fact that they were appearing to me seemed like proof enough to me. Wasn't it?"

"Wait for them to come to you . . ." I echo slowly. I start to feel something heavy pressing down on me. It's like Frick's hands on my skull again, but this time his hands are invisible, and made of iron.

"The angels appeared on the screen," Frick says, "and they told me I'd interpreted my visions wrong. They said the saved would not be lifted from Earth into heaven, as I'd expected, but that instead God would take their souls in their sleep. They said He would only take the True Believers, those who made the pilgrimage. They said they would bring the Believers here. That all I had to do was wait. And they did—some came weeks before the Rapture, and some appeared just hours before. But it had to be secret—this is what the angels told them. They had to make their journeys secret so the Non-Believers could not follow. Some nights, I worry it was too secret. Because hundreds came. But not all of them. That breaks my heart. Not all came. I don't know where they were, but they didn't come here.

"The angels said those who would be saved would have to sleep, that I would have to help them sleep, that I would have to make them sleep—"

Harp makes a noise beside me. I turn to her and see that she's crying, and even though I feel that unbearable pressure, the air around me weighing on me from all sides, I don't, I can't understand why yet.

"They said there was precedent for this. For sacrifice. So Adam and I, we served them wine that would make them sleep, and we watched them leave their earthly bodies."

Taggart falls backwards then from his sitting position, hitting his head on the floor. Peter doesn't notice. He has a hand in front of his mouth and he's staring at Frick in horror; his face pale. But I shake my head at him and Harp. I shake my head at Frick.

"You're lying." My voice sounds strangled.

"We—" Frick swallows. "We watched them leave their earthly bodies and then we burned the bodies. The angels

250

came on the screen and saw that it was good, and told us we would be rewarded. But still we wait and wait."

"No!" I say. "That isn't how it happened. That doesn't make any sense. There were holes in my parents' ceiling."

"They had to move in secret," Frick says, glancing at me nervously, "so the Non-Believers could not follow. And the angels saw that it was good—"

But I don't let him finish. I stride over to where he kneels, on the stone floor of the building in which he claims my parents were poisoned, and I punch him in the face as hard as I can. I've never punched anyone before and it hurts more than anything; immediately I feel sure that there are bones in my hand which are now broken. But I don't care, I don't care. I punch him again with my broken hand, and I kick him in the stomach. I shout, "You're lying, you're lying" as I kick him, and he falls to the floor, too, like Peter's father, both of them dead-eyed, hollow. I think of the gun in the glove compartment of my grandparents' car. If I had it in my hands, I know I would shoot this man, this man who says he killed my parents. But it's too far away and the pain I want to cause him can't wait for me to retrieve it. I kick him one more time, before Peter pulls me away.

"He's saying he poisoned my parents," I shout at him, struggling to get away. "Are you listening to him? He's saying he killed them and burned them."

"I know," Peter says. He holds my arms against my side. My hand throbs.

"He made them believe in him, and then he killed them, Peter!"

"I know. I heard him. But he's out of his mind, Viv. He's mentally ill. He didn't know what he was doing."

"He knew exactly what he was doing! 'Sacrifice,' he said!"

"It wasn't him, Viv. It was—I don't know, chemicals in his brain, or something; it wasn't him. But the person beating up a demented old man right now—that's really you."

I turn and look at Frick, lying on the floor where I left him. His green eyes fill with tears, as he stares up at the chandelier. He touches his face where I hit him. He looks old. He looks nothing like the man in the picture above my parents' mantle, the man they believed in. He looks tired and confused and small. I can't see him anymore then, because I'm crying so hard, and Peter pulls me into his arms and I can feel him taking deep breaths, trying to hold us both steady.

"My parents," I murmur into his shoulder. I think of the pictures of their baptism, in which their faces are so happy, so suffused with joy, but I can't picture those faces at all right now. I can see the shape of them, their necks and ears and collarbones, but their faces, I can't see. I can't believe Frick's story; I won't believe it. I'll come up with something else, some new story about how their lives ended, but I won't believe they ended here.

The light in the room changes suddenly. In addition to the hazy yellow glow of the chandelier, a fierce blue beam has suddenly been cast over Peter and I, over Harp, who lingers beside us, hazy-eyed, looking as if she wants to insert herself in the middle of our hug. We look up at the movie screen, which appears to have turned on suddenly. First the screen is nothing but blank blue, but just as suddenly it flickers onto a moving image: a white-walled room with no windows, a long table at which three people sit. It's a balding middle-aged man, a younger woman with her blonde hair pulled into a severe bun, and a third man, with light eyes and a high, sinister forehead. The men look strangely familiar to me. All three wear ridiculous white robes.

"Beaton!" the woman calls in a commanding voice. "Beaton, show yourself!"

Frick starts when he hears the voice, tries to drag himself up into a supplicant position. "I'm here!" he cries out. "I'm here! Is it time for my reward?"

"Your reward is nigh!" she booms. "But first—"

The woman stops abruptly. She squints and leans forward in her seat. "Is someone there with you?" she asks, her voice immediately losing its resonance. "Who are those—"

"Turn it off," the balding man says quickly. "Turn it off!"

There's a hectic moment where the picture goes a little scrambled. We can still hear the man screaming, "Turn it off! Turn it off!" and just before the screen goes blank again, a third voice tersely says, "Get someone over there! Now!" Then: nothing. Frick is kneeling, praying silently to himself. Taggart's still supine, though I notice that now his eyes are shut very tight. Harp turns to us.

"What the *fuck* was that?"

Peter wastes no time; he grabs us by our wrists and pulls us to the screen, until we're directly under it. He looks up, his eyes narrowed as though he's searching for something, then he nods and points. We follow his arm and see at the top of the screen a small black orb. A camera.

"I don't understand," I say. I'm still crying, but now it feels more like shock than anything. "Those were the angels? But those were just people . . ."

"I don't believe it," Peter says, shaking his head. "I mean, I *do*—of course I do. The Corporation. The Church of America Corporation. I think he just told us himself. People began to listen to him, and then the angels appeared. They told him to make it more about capitalism." Peter starts laughing, though it's clear he doesn't find this very funny. "They built up this company around him and used him for free marketing. They sold magazines and guns and survival kits and life insurance. All the Believers believed him because of sheer luck—bad things happened when he guessed they would—and because the Corporation kept him far enough away that nobody would figure out he was crazy. And when it came closer to the Rapture date, and they realized everything would fall through when it didn't happen, they *made* it happen."

Peter's theory is awful and impossible, but when I look at Frick and Taggart—I know in my heart there's truth in it.

"Holy shit," Harp says.

"Peter." I grab his hand with my good one. "If it's the Corporation that stuck him out here, they're keeping tabs on him. And they just said 'Get someone over there.'"

Peter's eyes go wide. "Okay," he says after a long moment. "Get out of here. Now."

Harp doesn't hesitate; she rushes past Frick, who is still praying, and towards the front door. But I stay where I am. I understand what Peter's saying. And I don't understand why.

"We probably don't have much time, Viv," he says.

"I know. Which is why we have to leave, now."

He presses his lips together in a grim line. He looks away, at Taggart, whose eyes are open again, but who otherwise hasn't made a noise or movement. "I can't just leave him here, Viv," Peter murmurs. "He's not well. Neither of them are. And the Corporation is taking advantage of them. They're making them do things they want to do. Look at him, Vivian. He's in shock, and he's all alone. I know, I understand what he is. But . . . he's my father."

I try to feel the empathy that Peter does when he looks at these two men, lost in their own little world in this big empty lodge, in the middle of the woods. But I have a fury in me that is bigger and wilder than any other emotion, including all the love I have for Peter. "Your father might have helped kill my parents," I tell him.

"I'm not asking you to forgive him," Peter says. "I'm just asking you to let me take care of him. I'm asking you to take the car and Harp and go."

"If I do that," my voice catches for a moment before I can continue, "we'll probably never see each other again."

"We might," Peter says.

"We won't." And when it feels like he's about to break down, like he's about to pull me close and kiss me, I take a step backward, wrenching myself out of his grasp. I don't say goodbye. I run.

"What is Peter doing? Why isn't he coming?" Harp asks as I reach the door, but I shake my head at her and motion for her to come along, and she does. We stumble out into the waiting dark, and at first I think I'll be relieved to be lost in it, somewhere the Church of America can't find me. But we don't have a flashlight between us. Harp starts down the path of crosses, but I grab her—and then immediately cry out, as I've grabbed her with my hurt hand.

"Viv," she hisses. "What is it?"

"Nothing," I say. "It's just—I think I broke my hand on Beaton Frick's face."

I can't see her face in the dark, but I know she's grinning. "Oh, Vivian Apple," Harp says. "You beautiful, crazy bitch."

"I don't think we should go down the path, Harp," I say. "I would guess that's the route the Church takes, and if they're sending someone here—"

"We don't want to meet them halfway," she finishes. "Right. Okay, so what do we do?"

"We have to go off the path and into the forest," I say. "I'm pretty sure the car is—" and I look around, trying to find my bearings. "I think it's over to our left."

There's a brief silence. "You're not giving me a lot to go on here, Viv."

"I know," I say, "but—"

I freeze, and so does Harp beside me. We can hear, not too far from where we're standing, the distant sound of an engine. I look out into the trees and see headlights dancing among them, far away but not far enough.

"Let's go," Harp says.

We climb into the trees. All the while I am thinking, *let him be okay, let him be okay, let him be okay*. Part of me wants to stay within the immediate area, to watch from

256

the darkness of the trees, to make sure Peter gets his father and Frick and himself out in time, before anyone tries to harm him. But he didn't want me to stay. He told me to go. And if I'd stayed—I have this sick feeling in the pit of my stomach, that I have to push down deep enough to ignore—I might have had to watch him get hurt again. Because what are the chances that Peter will be able to get two sick old men out of that lodge before the Church of America shows up? And what are the chances of them sparing his life once they find him there?

Harp and I stumble on through the forest. It's messy, dangerous work—we can't see the branches that trip us until we've fallen over them; I'm worried we'll run straight into the creek before we even hear it. We're taking it slow, stopping every twenty minutes or so to listen for the sound of footsteps following us, but we only hear wind and rushing water and our own frantic breathing. My hand throbs. At one point I run into a thin sharp branch and feel a wet streak of pain spread across my cheek. When I touch it my fingers come back smelling like blood. The temperature has dropped since we got here; it felt vaguely summery then, but now it's night and cold and though the running keeps my body warm, my nose is frozen. We can't stop. We can't sleep. We have nothing but half-eaten sandwiches in our bags, and we don't know where we are.

I start to lose my sense of time. I no longer know if hours have gone by, or only a few minutes. My legs ache, and all I can think is, *Peter, Peter, Peter*. When I trip over a rock and into the wet leaves below me, I stay there. I hear Harp's footsteps recede and it feels okay. *Let her keep going*, I think.

Let her be safe. I will get up in the morning and my parents will be making pancakes in the kitchen; Harp will be oblivious to my existence next door. Peter will be a dream so vivid, I'll still feel his kisses, the warmth of his skin. But only a dream.

I hear footsteps coming towards me. I roll onto my back and look up. We're in a clearing, and the moon beams down on Harp, who's leaning over me, her hair tickling my face.

"Are you okay?" Her voice sounds scared.

"I can't do it," I whisper to her.

I want her to understand, to leave me there. But Harp sighs and takes hold of both of my arms. She yanks me upright.

"Vivian Apple. This is *not* the time for dramatics, okay? I get it: you're tired, you're lost, your heart's broken. Well, suck it up. Because you're my best friend, and I love you, but we're not going to die in the woods together, okay? Not today. So stand up, goddamnit!"

There's no way Harp's going to successfully pull me to my feet; she's too tiny. I oblige her by standing up on my own. I remember then what she told me—only a few months ago, now, though it feels like years. That I'm the hero of my own life story. It isn't Peter, and it isn't my mother, and it isn't Harp. It's me. We stare at each other in the moonlight.

"Okay?" she says.

I nod. "Okay."

I don't know how long it takes us to stumble on the road, but eventually we do, and then we pray that the car is to our left and head that way along the overgrown road. I say nothing to Harp and she says nothing to me—we're exhausted, and we're also listening for the sound of a car behind us, for the Church of America to jump out at us from the trees, brandishing huge white crosses. But that doesn't happen. The sky begins to lighten and not long after it does, we see the tree lying across the road ahead of us, and my grandparents' car sitting right where we left it. We climb over the tree and Harp offers to drive. I toss her the keys. Before I get in, I stand by the door for a long moment. It feels exactly like it did in Winnemucca—I am watching a spot far down the road we've just traveled, waiting for Peter to emerge from the woods, bloody and chased, alive. But he doesn't come. The woods are silent but for the birds squawking in the sky, the sound of the ignition as Harp turns the key.

Chapter Twenty

I don't plan to fall asleep, but I do, and when I wake up the sun is shining and we're on the freeway. Harp is humming tunelessly in the driver's seat with her sunglasses on. When she notices me shifting about beside her, she reaches behind her into Wambaugh's cooler and pulls out the ice pack. She tosses it into my lap—it's not frozen anymore, but it's still cool.

"Put that on your hand," she commands, and I do.

"I can take over driving if you want a break," I offer, but Harp shakes her head.

"I'm in a groove," she says, "And anyway, we don't have too much farther to go."

I'm sleepy, and the events of the previous evening—really, the previous two months—are filtering slowly back into my brain, disorienting me. I can't remember where our next destination is, but I don't get a chance to ask, because Harp is holding something else out to me—a little wooden pendant hanging from what looks like dental floss.

"What is this?" I ask.

"I don't know," says Harp. "It was here in the pocket on the door. I was looking for gum and I pulled it out."

I look closely at the pendant—it's a thin sliver of chestnut brown wood, ending in an angled head. It looks, more than anything, like a tiny sledgehammer. *I have something for you*, he'd told me. I was supposed to remind him. I feel a sweet ache open up in the center of my chest and spread to my fingertips.

"Peter made it." I tell Harp. I put my head through the dental floss loop and touch the pendant where it hangs. "In Keystone, probably. That night we left Pittsburgh, he said the sledgehammer was a good look for me."

He didn't mean for it to be a message, but I take it as one. So long as I'm strong and brave, the version of myself he knew best, he will be okay. Maybe I'll never see him again. The rest of my life has no fixed end date now; it extends on and on in my imagination, forever. Maybe I'll spend the rest of it feeling my knees go weak every time I catch sight of a pair of blue eyes in a crowd. But as long as I'm always the Vivian he kissed two nights ago, the Vivian he gazed at with such satisfaction, Peter will be okay.

"Want to talk about him?" Harp asks, her voice more gentle than I've ever heard it.

I shake my head. "Not right now. Sometime soon, but not right now."

She nods, and takes a deep breath. "Then I think I need to say some things," she says. "Some things I've been meaning to say. If you want to say some things, when I'm done, you should do it. But first I'm going to say the things I need to say.

"First of all, I've been thinking it over, and I think it's possible Goliath is being bankrolled by the Church of America."

261

My mouth drops open. "*What?*"

Harp nods. "There was a lot of weird stuff about him that I couldn't figure out. The main one was, where all his money came from. He's our age, you know. And we're supposed to believe that one day this slacker stands up from behind his tweets and his partying and video games, and says, I'm gonna start me a commune? It makes no sense. I'd ask him questions like, how do you afford all this food, how do you afford these armed guards, how do you afford all this cocaine—did I mention that he had a pretty serious coke habit?"

"Uh, no, Harp. Weirdly, you left that out."

"Oh well," she shrugs. "Lust blinds me. Anyway, he had no good answers—like, not even rehearsed ones. When I asked them, he'd laugh nervously and then take his shirt off to distract me. And I'm sorry to say that trick *always* worked. Remember that bullshit explanation he gave for why they never did anything? 'They are the past, we are the future.' I think they were paying him to keep the resistance movement as passive as possible."

"'The Church created *me*,'" I say, remembering what Goliath had told us.

"Yeah!" says Harp. "Yeah!"

"Wow," I say. "I wish we could tell Peter that."

"I know." Harp is silent a moment before she continues. "There's another thing I have to tell you, and it's way harder for me to say, which is why I said that one first. I know I've been a brat for this whole trip, and I'm sorry. It was partially just general crankiness, but it was also—you and Peter, you both took this trip because you felt like your

262

family was still alive out there. And you both turned out to be right, didn't you? I mean, your first hunch was wrong, but it turned out you had family you didn't even know existed." She takes a steadying breath. "But I never felt like that. Never. I came with you because you asked me to, because I had nothing else to do. But I knew my family was dead. I had no spirit whispering in my ear that I'd find them out here. I saw Raj's body. I buried it.

"And I didn't mind, you know? I thought, I'm not going to win the missing parent scavenger hunt, no big deal. But every step closer we got to California, the more it felt like maybe you could. And if you did, where would I be? We aren't related; we wouldn't even have been friends if it weren't for Beaton Frick, have you ever thought about that? So maybe I thought I'd pull away before I got cut out. But I was kind of a bitch about it in the process."

"Harp," I say. "You know you're like a sister to me."

She smiles. "That's how I feel about you, too, Viv. Except neither of us would know, would we? Because neither of us have ever had a sister before."

I don't know what to say to Harp, in part because I fear and suspect that what she says might be true. If I had walked into the Believer compound last night and found my mother and father alive and waiting for me, what would have happened to Harp? She probably would have set off on her own in the opposite direction, and I would never have heard from her again. I would have fallen back into my normal, happy, placid life, and after a while I doubt I would have even felt her absence. I would have grown up and gotten married and had kids, and only occasionally

263

would I remember that for one crazy year leading up to and immediately following the Rapture, I had been friends with the extraordinary, wild Harp. If I had found my parents alive, that might have been enough for me.

Harp clears her throat. She's not done. "The thing is, I've realized how selfish that is. You have a chance to go out and find your family. How terrible a friend would I be if I tried to stand in your way?"

"But Harp, I didn't find my family. They're dead."

"They're not all dead," she says. "Here's the other thing I need to tell you. The other day, when I called Wambaugh? I also called Berkeley. They're closed indefinitely, obviously, but there was a lady working the phones there who was a total, delightful pushover. I faked some tears, told her I had to reach my beloved cousin, who was a student there, before the apocalypse, and she gave me Winnie's home address, no questions asked."

I've barely registered what Harp is saying when I glance out the windshield and see the Golden Gate Bridge looming up in front of us—solid and red and piercing the blue sky above. We're headed straight into San Francisco.

"I've told you from the start, Apple," says Harp, grinning at the expression on my face, my blank and happy shock. "I always, *always* have a plan."

I've never seen a city like the one we're driving through just a half an hour later, with its hills, its palm trees, the sun shining bright and clear and beautiful in the sky. It's the first place I've seen on this entire trip that I've been actually able to look at—for once I'm not anxious about where we're going next, or what we're going to do there. I'm glancing out the window at Thai restaurants, vibrator stores, gay couples walking hand-in-hand down the sidewalk. Harp is laughing hysterically at everything. She's so happy. "I wish Raj could see this!" she shrieks, and I laugh, because I was thinking the same thing. I was thinking of Raj and Dylan and Molly and Edie. I was thinking of Peter. I was wishing they all were here.

We pull up in front of a peach-colored apartment building facing a lush green park.

"This is it," Harp says, checking the piece of paper on which she'd written Winnie's address and glancing up at the number on the door. "Do you want me to come in with you?"

"Yes?" I say. "But I should probably do it alone."

"Look at that personal growth right there," Harp says, smiling at me. "It's beautiful to behold. Listen, I'll go park this thing and then meet you across the street when you're done, okay? Take all the time you need."

I want to throw my arms around her; I want to tell her how much I love her, that no blood-sister could approach anything nearing the hold Harp has on me, but she's clearly had her fill of sincere emotions for the day. She shoos me out of the car with her hands, and all I can do is I grin at her.

Winnie Conroy. Apartment 3.

I'm aware of my right hand, slightly purple, the cut on my cheek. I'm aware that my hair is messy and dirty and might contain one or two leaves. I ripped a hole in the knee of my jeans last night while we were running. Part of me thinks that when Winnie opens the door and I see her face, I will burst into uncontrollable tears. But still. Harp is right. Now that I know she's out there, I can't pretend she doesn't exist. I worry about the logistics of the buzzer—what do I say when she answers? "Hi, it's me, the half-sister you may or may not have known you have?"—but while I'm standing there, another tenant steps out, and I'm able to slip in before the door shuts and locks behind him. Then there isn't any point in turning back.

Hi, I think to myself as I walk up the stairs. *You may not know about me, but I'm your sister. You may not know about me, but we share the same mother, who by the way, was very possibly poisoned three months ago and then unprofessionally cremated. Yeah, I just met her murderer last night.* I'm standing in front of the door to Apartment 3 in no time at all, and I haven't come up with anything to say to her that is not totally crazy. I don't care, though—this is the new Vivian Apple, the hero of her own life story. I'm just going to wing it.

I press the doorbell and hear a shrill ringing inside. I hear the footsteps clattering down the hall. My heart begins to pound.

A young woman opens the door. She has my mother's red-blonde hair, the same smattering of freckles. This pretty, glamorous woman in front of me—this is my sister. She looks at me with polite concern, but I can practically hear the sirens going off in her head: I must look completely insane to her right now.

"Hi," I say. "Um . . . Winnie?"

"Can I help you?" she asks.

"Yeah," I say. "Okay. I don't know how to tell you this. Okay. So, you may or may not know about this, but—"

"Winnie?" calls another woman's voice from inside the apartment. Winnie turns, inadvertently opening her door a little wider, so I can see down the long hallway, to a room that a person in a bathrobe has just left. The woman has a towel over her head, she's drying her hair with it in this particular way—I have seen her do this before, a million times, and never once did I ever think it would break my heart the way it does right now. "Did the doorbell just ring?" the woman asks, and then she flips her red-blonde hair back and sees me standing in the doorway. She doesn't cry out, or even gasp. She smiles a little sadly.

"Hey, sweetheart," my mother says, like she's been waiting.

Chapter Twenty-One

"Where's Dad?"

I haven't even stepped into the apartment before I ask it. My mother—alive, wet-haired, living with her first-born in San Francisco—is like a ghost, floating down the hallway towards me in bare feet. But in the Technicolor reunion I've imagined for so many months, it's both of my parents, their arms outstretched, their eyes crying and laughing. This scene is off, distorted—my vision goes fuzzy at the edges.

"Sweetheart," my mother says gently. "You know where he is. He's been saved."

"No," I reply. "That's not right." I don't know why she's lying to me but she is; it has something to do with the Church, something to do with the Corporation. I hear Frick's voice echoing in my head: *They had to move in secret so the Non-Believers could not follow*. I push past Winnie, the dawning comprehension in her hazel eyes, and my mother, down the hallway and into the small living room, lit gold with sun. "Dad?"

There's an air mattress on the floor partially deflated, its sheets in a tangle; there are paintings of birds on the walls and a huge messy bookshelf. But my father's not here. My mother is hiding him away for some reason, the way she hid Winnie. I hear her rummaging through the closet behind me, and when she appears she has cotton balls, rubbing alcohol, bandages. She sits on the couch and pats the space beside her.

"Let me do something about your cheek, Vivian, honey."

"First tell me where my father is," I say. My heart is pounding at this boldness, at me telling my own mother what we're going to do now, at preventing her from mothering me.

"I've already told you, Vivian." Mom's gets a little tight, like she's about to cry. "He was saved. He's gone on to his eternal reward."

"How are you still lying, after everything that's happened? Are they making you lie?"

"Is *who* making me lie?" My mother shakes her head at me, confused. "What do you mean? I'm telling you what I know, honey; I'm telling you the truth."

I believe her—I know I have no reason in the world to believe her, but I believe that she doesn't know where my father is. My father is gone. My mother is here. I listen to the click of Winnie's footsteps on the hardwood floor behind me. I hear a heavy, ragged breathing and realize it's my own. I'm making a spectacle of myself, I know, bleeding and wild-haired in a stranger's apartment, staring down my mother, who looks very small and frightened in her bathrobe. And that's exactly how I want it. I am past goodness, past grief. I'm broken in a way I don't understand yet, and I'm going to make them feel it.

"You left me there," I say, "alone. You left me alone in that house with no money and no parents. You put holes in the roof and you let me find them. Do you have any idea what that was like? I saw those holes and it was like my entire history and future were being sucked up through them, and I was the only thing left, and I was nothing. And you were here? Were you here the whole time?"

Mom's eyes are glassy with tears. She nods.

"Well, that's great." My voice sounds thin and mean and I turn to look at Winnie. She's leaning against the doorway, staring at the floor, her expression unreadable. I'm seized with a sudden hatred, of her twee paintings and her sunny apartment and the fact that she stands there, cool and disinterested, infuriatingly adult. "How special for you two, to be able to bond like that. While I was hungry and tired and waiting for the plagues to start raining down. While my friends were getting beaten and murdered."

"Hey," says Winnie. She gazes back at me now. "Don't assume you're the only one who's been through something these last months. The apocalypse isn't something happening to you and you alone."

"Winnie," my mother murmurs, like a warning. The sound of her name in my mother's mouth makes my spine go rigid with jealousy.

"I know that," I say. "If you think I don't know that—"

"I think you're throwing a fit, and you have a right to throw one," Winnie continues. "But maybe let's calm down for half a second so your mother can get a word in. Don't you think she deserves it? Honor your father and mother, and all that?"

I laugh. "You *would* be a Believer. That's just perfect. You're the whole package, aren't you? The anti-Viv."

Winnie stands up straight. She's been snapped out of her calm; her eyes are burning. "Call me a Believer again, kiddo; I'm begging you. I would seriously *love* to hear you call me that again."

"Girls!"

My mother's voice rings out sharply in the echoing apartment and when I turn she points to the couch beside her. I find I don't even hesitate—I step forward, and sit down. She perches next to me and reaches for my hand, but I gasp in pain when she touches it.

"Vivian," she says, examining it. "I think your hand is broken."

"I think you're right, yeah."

"We should get it looked at."

"First, tell me the truth." I want to sound tough but I hear the begging in my own voice, the desperate, insistent pleading. "I don't care if it's hard; I've come all this way, and you owe me the truth."

I see a shadow flicker across my mother's face, and for a moment I think I've gone too far—she's about to yell, or shut me out. But just as suddenly the shadow's gone, and my mother takes a deep breath. She smiles sadly at me.

"Vivian, I don't know where to start. I messed up. I've been messing up my entire life. But I promise you that where you were concerned, I was always trying to do the right thing, the good thing.

"I was basically your age when I met your dad. You don't know how young that is, because you're still there. You've had this adventure now and so maybe you think you know all the answers. But, for me, I was seventeen. I was pregnant.

271

My parents had kicked me out of the house. I thought, *I'm going to die.* I thought it was only a matter of time. And then along came your father. He told me it was going to be okay; he was going to make it okay. Ned said it would be easy to be good because we'd love each other, because we'd be together. We'd be living for other people, not just for ourselves. It made sense to me then—it still makes sense—so I said yes, but the only thing I said was that I wanted to give up the baby. I didn't think I'd be able to look at Winnie without feeling like I had before Ned, that feeling of death, of waiting to die."

My mother glances up at Winnie but my sister stays impassive; she picks at the sleeve of her sweater like she doesn't even hear.

"But it didn't get easier," Mom continues after a moment. "I loved your dad; I loved the quiet life we had. But it always felt like I was playing a part. I felt like it would take so little—a fight with Ned, or too many glasses of wine, or a bad phone call with Grant and Clarissa—to turn me into that girl again. But it wasn't a small thing that pushed me there; it was you. After you were born, I had this feeling like, what have I done? Who was I to think myself capable of bringing this little person up in the world? Ned was so excited, but all I could think was that I was going to mess it up. I was going to care either too much or not enough. And what if you turned out like me? Wild, and unhappy, and hating us?

"If someone could have just shown me a vision of the future, of our Vivian Apple—from Day One, the sweetest and calmest and best of girls—I'd have relaxed. But instead

I panicked." She pauses and looks at me with a cringing, guilty expression. "I guess now's as good a time as any to tell you . . . I ran away for a while when you were nine months old. Your dad raised you alone until right around your first birthday."

She waits for my reaction but I say nothing—I'm not shocked by anything anymore, certainly not when it comes to the things I would never have expected my mother capable of.

"I went to New York. I tried to become someone new; I waited for it to feel right in a way that life at home hadn't. I knew I couldn't go back. Your father had saved me once, I thought; there was no chance he'd do it again.

"Of course I was wrong, and I should've known it. He tracked me down and asked me to come home. And I did, but I knew it would never be quite right. It felt like it didn't matter how much I loved you and Ned; it didn't matter how happy you both made me. I always felt like something was missing. Like a puzzle piece—the thing that would connect my old self to the new one. I could play the part of the good wife and mother, but I still didn't understand what I was getting out of it.

"And then the Church came along. I think it appealed to Ned, the idea of joining a church. He'd read about it online. That was right after he lost his job, remember? He was very depressed; he felt like he didn't know what his role was if he couldn't provide for us. He begged me to come to services and I thought—well, why not? I thought it was the least I could do, to go to this place where he thought he might find himself, when he'd spent his whole adult life trying to help me do the same. And the people turned out to be so nice, Vivian—I know what you think of them, and some of them can be a little much, but the people we met those first weeks were *so* nice. The women, especially; it felt like they knew just what I was going through. They got it, you know? That it was hard to figure out how to be the right kind of wife, the right kind of mother. They understood because they were trying to get it right, too, while they still had time. And the best part was that the Church gave you actual guidelines! They said, we know this is hard. Here's how you start. And for the first time, I felt like I was a good person. A person who was contributing to the world, making the person I loved best in the world happy.

"The only thing that bothered me then," she says carefully, as if not wanting to hurt my feelings, "was that you didn't want to be a part of it."

"Sorry," I say flatly.

"But, Vivian, I really don't understand," Mom says, and I can tell by her voice that she wants to. "It was always so easy for you. I feel like I never even had to teach you about all those things it took me until the Church to learn—sharing and hard work and kindness. Do you know I can never remember reprimanding you, until that last year? Any Believer who met you would attest to your godliness. So why did you never become one?"

It feels to me like the answer's obvious, but my mother stares at me with genuine curiosity. "Because I didn't Believe, Mom," I explain.

She waves her hand dismissively. "But that's just a part

of it, Viv. That's just a story you can take or leave. For me it was about feeling like a part of a community. It was about trying to be good."

"But that's not the kind of good I want to be," I say. I think back to the statues outside the Believer compound—the men proud and dignified, slapping fives with Lincoln; the women in a corner, over an open flame. "What the Church wanted from you wasn't goodness; it was meekness. And I know because that's what I've been for seventeen years. That's what you just called godliness. It's so much easier to be that—to read the guidelines and submit and obey, instead of actually dealing with chaos, or pain—but it's not what good is. When the Rapture comes, that's the life you're going to be satisfied by."

I've said something wrong. Immediately my mom's eyes well up.

"I'm sorry, Vivian," she says. "It's just that—well, you're forgetting that the Rapture *did* come. And I'm still here. And I'm not satisfied by any of it."

I feel a little thrill of excitement and fear, because we're right at the precipice of what I still don't understand. How did she manage to escape Frick and Taggart? How much does she know of what happened at the Believer compound? And if she's still alive, despite what she keeps insisting, does that mean my father is out there somewhere, too? I can't imagine how they could have gotten separated from each other; in what universe would my parents, who loved each other more than anything, let themselves be divided?

"How are you still here, Mom?" is the gentlest way I can think of to ask.

"I never made enough progress in my salvation," she explains, her voice catching and starting and stopping again. "I still had doubts. Sometimes I found myself thinking about the Church as Ned's religion, instead of my own. But—Vivian, the truth is I did something terrible. You're sitting here and you're already so angry at me—I can feel it, you know, you're just radiating heat—and you're going to be so much angrier when I tell you."

"What is it?" I ask, trying to sound gentle, like this isn't the case. But the truth is my mother is aggravating me even more than I think she realizes, wallowing in her mysterious despair, milking every minute of it. I think of the blue-haired girl she once was—what an exasperating drama queen that girl must have been.

"The Rapture was coming," she explains, "and we were counting down the days. Ned was a lot more excited than me. I spent a lot of time wondering whether or not it would hurt. About a month before it was supposed to happen, we got this letter in the mail, signed by Pastor Frick. He explained that he misunderstood his own vision. He said we wouldn't be Raptured from our homes. We'd have to be blessed personally by Frick at a special service at his secret compound. The Church had contacted pastors in every parish and asked them to send the letter to their most devout congregants." She can't help sounding a little smug at this. "The only catch was, we weren't allowed to talk about it with anybody—not any Non-Believer friends or family, not even other Believers. The letter explained that more people thought they would be saved than would actually be saved. If everyone knew about the special service, it could get awkward. So we had to make our way to California in secret.

"Ned was thrilled. It meant so much to him that our pastor would single us out. He booked our plane tickets within an hour of the mail being delivered—that was just about the last of our savings. And that made it real, of course, in a way it hadn't been. I started to think—what if we were wrong? What if we weren't taken? What if Ned was taken and I wasn't? Was I supposed to return to Pittsburgh alone? Raise you myself, with no money, without the guidance of Ned or the Church?

"But Ned told me to have faith, and I tried. He pointed out that my name was on the letter, like that meant anything more than the fact I was married to him. The tricky part was figuring out when to leave. We could tell which of our friends had been contacted because they started to leave town in the weeks before the Rapture—they'd say they were going to visit family one last time, or to one of the Seven Sacred Sites, but you knew what they were really saying. The Jandas just disappeared halfway through March. But we waited until the last possible moment, because we had you. You weren't around very much that month. You were spending most of your time with Harp. When you left that morning, I wanted to tell you goodbye, but I knew I couldn't. After you were gone, we put those holes in the ceiling. It killed us to do that, Vivian; you need to know that it killed us. Ned and I were both wrecks. But he said, and I believed him—you needed a trauma to learn the error of your ways, to come to Him. After that, a taxi picked us up and took us to the airport.

We flew from Pittsburgh to San Jose. At San Jose, a shuttle came to take us to the compound.

"Your dad fell asleep as soon as the plane took off. But I couldn't stop thinking. I don't know how to explain it. It was like, once we were up there, in the air, I just sort of shed every year that had passed between seventeen and now. I thought about all the things I hadn't done, that I'd given up to be with Ned. I'd never traveled anywhere. I'd never created anything I was really proud of. I'd only been with one man for over twenty-five years. All of this, I could live with, be happy with, even, but I believed I was entering my final few hours on Earth. And I just—I panicked, Vivian. I completely panicked.

"When he woke up, your dad said, 'Alright?' and I said yeah. We left the plane together. But he stopped in the bathroom right beside our gate. He thought I'd be waiting for him when he came out. But I ran." Mom starts crying again, and angry as I am with her, I know her heart is really broken. "I ran and left him there. I did that, to the man I loved."

I don't want to hear the rest of the story, and I don't want to imagine my father's half. I see him leaving the bathroom, sprightly with anticipatory energy, thinking he's about to go to heaven with the woman he loves. But she's gone. I can guess what happened next. Mom made her way up to San Francisco, tracked down Winnie, with whom she'd always stayed in some form of touch.

"Why didn't you call me?" I ask her.

Mom's face looks much older than I've ever seen it. "I was embarrassed, Vivian."

278

But I know there's more to it than that. Yes, it would have been embarrassing for her to have to return to Pittsburgh, husbandless, a runaway, a fallen woman, Left Behind. Certainly, though she'd have had no way of knowing it at the time, it wouldn't have been safe. But by running away first from me and then from my father, she'd also be able to recreate that aborted escape to New York. She'd be able to travel, meet new men, share a glamorous new life with her other daughter, the adult, the one who didn't think of her as mother. I can understand this. She was a year older than me when she married. She really believes that the world is ending. All she wanted to do was have some fun. But I can't forgive it. I try to find a tender spot in me with which to forgive her, but there simply aren't any left.

"And Dad never contacted you?" I ask.

Mom flinches, startled. "How would he have contacted me, Viv? It was only a matter of hours between the last moment I saw him, and the moment he was saved."

I say nothing. I want to tell myself a story. One in which my father survives, too. He leaves the airport bathroom and sees the empty space where my mother should stand, and he's snapped to his senses, just as I'd imagined he eventually would be. He heads on his own adventure. But what would that be? All this time I've spent stumbling over my parents' secrets, and still I can't see any clear alternative. My father was a born rule-follower, risk-avoider. I never thought he could love anything more than my mother, until he joined the Church. No. I'm tired of telling myself stories about how things did not happen. Dad got on the shuttle;

he drank the wine. Maybe he ended up somewhere peaceful, or maybe he's nothing but ashes now. In truth I've been mourning him from the moment he converted, the moment he became something strange and hard, something other than the kind man in glasses who never made me play soccer after that first, disastrous time. But this is a different kind of grief altogether. To know, for certain, that he's dead. It's a horizon I'll never reach. For now I'll bury it. If I don't bury it, I'll fall apart.

"Vivian?" Mom says, studying me closely. "Do you know something? Have you—did you hear from Dad?"

I have the story of last night on the tip of my tongue. I could tell her of the fate she unwittingly escaped, of the one to which her husband probably fell. In doing so, I could inflict on her more pain than I've ever caused anyone. I could make her feel what I feel. But I shake my head no. "Not a word," I tell her.

There's a shift in the room's atmosphere then. I can feel my energy draining away, my will to fight with either of these women stalled. I keep my eyes off the air mattress because every time I see it I feel a twinge. All I've wanted for three months is my mother. And some other daughter has had her instead. Winnie clears her throat and moves towards us.

"I'm sorry to do this," she says. "But I have to go to work."

"Of course, of course!" My mother wipes her eyes with the sleeves of her bathrobe and gets up to put her arm around Winnie. "Vivian, your sister works for a non-profit that finds temporary shelter for Left Behind babies—isn't that wonderful?"

It isn't Winnie's fault my mother sought her out, but that doesn't mean I have to like her. "That's so godly of you," I deadpan.

Winnie gives me a look I can't quite decipher—it's shrewd and maybe a little threatening. "You're welcome to stay here as long as you like, Viv. But only if you cut Mara some slack. She loves you like crazy, you know. Don't forget that you're the one she kept."

My mother's face goes a little pale at this, and a mild, uncomfortable smile stays on her face until Winnie walks down the hallway and we hear the front door shut behind her. Then she turns to me and the tiny smile becomes a huge, dazzling, fake grin. "I think we could both use some breakfast, don't you?"

In the kitchen, Mom rifles through Winnie's fridge and cabinets, taking out salt and pepper, butter and milk, and a carton of eggs. I feel weak, less with hunger than with the dizzying knowledge that I'm going to taste my mother's food again.

"I know that was a rocky start, but I think you'll get along with Winnie," Mom says as she prepares. "She's really sweet, and fun, too. Very bold, very opinionated. Nothing like your old friends from back home—no offense. But that Lara Cochran . . ."

"Lara Cochran's the worst, Mom. She was Left Behind though, did you know?"

"No!" Mom drags the word out in a delighted, gossipy way. She's cracking a ridiculous amount of eggs into the pan. "I didn't know that. It's very sinful of me to take pleasure in that, of course, but the Cochrans were a little much. Mrs. Cochran was—I guess the wording I'd use would be 'unintentionally sanctimonious.'"

I laugh, flipping through a cookbook Winnie has propped up on her kitchen table. "I think the wording *I* would use is 'heinous fucking bitch.'"

The room is silent except for the hiss of egg in the pan. My mother looks at me in horror. The sentence I've just said rings in my ears like an admonishment.

"Mom," I say. "I don't know why I thought you would find that funny. That was really inappropriate, I'm sorry."

My mother recovers, taking a short breath and smiling. "It sounds like Harp Janda has been rubbing off on you."

"Well, yeah. I've spent practically all my time with her for over a year now."

"Maybe now that you're here, you can take a little bit of a break." She says it naturally, like it's only a suggestion, but even though her back is turned, I know how serious she is. "I don't know her *well*, of course, but I know enough. She's a bit self-destructive, isn't she? She's a little too much."

I don't want to start a fight. Not now that she's back, and more normal than she's been in months. "A little," I begrudgingly agree.

"And anyway, you'll be busy, won't you?" Mom sets a plate of eggs down in front of me, procures from nowhere a grater and a block of cheddar cheese, which she now piles manically on top. "You'll be busy with me and Winnie. Me and my girls, together at last. Won't we have a nice time, waiting out the apocalypse together? Won't we be good influences on each other? Maybe after we get your hand

282

taken care of, we can head down to Valencia and buy you some cool new San Francisco clothes. Winnie is so stylish; wait till you see her. And maybe we can find a good bed for you and me to share—the air mattress is fine for one person, but now that you're here we'll have to get something more comfortable. Isn't this fun?"

There's a small part of me that wants to speak up, to tell her I won't blindly obey anymore, that I'm Vivian 2.0. But she's offering scrambled eggs, medical attention, new clothes, a soft bed. I savor the wave of calm that spreads over me as I nod and nod and nod.

Chapter Twenty-Two

"Now then," Mom says when I've finished my eggs. "We're not waiting a second longer to get that hand looked at. Okay? Let me get dressed and then we'll go."

"Okay." I follow my mother into the living room, where she digs around in a pile of clothes I don't recognize. She hadn't brought a suitcase to San Jose, I realize—she didn't think she'd need more than one outfit. Mom pulls out a blouse, a long black skirt. I realize that despite Winnie's stylish influence, she's still dressing Believer. She heads to the bathroom, in which she'll change, but I take a step towards her. "Mom?"

My mother turns to me. Her gorgeous hair is drying curly down her back. She's getting dressed so that we can spend time together, all the time we have left in the world. But I can see in her eyes just the slightest hint of apprehension, and I know that even as she loves me—and I have no doubt that she loves me—she's still trying hard to play the part. I take another step towards her and she stiffens, but then I put my arms around her.

"I love you so much," I say.

Mom's body relaxes as she wraps her arms around me, too. "I love you, too, sweetheart."

*   *   *

I leave the apartment while she's still in the bathroom, not giving much thought to what she'll think when she finds I'm not there. If she's close enough on my heels, she'll see me walking across the street, into the sun-drenched park, which is filled with homeless men and dogs and topless women, dudes making out on benches. I head up the park's gentle slope, and then I spot her. Harp's lying on the grass with her jeans rolled to her knees; she's folded her shirt up to bare her stomach. Her eyes are closed, but they pop open when she hears me approaching.

"All that shit in my suitcase," Harp says, "and I forgot to bring a bikini."

"You know you're already pretty tan, right? Like, I don't really see how you could get much tanner."

"I'm allowed to participate in whatever cultural beauty practices I want, Viv. This is *America*."

I sit beside her and laugh. I watch the front door of Winnie's apartment building. Harp sits up and follows my gaze, but for a few long moments says nothing.

"So?" she says finally. "What's Winnie like?"

I shrug. "Pretty, hipster-y. Kind of a know-it-all. Maybe a little Believer-lite. I didn't talk to her that much, really. My mom's there."

"Oh," says Harp, and then she says, "*Ohhhh*." And then it seems like she doesn't know what to say. "She escaped, then?"

"She never made it to the compound," I explain. "She ran out on my dad at the airport."

"Mrs. Apple. So punk rock." Harp tries to sound impressed, but it comes out sounding mostly sad. The apartment door still hasn't opened. For the first time I notice that the sky is weirdly pink, like it's sunrise or sunset. But it's mid-morning, a couple of hours until noon. All of the sudden, Harp stands up.

"Well, I guess that's that," she says. "I should probably hit the road, then."

I stand up with her. "Yeah?"

"Yeah. I mean, right? You thought your mom might be alive and here she is. You found what you were looking for. I think it's really, really great, Viv." Harp frowns as she says it, but I know she means it. "But I can't stay here. I don't have anything keeping me here. And anyway, it's fucking *expensive*."

"What are you going to do now?" I ask her.

In a lot of ways, Harp's face is different than it was last July, when we first became friends. It's more serious, and so tired, and much harder. But now she gets a trace of an old mischievous look in her eye. I didn't realize how much I missed it until I see it now. "Well, there are a few things that still bother me. Goliath, of course. But also the number of people missing. Frick said that only hundreds showed up to the compound, right? But the news said three thousand missing, from the very beginning."

"You're going to find a few thousand unaccounted-for Believers?"

Harp shrugs. "I'm going to *look*, anyway. But the *main* thing, obviously, is that everyone still thinks the apocalypse is on its way, don't they? And I guess I feel like I have a moral obligation to correct them. Like it's my duty. As an American."

"All of this," I point out, "will be ridiculously dangerous."

"Naturally," says Harp. "But that's what makes it fun. Do you mind if I take the car?"

I shake my head. "Not at all."

"Thanks." Harp nervously jingles the keys in her pocket. "I was thinking I'd try to find Peter, too. I think he could probably use the help. I can figure out some way to let you know, when I know he's okay. Would that be weird for you?"

I take one last look at the door of the peach building. It's still shut. By now my mother must have stepped out into the hallway and called my name. I know it won't be for her like it was for me, staring up at the holes in the ceiling. I know I'm giving her a gift. Harp watches me, waiting for an answer, waiting for the second where she can leave.

I shake my head. "No," I say. "I don't think that would be weird. Let's go."

A grin spreads slowly across Harp's face as she understands. She tries her best to suppress it. "Viv, come on. Be serious. You should stay here, with your family."

"My family isn't here," I say, shrugging. "My family is wherever you and Peter are."

Harp drops her head back at this statement and groans into the air. "Jesus, Viv. How much money did we have to waste on gas before you came to *that* conclusion?"

The sky above us is red as flame, and there's a thick silver fog rolling slowly in from all directions. I'm tired and confused and afraid. But I have Harp, and I have the truth. The one thing I know for sure is that I've never been more powerful. My best friend smiles at me and takes my unbroken hand. She leads me up the hill, to where the car is parked, and we head out into the dying world to find Peter.

Acknowledgements

Thank you to the *Guardian*, Hot Key Books, and the judges of the Young Writers Prize for believing in this book. Particular thanks to everyone at Hot Key for their passion and support, and especially to Emily Thomas for her sharp eye and her guidance.

Thanks to the friends who read early drafts and responded with smart feedback and sometimes hysterical enthusiasm—Salvatore Pane, Kimberly Townsend, and Alice Yorke; and to the teachers who taught me how to put writing at the center of my life—Jack Shea, Cathy Day, and especially Jerry Williams.

Thank you to my wonderful, funny, loving, supportive family, especially my parents, who taught me to appreciate stories, and from the beginning have never treated Professional Make Believe as anything but a logical career choice.

Most of all, I am beholden to Kevin Tassini for a news-paper article, a cross-country road trip, and five years of his singular, unwavering belief in me. I don't know that I can ever repay this debt, but I'm happy to spend the rest of my life making the attempt.

Katie Coyle

Katie Coyle grew up in Fair Haven, New Jersey and has an MFA in Fiction from the University of Pittsburgh. She lives in San Francisco with her husband, and blogs at katiecoyle.com. This is her first novel.

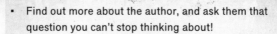
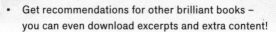